# DRUG AFFAIR

## RICK POLAD

**CALUMET EDITIONS**
Minneapolis

**CALUMET
EDITIONS**

Minneapolis

THIRD EDITION 2026

10 9 8 7 6 5 4 3

Cover and interior design: Gary Lindberg

ISBN: 978-1-960250-46-9

*To friends... gifts more valuable than gold.*

## Other Spencer Manning Mysteries

# DRUG AFFAIR

## RICK POLAD

# Chapter 1

We were all sitting in the beach room of Mrs. Margot's multi-million-dollar house in Kenilworth. An all-glass wall overlooked a private beach and, farther out, slight swells on Lake Michigan. White, fluffy clouds drifted across a blue afternoon sky.

I had never met Agent Thward, but his reputation had preceded him. He was a big man who had two modes of operation, depending on where on the social ladder you were. Mrs. Margot, living in the highest income congressional district in the country, was on the top rung. He worked out of the Chicago FBI office, and word on the street was that he was far better suited to being a guard on a chain gang. The people on the bottom rungs could testify to that. He had one personal chink in his tough guy armor—his first name was Pegasus, and behind his back people called him Peggy. Some had called him that to his face. A few of those had regretted it. I wasn't going to call him anything. He wore an off-the-rack tan suit with a jacket that was too tight across the shoulders.

Besides Thward, Mrs. Margot's lawyer, Mr. Malbry, looking every bit the part of the fee he was surely charging her, and the chief of police in Kenilworth, Sawyer, who smiled a lot and was probably more concerned about campaigning than solving crimes, were also there.

But then, crimes weren't allowed in Kenilworth, just an hour north of Chicago but separated by the stuff of fairy tales. You could barely get a glimpse through towering trees of the huge mansions that were guarded by wrought iron fences and gate houses that were bigger than most houses in the city.

With finger sandwiches on a silver platter and a well-stocked bar tended by a barkeep, one could have the feeling that we were there to discuss something other than the arrest of Mrs. Margot's son, Reynolds, on drug charges. Crimes in Kenilworth were handled with kid gloves... and somewhere along the way was the pull it took to buy the presence of an FBI agent. I figured he wasn't there to help the state make its case.

I was part of the crowd because I had performed miracles for a friend of Mrs. Margot a few years back, and she was hedging her bet with her influence. If her money couldn't buy it, and she needed a miracle, I was on the sidelines.

Reynolds, eighteen years old, had been arrested a week ago on the west side of Chicago for selling heroin from his BMW. He was charged with possession and sales. He had somehow thought it would help to repeat over and over again that he wasn't a user to the arresting officer. So far it hadn't helped. He had been released on a very high bond and was awaiting trial like everyone else. The atmosphere in the room wasn't tense, like it should have been for a young man facing serious prison time. Mrs. Margot was entertaining guests as she had done hundreds of times before at hundreds of cocktail parties for some event or another. I wondered where the tension was. It should have been there.

I just sat and listened and watched the clouds as everyone else told Mrs. Margot what a shame it was and that they were sure it would all work out. As the clouds drifted by, I realized that this not only *appeared* to be a cocktail party—it was. And it was obvious that this wasn't their first meeting. I hadn't been invited to that one... one where something had been worked out. And the parties that had worked it out were in this room eating finger sandwiches. The reason for the lawyer was obvious, and the chief of police was probably expecting a large donation for his campaign.

That left Thward. I turned to look at him. He had a permanent smirk on his face... he was enjoying this audience with money, knowing he was the top dog in the room. But he wasn't a man I would trust or would want to be in a dark alley with. If I wanted someone who would have my back, it wouldn't be him. All I knew about him was from his reputation, and that wasn't good. But I *did* know that he was the reason why there was no tension in the room and no worry on Mrs. Margot's face. Whatever had been worked out had been worked out with *him*.

I looked around the room and saw a photo of a young man on a table in the corner. I assumed the man was Reynolds. I had no sympathy for drug dealers, but I suddenly felt sorry for Reynolds. He had been thrown to the feds… by his mother. And I couldn't help wondering if it was out of concern for her son or her reputation that she had made her deal with the devil.

\*\*\*

By the time they had all started to leave I had pretty much decided there was nothing there for me to spend time on. Reynolds had been caught red-handed. The cops wouldn't have to do much work on this one. I got up to leave with Chief Sawyer, and Mrs. Margot asked me to wait for her in the den. She pointed across the hall.

It was a rich man's den with a large wooden desk, built-in book-cases, thick carpeting, and leather chairs and couches. There was a lot of purple. Northwestern wasn't too far down the lake front. I wandered around the room and looked at photos and awards, then sat down on one of the couches and listened to polite chatter in the hall. When they had all left, Mrs. Margot came in and sat next to me.

"Thank you so much for coming, Mr. Manning. Babs speaks very highly of you. May I call you Spencer?"

"Sure, but I don't see how I can help here, Mrs. Margot. I—"

She smiled, moved so that her leg was almost touching mine, and said, "Please, call me Jeanne." There was a sultry hint to her voice that made me nervous.

I nodded. But I wasn't going to call her Jeanne. I shook my head. "I'm an investigator. I look into things that don't make sense… look for the truth in fields full of question marks. There are no question marks here. We already know the truth."

Closing the distance between our legs, she put her hand on my thigh and said, "But maybe you could find something that would make it not quite so bad. He's really a good boy. He's just lost his way after his father died a few years ago. I haven't been able to..."

I tried to feel sorry for her, but there was no sincerity in her words, and I didn't feel comfortable with the seductress. I moved to my left, putting some space between us, and again tried to explain the situation, but she got up and walked to her desk and came back with her checkbook. Evidently that was the next strategy if the hand on the thigh didn't work. She sat back down, opened the book, and started to write. I stopped her.

"Mrs. Margot, save the check. I don't want your money." She looked shocked. I wasn't fazed by shocked... concerned would have been nice.

"Look," I said, "I hope it all turns out well, but I just don't see how I can help. There's just nothing—"

The first break in her wall of composure stopped me. Her forehead wrinkled, her eyes narrowed, and there was a hint of fear.

I turned on the couch to face her. "You seem to have some deal worked out here with Agent Thward, and you have the chief of police sitting in your house. My advice would usually be to get a good lawyer, but I assume you have already done that."

She took a deep breath. "If you can measure good by expensive, then I guess I have."

I shrugged. "Then what do you want from me?"

She looked across the room and out the windows, and it was a good minute before she responded. After another deep breath, she said, "The one thing all those people can't give me and my money can't buy... someone to look after my son... someone to make sure all this will be okay." She paused and took a quick breath as her eyes welled up. "I've tried, and..."

I wasn't interested in the Mrs. Margot who had been on display for the last hour. But she had traded places with Jeanne. There *was* a mother in there somewhere… or was she just a good actress?

I covered her clasped hands with my right hand. "I'm not promising anything, but I'll look into it."

Now the tears ran, and she took my hand. "Thank you. What will you do?"

I shook my head. "I have no idea. But I'd like to talk to Reynolds at some point. Would that be all right?"

"Of course."

"And I need to know what's going on with the FBI."

She shook her head. "I'm not real sure. My lawyer, Mr. Malbry, has been dealing with him. They want help with something and are willing to drop the selling charge if he cooperates."

"That's all you know?"

She nodded.

It wasn't hard to figure what they wanted help with. Convicting a rich kid from the suburbs wouldn't get Thward much, but getting whomever was next up the ladder would. And that ladder would eventually lead to the Prophets, the top gang in Chicago. A large portion of their money flow came from drugs, and that flow reached way past the city limits of Chicago.

"Okay, I'll need to have a chat with Mr. Malbry, but he may not be too happy about my getting involved."

"That's no problem. I'll remind him who's signing his checks. I'll make a call when you leave and tell them to expect a call from you."

Mrs. Margot was back, but Mrs. Margot, and evidently her checkbook, did have some value.

She got up, went to her desk, and came back and handed me his card—Keats, Malbry, and Jennings, Ltd. imprinted on a white linen card. She picked up her checkbook.

I stopped her again. "I still don't want your money. I'll look into it, and if there's anything I can do, then we'll talk about money."

She looked surprised. "I assume you need to make a living, Spencer. I don't want you spending time for free."

I smiled. "Be careful about assumptions. I don't need to make a living. I can be picky about what I do, and I don't take cases I don't believe in. But I have a few charities that never turn down donations, so we'll talk if anything comes of this."

She looked like she wanted to ask questions, but she just nodded. "Well, let me know if you need anything. Do you want to talk with Reynolds now? He's in his room."

"No. I'd like to get some information first. I'll let you know."

"Okay. You have my number?"

"I do."

I put the card in my shirt pocket and stood.

"Thanks for coming, Spencer. I'm glad you're helping." She put out her hand.

I shook it and said, "Like I said, I'll look into it, but I think you have all you can expect to have going for you already."

"Well, even if you just confirm that, I'll feel better."

"Okay. I'll be in touch."

She walked me to the door and looked surprised when she saw my baby-blue mustang. As soon as I had turned into the driveway, I had felt out of place. But I was surprised by what she said next.

She looked wistful as she said, "My father had a '66 Mustang. His was green. Is this a '66?"

"It's a '65." I touched her shoulder and walked to the car. As I drove out the long drive I glanced in the mirror. She was still standing at the front door, and I had the feeling she wanted to wave goodbye. I felt sorry for her but was also wary. There was something about Mrs. Margot that wasn't quite right.

As I pulled out of the drive and headed south I glanced at the for sale sign in front of the house across the street and wondered what the price tag was. Wondering was all I could afford.

# Chapter 2

Wednesday night was gin night with Stosh. I headed south on Sheridan and took Lake Shore Drive to Montrose. Twenty minutes later, I pulled into Stosh's drive where my Mustang was more at home. It was just a little after four. I had two hours to myself. I set up the card table and settled into the recliner with a book on Chicago crime history. Stosh probably had a bigger collection than the library.

Somewhere in the midst of thumbing through the book I had fallen asleep. The sound of his car door closing woke me up, and I had the book open when he walked in the door.

"Hi, kid. Sorry to ruin your nap."

"Wasn't napping. I've been catching up on crime."

"Right." He hung his holster on the coat rack and said he'd be right with me.

I heard the water running in the bathroom and the door open.

"I want to hear about your trip up north, but I'm starved," he said. "Let's go get some Italian."

I set the book on the table and pulled the recliner to vertical. He drove.

I filled him in on Mrs. Margot and her son at Bella's, a small neighborhood restaurant. We ordered lasagna and spaghetti. I told him about the afternoon tea party and Mrs. Margot's attempt at seduction.

"Be careful with that one, Spencer."

"What do you mean?"

He took a long drink of Peroni and sighed. "It's a different world up there behind those brick walls. When you put a lot of money and good looks together you get women who make great lovers and expensive wives. And they're very good at both."

I smiled and said, "I'll remember that. But I'm not in her league."

"The league has a wide net, Spencer. I'm saying to be careful."

"Noted." I took a bite of bread and said, "And then there's the drugs."

He shook his head. "I never get used to these kids getting mixed up with drugs. People think it's a city problem... bad neighborhoods. But it's just as bad out in the suburbs, maybe worse because there's more money."

I took a drink of Peroni. "Just fancier cars. And it's a government problem."

"How so?"

I shrugged and swirled my beer. "It's all about what they're willing to condone. Look at Prohibition. That was a disaster, except for Capone and friends. The government lost a billion dollars a year in tax revenue, spent millions trying to enforce it, and the tainted bootleg liquor killed thousands. Great idea. The numbers are even higher today with drugs. Control it and lots of negatives turn to positives."

"Ah," Stosh replied with a smile, "but the people who would be responsible for that are making fortunes from the illegal market... and they include law enforcement and politicians. So why would they want to change it?"

"Yeah, government for the people only lasted until politicians found they could get rich off of it."

Stosh was still smiling. He was used to my soap box proclamations. "Where was Reynolds arrested?" he asked.

"West side... Madison Avenue."

"Fourth precinct."

"Who do you know over there?"

"Lieutenant Graves."

"Would he share?"

"Sure. He owes me. Let me know what you want."

The food arrived. I watched it steam and said, "I'm not sure what I want. At the moment just a look at the arrest docs. Don't know what I can do to help, but it seems to make his mother feel better that I'm even willing to look into it."

He cut into his spaghetti. "I wish Thward wasn't involved in this."

My eyebrows went up. "Do you know more about him than I do?"

"That depends on what you know." He wound spaghetti on his fork.

"Just the street rep... the bit about the chain gang. Has a tough guy reputation, but he was all manners up in Kenilworth."

"Yup, not saying he's stupid. He knows how to act around money."

"Yeah, he was all politeness and smiles."

Stosh gave me a serious look. "Unless you have another tea party, that's the last time you'll see those smiles. Be careful of him."

We ate and drank for a couple of minutes. The waiter brought more beer.

"Why do you wish he wasn't involved?" I asked.

"He gets results, but he's willing to sacrifice people to do it. I'm guessing he made some kind of deal about the kid."

"Yup, but evidently with the lawyer. Mrs. Margot told me to talk to *him*."

He nodded as he ate. "He doesn't care about the kid... he wants the top of the ladder, and despite his record of arrests, he hasn't been successful with that." He took a bite. "By the way, neither have we."

I took a deep breath. "How long has he been around?"

"He's been in Chicago for about six years. In the Bureau... no idea."

"And he's still on the street?"

"Yeah, he's not political... doesn't play the game. And I think he likes the street. Gives him some power he wouldn't have behind a desk."

We both ate.

"Is this about the Prophets?" I asked.

"Sure, almost everything is at some point."

"So if the kid gives up his supplier that's going to help?"

"Probably not. The couple of layers below the top are taken care of."

"What does that mean?" I took the last bite of lasagna. "If whoever supplies the kid doesn't give up the next person they're going to jail."

He shrugged. "Maybe... maybe not. They've got the best lawyers in town. Even if the state gets a conviction it won't be much. And when *whoever* gets out of jail there's a nice chunk of money in his bank account."

"Hard to fight against that," I said.

"Yup."

"You want dessert?" I asked.

"Cherry pie at home."

"Sold. I wasn't impressed by Chief Sawyer," I said. "Seemed more like a politician."

He sighed as the waiter cleared the table and asked if we wanted dessert. We declined.

"Those positions are political. It's all about keeping your nose clean and raising money. Making it look like he's protecting the kid gets him a nice check."

"So where does he fit into this?"

He shrugged as the waiter dropped off the check. "He doesn't. It's all going to happen with the fourth precinct and the FBI..." He emptied his glass. "And not so much the FBI as Thward."

"What does that mean?"

He shrugged and reached into his pocket. "He tends to be a lone wolf... operates pretty much on his own. He's been written up several times for the way he does things."

"Then why is he still around?"

He smiled at me like one would at a child who just asked a silly question. "He does get criminals off the streets."

I thought about that for a second without comment. "And then there's the lawyer."

"That goes without saying."

We each left a twenty on the table and headed for the car.

***

After two pieces of pie each, we played some gin. After the first hand I reminded him of the new doorbell rules. The odds were pretty good that a person looking to put a bullet into him wasn't going to come to the door again, but the new rule was to look out the window before opening the door.

As I dealt, he said, "So, kid, where do you wanna have your birthday party?"

"I've told you six times I don't want a birthday party."

"And I've told you six times that's a lotta crap. Thirty is a big year. You need to celebrate."

"The big year is exactly the problem." I picked up my cards. "Thirty years, and what have I done with my life?"

"Maybe you could ask the people who are alive because of you."

I picked and discarded. "It's my birthday. I cannot have it if I want."

He just gave me a look and drew a card.

It was a quiet night after that, and I went home three bucks richer.

# Chapter 3

Thursday morning, I joined the stop-and-go traffic on the Kennedy Expressway and drove to the fourth precinct headquarters on Randolph. I couldn't help thinking I'd rather be driving up to my cottage on Moonlight Bay on this beautiful early-spring day. Before I left I called Carol and asked her to set up an appointment for Friday with Mr. Malbry.

Stosh had made a call to the fourth precinct, and I was meeting a Detective Bast at ten. He was the head of the detective team. I was five minutes early. An officer showed me to Bast's office. The man occupying it stood up, held out his hand, and introduced himself. As he gestured to the straight-back chair on the back side of the desk, I got an unexpected greeting with a smile.

"Spencer Manning. You've become almost a household name around here." That's not usually a good thing for a private detective to hear from a cop, but this time was different. He continued. "You've done some great work over the last few years, but I would expect that, given who your father was. My sympathies about your folks."

I nodded and thanked him.

"My colleagues told me to get some back story on the mob frame. Talk about a cold case. You should write a book."

I laughed. "Maybe when I'm old and gray."

He leaned back in his chair. "So, Lieutenant Powolski said you were interested in the Margot case. I've gotta admit, that has me curious and wondering if we missed something."

"Why is that, Detective?"

He shrugged. "Call me Charlie. Until I got that call it was pretty open and shut. Kid caught red-handed, plenty of evidence, the feds drooling. But you wouldn't be involved if it was that simple. So I'm wondering what we missed."

"Not a thing."

He looked confused. "Then why *are* you involved?"

"To tell you the truth, I have no idea."

He still looked confused.

"Well, I do, but it's nothing that has to do with your case. I did a job for a friend of Mrs. Margot. She raved about me, and Margot asked me to take a look at it. Said it would make her feel like her son was getting the best she could hope for."

"So you're looking for a favor?"

"Not at all. Just looking. She tells me there's some deal in the works with Thward, so she's getting the best she's going to get already."

Another detective came in, and Bast introduced me. He dropped a file on the desk.

"So, what do you want from me?" he asked.

"Just background. Whatever you can share."

He took a cigarette out of a pack and rolled it slowly between his fingers. "That's not much. It was 10:20 on a Wednesday night on a run-down block on Madison. The feds and us had surveillance that night from inside an apartment across the street. A BMW pulls up and parks at the curb. After ten minutes the customers started showing up. We got video of three buys before we stepped in. The kid didn't cause any trouble. The only thing he kept saying was he didn't use the stuff... like that made it okay."

"How did he act?"

"Tried to be a tough guy, but he wasn't good at it. There was fear behind the words."

"A rich kid pushing drugs in a poor neighborhood." I shook my head.

He let that sit for five seconds. "This kid isn't going to win any awards for civic responsibility."

I agreed.

He still looked confused. "So…?"

"Yeah, I know… why am I here?"

He nodded.

"I haven't met the kid, and I gotta say I don't really want to. But somewhere inside Mrs. Margot's checkbook there's a mother who is worried about her son. I'm here because it makes her feel better."

He took a deep breath and let it out slowly. "Okay. You wanna see where he was arrested?"

"Sure, if you'll give me the address."

"I'll do better than that. Let's go… we'll take my car." He stuck the cigarette behind his ear.

I liked that idea. I was planning on seeing where he was arrested, but I wasn't happy about driving my Mustang through the west side of Chicago.

As we stood, his phone rang. He answered it and held up a finger. I turned and looked at the wall to my left where various certificates and plaques were displayed. Among several commendations was a degree in Criminal Justice from Northwestern. Next to that was a plaque that named him as president of Alpha Epsilon Pi fraternity in 1975.

He finished his call, and we walked to his car. When we got to the lot, he pointed to a crowd and said, "I wonder what's going on over there."

"Looks like my Mustang has some admirers," I said.

"Your Mustang? Let's take a look."

"Hey, Bast. Take a look at this beauty," one of the officers said.

"Pretty sweet. I've got the owner here. Maybe he'll open her up."

I walked over and said, "She's open. Help yourselves." They did, and the crowd spent a few minutes admiring my baby. The crowd broke up, and we walked across the lot to Bast's car.

"You don't lock your car?" he asked.

"In a police lot?"

He laughed. "Especially in a police lot."

"I try to have faith in human nature."

"Really. With what you do for a living?"

"*Because* of what I do for a living."

As he unlocked his car he said, "It's your Mustang."

As he was backing out I asked, "Are you going to smoke that?"

"What?" Before I could answer, he laughed and said, "Oh, the cigarette. I'm trying to quit. It helps me just to hold it."

"And you don't light up?"

"I usually give in once a day. But that's down from two packs, so I figure I'm way ahead of the game."

"I agree. Good for you." I had never had a cigarette and had no desire to. Breathing in smoke just didn't make much sense. But never having tried it, I had to admit I didn't understand the addiction. And I never would.

\*\*\*

The neighborhoods deteriorated the farther we drove west. Mixed light commercial and apartment buildings changed to boarded up buildings, most of which looked empty. Bast stopped halfway down a block in front of a three-story brick building with a lot of boarded up windows. Next to that on both sides were empty lots full of debris. There were no other cars on the block.

"This is where he was parked," said Bast.

I took a deep, slow breath and looked around. "I have a silly question."

"Probably already been asked."

I nodded. "What's a rich kid from Kenilworth, who has plenty of other rich kids from Kenilworth to sell drugs to, doing down here?"

"We'd all love to know."

"Any ideas?"

"A couple. Could be whoever was supplying him wanted to do some business here."

A cherry-red Chevy in showroom condition sped by, making a lot of noise.

Bast shook his head. "They live in squalor, but somehow they have money for hot cars and drugs."

"But why would dealers want to sell drugs here when they can probably get more money for them on the north shore?"

"Beats me. I'm not privy to the business plan. My guess would be it has something to do with prostitution. I'm guessing a reduced drug price is a loss leader of sorts."

"Yeah, just part of a bigger picture. What's your other idea?"

"The kid just did it for the kicks. You aren't a player in the drug culture unless you're working the west side of the city."

I shook my head and watched an old man pushing a shopping cart full of probably everything he owned in large, black plastic bags. "It's all so sad."

"Yup," he agreed. "The kid has everything going for him, and he ends up here."

"Well, almost everything…" I said.

"Almost?"

"Everything but whatever made him start with drugs and come here… excitement, danger, whatever pushed that button for what was missing."

We were quiet for a minute, listening to the police radio.

"Do you know what the deal is?" I asked.

"Nope," said Bast. "Thward is never very talkative. He doesn't think much of us lowly cops on the city payroll. We'll find out when the district attorney gets involved. At the moment, it's between Thward and the lawyer."

"Who I'm going to have a chat with."

He smiled. "Good luck with that. I have a feeling he'll be as talkative as Thward."

"I'm betting he'll be as talkative as the lady who is writing the check tells him to be."

Bast laughed. "You may have a point there. Listen, Spencer, I'd appreciate working together on this."

"No problem, Detective. If I find out something, you'll be the third person to know."

He laughed again but didn't ask who the first two were.

He drove back to the station and pulled in next to my Mustang. We agreed to keep talking.

\*\*\*

I had a date to pick up Rosie at the station at six. Her car was in the shop, and she had taken the bus to work. She had changed clothes for dinner. It would be our last one for a month. She was leaving Friday for training in California. She wouldn't tell me anything about it. She said she couldn't. Made me wonder what it was. I'd have to grill Stosh. I filled her in on the way to McGoon's. Jack gave us a wave from behind the bar, and Nathan showed us to our usual table and said the Guinness would be right up. Jane brought two glasses a couple minutes later, and we both ordered steak, medium rare.

As I wiped the foam off my lip, I said, "So, the question of the day seems to be why a rich kid from Kenilworth is selling drugs on the west side of Chicago."

She smiled and set down her glass. She had managed to take the first drink without ending up with a foam mustache. She was very well-mannered. "Well, that's one of the questions. Another might be where he got the drugs. And that one we're much more interested in."

"Yeah." I took another drink. "Maybe they're related."

She shrugged. "Maybe, but I'll leave *your* question to the therapists."

"Do you know Bast?"

"Yup."

"What's your take on him?"

"I like him. He's always been straight with me."

"He was with me too. But he doesn't have much to share at the moment. His attitude might be different when he does."

She slid her glass back and forth in the moisture on the table top. "Might, but I'd guess not. If you're up front with him he'll be the same."

"That'd be refreshing. Hardly what we got up in Green Bay."

She laughed. "You mean after you had been caught breaking into a business and—"

"Hey! I didn't break in. I—"

She was still laughing. "Yes, we all know. But you see my point."

Jane arrived with the salads, and we both took a bite.

"Have you run into Thward?" I asked.

"A few times."

"And?"

"And I'd rather not run into him again. What's your opinion of him?"

"Seems slimy," she said.

"Amongst other things. We call him the chameleon… changes his personality in seconds depending on who he's talking to and what he wants."

"But I hear he gets results."

The steaks arrived.

As Rosie cut into hers, she said, "He does, but people get thrown under the bus. Then he gets in and drives over them. Don't trust him."

"Wasn't planning on it."

We ate and talked about the Cubs for a few minutes.

"What's your plan?" Rosie asked.

"Two people I need to talk to… the lawyer and the kid. I don't know which I look forward to least."

"Yeah, doesn't sound like fun. I'm betting if there are any surprises they'll come from the kid. You know what you're going to get from the lawyer."

I agreed. "If it wasn't for Mrs. Margot's phone call I wouldn't even get in the door."

We finished eating and moved to the bar where we had another beer and chatted with Jack. He wanted me to tell him again how I had brought Stosh back to life.

\*\*\*

**W**hen I got home I called Paul and gave him an assignment. I had a team of surveillance people, but I only needed one, and Paul was the best in town. I brought him up to speed and told him I was going to meet with Reynolds on Friday for lunch and would be shaking the tree and seeing what the kid's reaction would be. The house across the street was a perfect spot to sit and watch the Margot house. Being for sale, a car in the driveway wouldn't attract attention. The front of the house was lined with trees, so he could park out of sight and watch. If the agent showed up he'd have a story ready.

# Chapter 4

**M**albry's office was in a two-story building made out of gray stone a block from the railroad station in Kenilworth. The rent would be more than I could afford, just because it was in Kenilworth, but the high-rent buildings were closer to the tracks. Before I left the house I had called Mrs. Margot and confirmed that Reynolds would be home for lunch. I got held up by a train and walked into Malbry's office two minutes late. His secretary smiled and said it was no problem. He came out of his office to greet me.

"Mr. Manning, we meet again. Please come in."

I had the feeling he was the spider, and I was the fly. There was a nicely stocked bar in the corner, but he didn't offer anything. Before noon maybe.

"What can I do for you?" he asked with a smile.

He knew why I was there, but I'd play the game.

"It doesn't take a genius to figure out that with Thward at the party there's some deal in the works. Mrs. Margot confirmed that, but all she knows is they'll drop the sales charge."

Still smiling, he said, "That's true."

"In exchange for what?"

"I don't think that's something—"

I held up my hand. "I figured you wouldn't. A phone call might get that straightened out." I had thought I'd at least get through the first five minutes without playing that card.

"No need to get testy. If I may ask a question first."

I nodded.

"What exactly is your involvement?"

"Exactly… not much. Mrs. Margot would just like me to make sure her son is getting a fair deal and that everything is kosher."

He nodded slowly and wasn't smiling anymore. "And you figure that means you get inside information."

"I'd hardly define it that way. In order to do what she wants, I need to know what the offer is."

"And you're going to do what with that?"

"Nothing besides note it and be able to tell her whether it's fair or not."

"And you're an expert on federal cases are you?"

"I don't see where this needs to be contentious, Mr. Malbry. It's as simple as I explained. I don't need a law degree to be able to assess fairness."

He stared at me for ten seconds. I stared back.

"Okay, they've offered to drop the selling charge and go with possession of a controlled substance. But they want some jail time."

I shifted in the chair and crossed my legs. "That doesn't seem like a very good deal."

"He faces twenty years on the selling."

"Right, but a first offense for possession gets him probation."

"But there's the selling charge."

"Which they're dropping. I'm missing something here. What's the trade?"

"Reynolds gives up his connection," he said. "They want the pipeline."

"Of course they do, but I'd think that's worth probation—no jail time."

"We're still talking."

I just looked at him. There was something wrong here. It seemed to me Mrs. Margot could get far better representation for far less money. I thought I might have the chance to tell her that.

"Is Reynolds willing to talk?"

He took a deep breath and let it out slowly. "Not so far."

"You've tried?"

"He's been in here twice, once with his mother and once without. Either he thinks he's invulnerable or he thinks he has protection." He shook his head. "I tried to tell him whoever sold him the drugs was only going to protect themselves, but he was sure about it."

"So he doesn't want the deal?"

"Not as of this moment."

"And I assume you've explained he doesn't have a prayer in court."

"Yes. There aren't any loopholes. I explained that, but he's a bit cocky. Have you met him?"

"I'm heading there after this."

He nodded. "Well, maybe you can talk some sense into him. Listen, Mr. Manning, despite what you think, I'll get the best deal for the kid that I can. We can end up with probation, but he has to realize what he's up against and agree to talk."

"I'll see what he has to say. Maybe he's afraid. These aren't people who care about what happens to him."

"No. It's too bad he didn't think of that before he started all this."

"Nobody thinks they're going to get caught. Has he told you why he did it?"

"No. He's not saying much of anything. Just said it sounded like something to do. He did say he had friends who were making a lot of money, so why shouldn't he?"

"Hmm. Did he say who the friends are?"

"Nope, that's it."

"Okay." I pulled a card out of my shirt pocket and handed it to him. "If there's anything I need to know…"

He took it and set it on the glass top of the desk. "Certainly."

I was sure he meant that, but I was also sure that what I needed to know was a judgment call. His judgment would be that there wasn't anything I needed to know.

We parted with a handshake, and I left hoping I'd never have to go back.

\*\*\*

There were cars in the driveway of the house across the street... a BMW and a Cadillac. I was tempted to go in and have a look around, but my Mustang would have had to cower in the drive. Mrs. Margot's maid answered the door and cheerfully showed me to the beach room. She said Mrs. Margot would be right with me, and lunch would be served in fifteen minutes. I stood by the windows and watched gulls playing in the waves. The sun was directly overhead, and everything was bright and without shadows. There were place settings for three on the glass table on the curved stone patio.

A few minutes later, Mrs. Margot walked in with Reynolds and introduced me. The kid held out his hand, but he didn't say anything, and the look he gave me was from someone who was planning to keep it that way. He was a bit on the scrawny side with shaggy, brown hair and was trying his best to look like a tough guy. Dad had told me never to turn down a free meal, so if that was all I got...

Mrs. Margot was all smiles and cheery... too cheery. She was trying to make up for her son, but that would take more than she had. She told me we were eating outside and led the way out via the glass doors. Throughout the meal, she made small talk, which mostly consisted of the family history. Mr. Margot's father was a stock trader and had left a large fortune. His son had carried on in his footsteps and had continued the magic. They had been married for twenty-five years before he died from injuries suffered in a car accident. Reynolds was their only child. I think Reynolds grunted once when his mother asked him a question, but I wasn't quite sure.

When we were done eating, the maid cleared the dishes and brought dessert... Boston cream pie. Mrs. Margot told me it was Reynolds' favorite. She said she needed to write some letters and left us alone. Reynolds ate the pie, but it didn't seem like he was enjoying it. I wouldn't have either, given the situation.

I swallowed a bite and asked if he wanted to talk about that situation. He did look at me briefly but didn't respond.

"There are people here who are trying to help you, Reynolds," I said.

"I don't need their help."

"I disagree, and I think you could use a friend."

He laughed. "If you mean you, the only reason you're here is because my mother writes checks with lots of zeros."

"Your mother hasn't paid me anything."

He laughed again… harder this time. "Maybe not yet, but she will. You're not in this for nothing."

I started to respond, but he stopped me. "Money talks, man. It's the universal language."

I set the fork down on the plate and washed the last bite down with water. "I can understand why you would think that, but there are exceptions to your rule."

"Right. And I suppose you're one." He stared at me. "I don't need your friendship. You're no better than all the rest of them."

I wasn't sure what that meant and said, "Look, kid… I'm trying hard to like you. Help me out a little bit, would you?"

He banged his fist on the table. "I didn't ask you here, and I sure don't need you to like me or help me. I already have people who will take care of me."

"Like the ones who sold you the drugs?"

"You don't know anything about that, and I don't have to tell you!"

I saw the maid at the door. She was waiting to get the dessert dishes and looked frightened by his outburst.

"No, you don't have to tell me. But those people aren't your friends. They're just using you."

"You shut the hell up!"

"Do you know your lawyer is talking a deal with the feds?"

"Of course he is. That's what money is for… to buy lawyers who make deals."

"So there *is* something useful about your mother's checkbook?"

He just glared at me without answering.

"And that would involve you giving up some names."

More glaring. "I'm not stupid. Do I look like I want to die?"

"You willing to do jail time, Reynolds?"

He laughed again. "That's what this is all about, man. Haven't you been listening? Money buys no jail time."

I shrugged. "Maybe. Maybe not. The feds want more than money. There aren't any sure things when you stand up in court. Do you know what they'd do to a young kid like you in jail?"

I thought I saw a momentary break in the tough guy act, but it was fleeting.

"Well, it's a good thing I won't have to find out," he said with a cocky attitude. "That's why the legal gets the big bucks... to know if there's enough money I won't be doing any jail time."

I shrugged again. "What were you doing on the west side, Reynolds?"

"That's a pretty dumb question. What was I arrested for? I wasn't selling Girl Scout cookies."

"I guess I wasn't clear. I know what you were selling. Why were you selling it *there*?"

He smiled. "You're pretty dumb for a big deal private dick. It's all part of the game."

"What does that mean?"

"It means you're not as smart as my mother thinks you are. Now, if you're done with your pie, I've got things to do."

I pulled a card out of my pocket and laid it on the table. "If you ever need a friend, call me."

He got up and walked into the house, leaving the card on the table. I left it there too.

The maid gave me a worried look as I walked into the beach room. Reynolds wasn't fooling her... he probably never had. She felt sorry for someone, but I didn't know if it was him or his mother... or me. I guessed it didn't matter.

***

**A**s I was fixing dinner, I got a call from Paul. Reynolds had left twenty minutes after I did in his BMW. He drove into Glencoe and met a kid at a coffee shop who appeared to be about the same age as Reynolds. Paul described him as about five eight, short blond hair, medium build, and well-dressed casual. He sat at a table next to them and could easily overhear their conversation. They were talking about the next dare. It was the other kid's turn. Reynolds said he'd come up with something even bigger than last time. The other kid drove an Audi, and Paul gave me the license number. Reynolds had gone home after the meeting.

Paul asked if I wanted him to continue, and I told him I wasn't looking for constant surveillance… just cover as much as he could for a couple days.

When we hung up I called Stosh and asked him to run the plates. He said something about taxpayers' money, and I reminded him that I was a tax paying resident of the city. So he said he'd run the plate if I'd bring the beer for our Saturday lunch. Sounded like a fair trade to me.

# Chapter 5

I walked in with a six-pack of Schlitz, took two out, and put the rest in the fridge. Stosh had the pastrami on a plate on the counter with all the fixings. I always ate a light breakfast on Saturdays in anticipation of lunch. We ate in the living room. The Lead-Off Man with Vince Lloyd, the intro to the Cubs game, was on WGN.

When we had finished eating, we cleaned up, and I got out the cards. Stosh came in from the kitchen, sat down, and slid a piece of paper across the table. On it was written the license plate number Paul had given me.

"No luck?" I asked.

"Turn it over."

On the other side was a name—Robert Nadem. I looked up at Stosh with raised eyebrows.

He answered my unasked question. "Yes, *Senator* Robert Nadem."

"Well, that sweetens the pot."

"You could say that... along with a few other things."

"Like drugs and money wasn't enough. Now we throw in politics."

He picked up the deck and shuffled. "First of all, you have no idea what those two were talking about. Second—"

"I don't? The first thing the kid does after I put the fear of God into him is run to the senator's son. And they want to up the ante on the dares. What do *you* think they were talking about?"

He shrugged and started to deal the cards. "Who's taking Beckie Smith to the movies tonight?"

"Sure." I picked up my hand. "What's second?"

As he fanned his cards, he asked, "What?"

"Before you were interrupted you said 'second.'"

He discarded a ten and scrunched his forehead. "I don't remember."

I picked up the ten and discarded a three. "Well, try this. Reynolds said he was on the west side because it was part of the game. Any idea what he was talking about?"

He picked up a card and smiled. "Gin!"

I counted my points and picked up the deck.

"The gang needs drugs moving on the west side," he said. "They need to get the new kid involved. I'm guessing it's an initiation. He's the new guy on the block. It's like the frats doing crazy damned things to pledges."

"Could be," I said, "but the stakes are a bit higher."

"Just a bit."

I dealt, and Stosh won the hand.

"I don't know what I can do about this situation," I said.

"The drugs or your lousy gin playing? Or your birthday party."

I ignored him and watched him deal. "Drugs."

"Well, you're not going to do anything about drugs. The people that matter don't want that problem fixed. Your client is another story."

"What are you talking about? Who matters? The drug cartels? The gangs?"

He laughed. "I guess they matter at some level, but the problem isn't being solved, because people with a lot of money and a lot of power don't want it solved."

I drew a queen to add to my pair. "And why wouldn't they want it solved?"

"Were you not here when I mentioned lots of money?"

"It's not investing in real estate… it's drugs. People are dying."

"Yup. But did I mention the money?"

I picked up another queen. "Okay, I get it, but that's disgusting."

"It's the way of the world, Spencer."

I took a deep breath in and let it out slowly. "Maybe, but I'm not trying to fix the world. I'm just trying to help one kid."

He laid down his cards, but this time he wasn't smiling. "Not a bad way to fix the world… one kid at a time."

"And that's the other problem. I got nowhere with him. He doesn't want to be fixed or helped. He says he already has people to take care of him… and now we know who that is. And even if he did want my help, I'm not a babysitter. All I could do would be to suggest he get some professional help. But since he doesn't take the drugs he sells, I'm not sure what help that would be. Thward and the lawyer are working out a deal. I can't do anything there. So what's there for me to do?"

"Not much."

I picked up a new hand. "All I can do is stay on top of what the deal is and whatever else is going on and nod politely and tell Mrs. Margot all is as good as it's going to get."

"Looks that way. Easy money."

"It would be if I took it."

Before drawing a card, he said, "Gin!"

"Damn! Let's play Go Fish."

I shuffled. My luck had to change. "What are the chances Thward would talk to me?"

"Pretty good as long as Mrs. Margot and her checkbook are looking over your shoulder."

"What are the chances Senator Nadem would talk to me?"

"Zero. He wouldn't even let you wash his car."

I thought maybe he would. "You think his kid is involved?"

"I don't think, kid. I just—"

"Yeah, I know. You collect evidence and follow the rules. But I get to think. If he wasn't involved in the drugs, he's someone Reynolds thinks is his friend and will protect him because of his father."

"Could be. Could be not. That's the trouble with thinking."

The hands evened out for the rest of the afternoon, and the Cubs had beaten the Cards. But I was into Stosh for three dollars and twenty cents. By five we had talked me out of a job. I'd have a chat with Mrs. Margot and tell her everyone was doing what they were supposed to do, and I had nothing to add. I didn't mind that decision at all. I didn't like the kid, and I wasn't fond of wasting my time. And I didn't mind not having to talk to Thward. That guy made my skin crawl.

"I think I've taken enough of your money, kid." Stosh pulled the cards together. "You still working out?"

"Not as much as I'd like. Make it to the gym maybe once a week and run a couple times a week, but still a well-oiled machine." That was nothing like my old routine of running almost every day and working out at the gym three times a week. I was putting on a few pounds, losing some muscle, and probably a few tenths of a second on my punches.

"Don't kid yourself, Spencer. It takes routine to keep in shape."

"I still got it, Stosh."

"Hope you don't have to find out."

As I slid the cards back into the box I asked, "What's up with Rosie going to California?"

He smiled his sardonic smile. "That's driving you nuts, isn't it?"

"What is?"

"The fact that you don't know, and Rosie won't tell you."

"How do you know she won't tell me?"

"Because I know Rosie."

"So what's the big secret?"

"Just business, the kind we don't tell anybody about."

I set the box on the table. "I'm not anybody."

He was still smiling. "You are today, kid."

I gave up and paid the man.

When I got home I called Paul and left a message on his machine to end the surveillance and send me a bill.

# Chapter 6

I met with Mrs. Margot at ten Monday morning and told her everything was going as well as it could for Reynolds, and there was nothing further I could do to help. Mr. Malbry had things under control, and it was very likely Reynolds would get probation as long as he cooperated. That was the wild card in the game, but I didn't tell her that. She wouldn't have been able to help—it was obvious she held no influence over Reynolds.

I went into the office every day and tried to look important. I practiced darts and chatted with Carol, who was becoming more comfortable with getting paid when there was nothing to do. Once in a while the phone rang, and I had to tell people I didn't do marital work. Sometimes I didn't go in until three, so I could play darts with Billy.

The week went by quickly. I was in the office Friday morning, considering taking a trip up to Door County and spending the weekend at the cottage and inviting myself to dinner with Aunt Rose. Carol thought it was a great idea… she was getting tired of babysitting me. I was going to call Aunt Rose and tell her I was coming when the phone rang. I considered leaving in a hurry, but I didn't make it. I saw the button on my phone flash, and Carol stepped into my office and said Detective Bast was on line one. She gave me a sad look.

I punched the button. "Hello, Detective."

"Spencer."

"I was just going to take the weekend off, so be careful what you say."

"You can still do that, but I have some news."

He paused, and I didn't ask. I figured he'd tell me.

"A patrol car found a body this morning on Madison Avenue."

Another pause filled with silence.

"Reynolds Margot."

I stared at the wall. Something had gone terribly wrong.

***

An hour later I was sitting in Bast's office. Reynolds' body had been found shortly after dawn, just inside an alley, twenty feet from where he had been selling drugs. He had been shot in the head. The Prophets' gang sign, a raised fist, had been painted on the brick wall next to the body. The message was clear… Reynolds wouldn't be doing any talking.

"Let me know the caliber when you find out," I said.

"Sure. Small… likely a .22, the gun of choice for a gang hit. Enough power to get in but not enough to exit. Makes a mess along the way, but we cops love them… easy to find the bullet."

"Was he shot in the alley?"

"Plenty of blood."

"Where do you think this went south, Detective?"

"Any number of places. The Prophets' message is pretty clear… it's their turf. If the kid was going to talk, it's hard to tell what rung on the ladder took care of the problem."

"I'm not saying this has anything to do with the murder, but I had a chat with Reynolds a week ago. It didn't sound to me like he was planning on talking."

"Yeah, well, perception is all that's needed. Once the feds are involved, these people make some assumptions and don't really care if their assumptions are correct. The gangs have their own set of rules."

I sighed and shook my head. "I guess this is a rhetorical question, but how do you handle the gang problem?"

"It's not totally rhetorical. One kid at a time. The gang unit doesn't just arrest them. They actually spend more time trying to reach the kids who aren't in gangs yet... after school programs, sports programs. We need them to join *those* gangs. If we can give them another option, the gang option isn't effective. There's a verse in Proverbs, twenty-two six if memory serves me, that says something like if you train a child the way he should go, then when he's old he won't depart from that."

I nodded. "That's pretty deep for a cop."

He laughed. "It's the battle cry of the lady who runs the gang unit. There's a banner hung in the rec center where she performs her miracles with that on it."

"A lot of truth in that. But, if *I* remember correctly, the Hebrew translation is more of a warning. The King James version changed it to advice."

"What do you mean?"

"It reads more like... if you leave a child to his own ways he'll continue those ways as an adult."

"Wow. From a PI?"

I smiled. "I read a lot." I let that sit for a moment. "There's something else." I waited while he gave instructions to another detective who dropped a file on his desk. "I put an operative on the Margot house. After my meeting with Reynolds, he left and met someone at the local coffee shop who looked to be about the same age as him. My op got the license plate. The car is registered to Senator Nadem."

He didn't try to hide his surprise. "This keeps getting better. You think the senator's kid is in on the drugs?"

"Hard not to."

He sighed. "Yeah."

"What's your plan?" I asked.

He raised his eyebrows. "I might just retire."

I laughed. He didn't.

"I've got a call in to Thward," he said. "This was in his lap."

"Yeah, good luck with that."

He straightened in his chair and arched his back. "This job usually sucks, but sometimes it sucks worse than others."

"Where to from here?"

"The same as any other murder. But don't get your hopes up… there are a lot of gang hits in the unsolved drawer. They don't make many mistakes, and nobody talks… everybody's afraid. It's a damned shame… the kid had no idea what he was getting involved in."

"Maybe the senator's kid knows something."

"Could be, but I won't be asking."

"And why is that?"

"Because it'll take a judge and twelve lawyers to get an interview with a senator's son. And by the time they run out of stalls nobody'll care anymore."

"Nice system you've got there. I'm usually glad I'm not part of it. Are you talking to Kenilworth?"

"Yes, we had a brief chat this morning."

"Cooperative?"

"So far, but who's running the show hasn't come up yet." He rubbed his forehead.

"Have you talked to Mrs. Margot?"

He shook his head. "Nope."

"Wouldn't that be part of the process?"

"It would if it wasn't Kenilworth. It's like a different country up there. You in on this?"

"Nothing else to do at the moment," I said. "You think Thward will talk to me?"

"He barely talks to *me*, and we're supposedly on the same side."

"One could make the case that he got the kid killed," I said.

"That kind of thinking makes people disappear."

I laughed. "I'm not worried. I've got nine lives, and I've only used a couple."

"I'll read about it in the paper. What's your plan?"

"Talk to Thward and see if I can have a chat with the senator's kid."

He rolled his eyes. "You like challenges, don't you?"

"So you're out of this. Not doing anything?"

"Odds are this is gangs, and the Prophets are on top of the list. We'll put some pressure on them and see what happens."

"Seems like the thing to do."

"Maybe, but not so easy. I have to be wary of Thward. I've stepped on his toes in the past. Didn't turn out too well for me."

"I thought you were on the same side."

He laughed. "Only on paper. Out on the street, egos get involved, and guys like Thward strut around like big shots."

I shook my head, got up, started to leave, and then turned back and sat. "Who's the lady who runs the gang unit?"

"Benny Landez."

"Benny?"

"Short for Benita."

"She's good at it?"

"The best. The kids love and respect her. She's got a heart of gold but can be tough as nails, and she doesn't take crap from anybody, including the bureaucrats who talk a good game but just give her excuses as to why there's no money."

"Sounds like a good person to have on your side. I'd like to talk to her. Can you set it up?"

He opened a drawer, pulled out his business card, wrote an address on the back, and handed it to me. "She's at the rec center in the basement of St. Agatha's from nine in the morning until whenever. Give her my best."

I nodded. "Will do." I stood. "We still sharing information?"

"Until I get told not to."

"Good enough. I'll be in touch."

*** 

I decided to take a drive up to Kenilworth and offer my condolences, but first I called Carol and asked her to see if I could get an appointment on Monday with Agent Thward. When I got to Margot's house, there were three expensive cars in the driveway. I rang the doorbell, and the maid answered.

"Good morning, sir. Please have a seat in the study, and I'll tell Mrs. Margot you're here." She gestured toward the room ahead and off to the left.

I sat on a red leather chair and tried to ignore the message from my hungry stomach. The walls were paneled in a dark wood. One wall was built-in bookcases, floor to ceiling. A large wooden desk was opposite the books. The top was clear except for a lamp. The double doors were open, and I could hear muffled voices. I stood when Mrs. Margot came in ten minutes later with red eyes.

"Oh, Spencer, thank you for coming."

"I'm so sorry, Mrs. Margot."

"Please… Jeanne."

"Jeanne. I'm sorry about your son."

She led me to the couch, and we sat. Her eyes filled with tears. "Now I've lost them both. I…"

Her voice trailed off as she cried. That was something money couldn't fix.

She wiped her eyes with a handkerchief and said, "What kind of world do we live in, Spencer? Who would kill a boy who…?" She was trying to find answers where there were none.

I looked around the room. She had a beautiful house that was filled with sadness. She took my hand, and I held hers.

Her eyes filled with tears again. "Why…?"

I didn't have a lot of good answers, but said, "He got involved with some bad people, Jeanne. He was just in the wrong place at the wrong time."

"It's all my fault. If I had just…" She tried to compose herself. "Will they find who…?"

"We're going to try."

"We're? You're going to help?"

"I am. I've got a soft spot for kids."

She squeezed my hand tighter. "Thank you, Spencer. I'll write you a check."

I shook my head. "No need. At some point, if you want to, you can write a check to a charity to help with the drug problem. We'll talk about that later."

She wiped her eyes again. "Certainly, but I'd like to help. Is there anything I can do?"

"Are you up to answering a few questions?"

She took a deep breath and nodded.

"When was the last time you saw him?"

"Last night at dinner."

"Did he seem upset about anything?"

She looked like she was struggling to remember and shook her head. "Nothing out of the ordinary."

"Did you talk?"

She looked down at her hands. "We don't talk... didn't talk much. He did say he was going out. I asked where and who with. He gave me a disgusted look and just said with friends. I asked him to be home by eleven, and he said he would. When midnight came, I..." Her eyes started to water. "I called the police."

She dabbed at her eyes with a Kleenex.

"What time did he leave?"

"About eight thirty."

"Tell me about his friends."

She looked confused. "What do you mean?"

"Who did he hang around with? What did they do?"

She shook her head. "I don't know. He never mentioned anyone in particular."

"He didn't talk about his friends, or say where he was going?"

"No, he was just going out." She looked even sadder. "After his father died, I thought I should let him do whatever made him happy. I didn't want to be a prying parent."

I wanted to point out that there was a difference between prying and caring, and maybe that was why she had lost her son, but I kept it to myself. She was having enough trouble facing it without my hitting her over the head with it.

"He didn't introduce you to friends who came over here?"

She looked at me with vacant eyes, forlorn and hopeless, and didn't answer for about a minute. Then, very quietly, she said, "No one ever came over here."

I could see she was coming to grips with how odd that was.

"I never thought... I was too wrapped up in my own life, trying to keep together what we had left. I..." She wiped her eyes.

I put my arm around her shoulder. "A girlfriend?"

She slowly shook her head. "No... no one." Her crying turned into sobs, and she put her head on my shoulder. I knew she had just figured out what she should have done differently. And perhaps she realized she had everything a person could want except for one thing... time. Time to spend with her son, time to fix what had gone so wrong. And I also knew I was probably the only friend she had who knew that mattered. I wanted to hold her forever... because I had a feeling I was all she had left. But I had a job to do, and maybe my doing my job would help her.

When she calmed down, I said, "I have one more question."

She sat up and nodded.

"Do you know Senator Nadem?"

"Yes. We've been involved in some of the same charity events, and I've contributed to his campaign."

"Do you know his son?"

"Mark? I've met him. Why do you ask?"

"Did Reynolds know him?"

"I think he did. But Reynolds didn't want anything to do with what he called the *establishment*." She gave me a puzzled look. "Why do you ask? Do you think he had anything to do with this?"

"Just wondering. His name came up last week, but it was probably nothing."

I told her I'd stay in touch and wished her well. But I knew it was going to be quite a while before she was anywhere near well. I let myself out.

# Chapter 7

I took the scenic route down Green Bay Road to Lake Street and jogged over to the Edens Expressway. At a little after two, traffic was just building into rush hour as I merged onto the Kennedy Expressway and made my way down to Ogden Avenue, where I exited west and made my way to St. Agatha Catholic Church on the west side of the city. I pulled into a small, almost empty parking lot and parked in front of a statue of the Virgin Mary recessed into a stone wall.

One thing I had always found amazing about Catholic churches was that the doors weren't locked during the day. I understood the principle. Those who sought the peace and quiet of the sanctuary were given access, but I was in the crime business, and this was the west side of Chicago.

I walked around the front and up the stone steps. A man wrapped up in a navy-blue blanket sat with his back against the wall on the parapet to the left of the steps. He had a beard and long hair and looked like he needed a bath. He appeared to be asleep. I tucked a ten-dollar bill between his hand and the blanket.

As I pulled open one of the large wooden doors, I heard organ music. The door closed behind me, and I walked through the narthex, separated from the pews by marble columns. Sunlight brightened the vivid colors of the vertical stained glass windows on the west side of the sanctuary. I walked to the second row of pews and sat on the aisle and listened to the music. I got a glance and a smile from the man at the organ.

When he finished with a long-held majestic chord, he walked down the four steps and asked if he could help me.

I stood. "Yes, but I enjoyed the concert. What was that you were playing?"

"It's a Bach chorale prelude for part of Sunday's Mass."

"You play beautifully."

"Thank you, but what can I help with?"

"I'm looking for Benita Landez."

He smiled again. "Ah, yes, but no one calls her Benita. She prefers Benny."

I smiled.

"If you go back toward the street, you'll see stairs on your left that will take you down to the basement. Just follow the hall. You'll find her."

I thanked him and headed back up the aisle. By the time I got to the stairs he had started playing again. Another thing I found interesting about Catholic churches was the drastic change in environment from the sanctuary to the basement. Stained glass windows, marble columns, and carved wood quickly changed to concrete, linoleum tile, and cinder block... from exalted to functional. St. Agatha's was no different. And at the bottom of the stairs was a sign on the wall showing the way to the bomb shelter. I didn't recall a bomb shelter in our church when I was a kid. I followed the sound of excited voices down a long hallway. Almost at the end were double doors on my left that opened into a gym area where there was a game of volleyball going on. There were six kids on one side and seven on the other... three more girls than boys. Two boys were playing chess on a worn-out board against the back wall. The banner with Benita's battle cry was hanging five feet above their heads.

Standing on the other side of the room was a woman about my height in jeans and a plain sweatshirt with long, dark hair pulled into a ponytail and a whistle in her mouth. Even covered by a sweatshirt, she looked like she was all muscle. She looked like she could hold

up a car with one hand while she changed the tire with the other…
not someone you'd want to mess with. She glanced at me when I
walked in, but made no attempt to investigate the intruder. I watched
the game for a few minutes and then walked around the back of the
court to her side. As I came up to her she blew her whistle and de-
clared a hand foul on the net against a boy with glasses. He rolled his
eyes, and a teammate threw the ball to the other side.

Benny turned to me and said, "I'm Benny Landez. Can I help
you?"

"I'm told you can." I introduced myself and handed her my card.
"I met with Detective Bast this morning, and he gave me your name.
If you have time to chat for a few minutes, I'd appreciate it."

If I had been her I would have asked what it was about. She
didn't. I assumed mentioning Bast's name told her all she needed to
know for starters.

She waited until the ball rolled out of bounds, blew her whistle
again, and announced she'd be back in a bit and to carry on without
her.

"My office is just down the hall. Please come with me, Spencer."

\*\*\*

Her office was across from the kitchen. It was spotless and empty.
As I walked into her office, I couldn't help noticing the walls that
were covered with the pictures of kids of all ages. She sat at one of
the functional wooden chairs on the door side of her old wooden
desk and motioned me into the other.

"So what brings you to our little corner of the world, Spencer?"

Up close she didn't look quite as tough as she had in the gym.
There was a welcoming look to her face, and her eyes, as dark as
her hair, sparkled. I wondered about the stories hidden behind those
eyes.

I took a deep breath and sagged back into the chair. "A young
man was killed this morning. His body was found in an alley on
Madison Avenue."

She sighed and shook her head. "I'm sorry. Unfortunately, that's not something new around here. But why are you involved?"

"This may be something new. He was from Kenilworth."

Her eyes widened in surprise. "Someone you knew?"

"Reynolds Margot. I've been working with Detective Bast and his mother on a drug charge against him. He was arrested a while back for possession and distributing."

"How did this end up on Madison Avenue if he was selling drugs up in the suburbs?"

"He had been arrested on Madison Avenue. His body was found in the same place where he was arrested."

She shook her head. "I guess I shouldn't be surprised anymore by things that happen on the streets, but I am. How sad. My life is spent with kids who have nothing and are looking for a way out of the hole they're growing up in, through no fault of their own. I try and show them a way out. It's so sad sometimes that I can't even cry anymore. But it may be even sadder when a kid who has everything ends up down here."

"Well, not quite everything."

She looked thoughtful, then said, "No, I guess not. I'll tell you his story. A kid whose parents shower him with money and a fancy car but can't spare the time to pay attention to him... a kid whose friends get the same... a kid who is looking for thrills and excitement... and a kid who has everything but the only thing that matters—someone to care."

I folded my hands in my lap and said, "Sounds like you knew him."

She nodded. "I've heard enough stories. But usually the suburbs stay out of this neighborhood. I—"

"Excuse me, Miss Benny." A boy of about twelve had peeked into the room.

She smiled at him. "Yes, Scotty."

"We're done with the game, Miss Benny. Can we have snacks?"

"You certainly can. They're all ready on the table. Just start without me, and I'll be there in a few minutes."

"Thank you, Miss Benny."

I marveled at Scotty as he grinned and waved.

I shook my head. "That's the most polite boy I've ever met. Are they all that polite?"

"They are," she said with a proud look.

"Parents… or you?"

"Well, usually not parents, and not really me anymore either. It was me in the beginning, but the older kids who have been here a while set a good example."

"I'm amazed. You've worked a miracle."

"I've had help, and it's really not that hard. Everyone needs someone to look up to… to feel important. And if they don't have anyone, and a lot of these kids don't, the gangs fill that need. We just give them someone to look up to. The older kids give them that role model."

"And so do you."

She nodded. "To a certain extent, but it means a lot more coming from someone their own age."

"So if this is so successful why is there a gang problem?"

"Because it's not that successful."

"But if all the kids in that room—"

She held up her hand. "Yes, a 100 percent success rate with the kids in that room. But look at how many kids are on the street."

"So where's the problem?"

"Getting them in here. What the gangs offer is a lot more exciting."

"So how do you deal with that?"

"One step at a time, one kid at a time, Spencer. I take great joy in the fifteen kids who are in that room… and every new kid who comes in the door."

I let out a long breath. "One kid at a time." I shook my head slowly. "There are fifteen kids in that room and so many more out on the streets. It just…"

My dejection must have showed, because she said, "I learned a long time ago that if I didn't accept that I couldn't solve *all* the problems, I wouldn't be able to solve *any*. Those fifteen are my miracles."

"You're quite a person, Miss Benny."

She laughed. "Like I said, I have help. So, you still haven't told me why you're here."

I sat up in the chair and stretched my back. "I started out trying to help with the drug charge."

"There was some question as to his guilt?"

"No. None. But as a favor to his mother, I said I would look into it. She just wanted to make sure he would get everything that was due him as far as the system was concerned."

"Understandable. So…?"

"So, now it's murder, and she'd like to know who did it."

"And Detective Bast?"

"We're working together."

"He's a good man. He's sent several kids our way whose alternative was jail. He thinks I can help somehow."

"The Prophets gang sign was painted on the wall where Reynolds' body was found. Bast suggested I talk to you."

"I see. But what can I do?"

"Just keep your ears open. If you hear anything call one of us."

She smiled. "Which one?"

I smiled back. "I guess that depends. I'm a lot better at things that don't have to follow the rules, and I can poke into places Bast can't." I didn't know how she would take my admission… we were in a church after all.

She smiled. "I've been known to break a few rules myself, Spencer. Sometimes it's the best way to get things done."

Another kid peered into the room.

"I'll be there in two minutes, Jaimie."

"Okay, Miss Benny. I just wanted you to know we saved you a snack."

Benny beamed at her. "Thank you!"

"I need to get back, Spencer. I'll certainly keep my ears open and get ahold of you if need be. But I'm not out on the street much.

I spend most of my time in here with the kids. But there is someone else you should talk to."

"Who would that be?"

"Sister Katherine."

"Sister…?"

She smiled. "Katherine."

"Yes… I just… A nun?"

"Most sisters are."

I smiled. "How is she connected to you?"

"Well, we *are* in a church, Spencer. She appeared here soon after Father Brown agreed to let me use this space in the basement."

I nodded and then gave her a puzzled look. "*Appeared?*"

She laughed. "Yes, it was all quite mysterious. I've learned not to question the workings of Sister Katherine. About six months ago she just kind of started showing up where kids needed her and bringing them to me. I consider her a gift from God. She knows a lot more about what happens out on the street than I do… perhaps more than anyone."

I shrugged. Who was I to argue? "And where do I find this miracle?"

She smiled as if she were forgiving me. "If you need her, she'll find you."

I opened my mouth to say something but quickly realized I didn't know what to say. I slowly closed it.

"I need to get back to the kids, Spencer. I enjoyed meeting you. I hope you find who killed Reynolds. I'll say a prayer for his soul and his mother."

We both stood, and she shook my hand.

"It was a pleasure meeting you also, Benny. But I leave with more questions than I came with."

Her eyes sparkled with mischief and wonder. "That's not uncommon here. I hope you find the answers. And remember… one step at a time."

"Thank you."

I watched her walk away as she headed back to the gym, then turned and walked in the opposite direction, wondering what had happened and how I was going to find Sister Katherine. And as I got to the stairs I remembered... *one step at a time*.

# Chapter 8

The organist had left, and the church was quiet enough to hear scurrying mice. I was sure there were some in there somewhere seeking refuge from the chilly early-spring nights. When I was a kid I had spent many hours just sitting in our empty church. I enjoyed that alone time more than when the church was full of people. The late afternoon light was dimming, and the effect on the stained glass was subdued. But the atmosphere was as ethereal as I remembered it. There was still something peaceful and magical about an empty church.

I headed for the door but stopped and took a seat on the aisle in the second pew and thought about Mrs. Margot and her son and the sadness of the world Benny was trying to fix. I didn't understand drugs… I had never tried them and had no desire to. I did understand the escape drugs and alcohol provided, but at what expense? What I knew nothing about was the addiction. What was there that made someone willing to steal from their friends and families and even kill to get that next fix?

I knew the problems were nothing new… they just changed over the years with new drugs of choice. And maybe they'd never be fixed. But that wasn't going to stop me from trying. Benny welcomed one kid at a time, and I could only fix one thing at a time. One step would turn into two, and maybe two would turn into three.

I didn't know how long I had been there and realized I may have dozed off when a voice from behind woke me. It was calm and soft, like the coo of a dove.

"Can I help you?"

Only half awake, I at first wondered if it was an angel. I didn't know then that I would find myself wondering that for a long time.

I turned and found a petite woman with short brown hair, bright blue eyes, and a cherubic face lit up with an endearing smile. She was wearing a white cotton blouse and faded jeans and looked like she was about sixteen.

"I'm looking for Sister Katherine. Would you know where she is?"

She sat in the pew in front of me. "I would." She reached over the back of the pew, and I took her hand.

"What is it you need from me?" she asked.

I dropped her hand and said, "*Me?* You're Sister Katherine?"

She laughed, a soft musical sound like muffled bells. "I am."

I was flustered. "I'm so sorry... Sister, I..."

"No need to be sorry. I surprise a lot of people."

I smiled back. "Well, you did do that." I looked at her with my head cocked.

"What?" she asked.

"I'm pretty sure I've never shaken hands with a nun before."

"Well I'm happy to be your first, but I'm sorry to hear that."

"The nuns I grew up with were not exactly like you. The closest I ever came to a nun's hand was when she had a ruler in it."

She laughed. "And how many times did that happen?"

I smiled at her and asked, "You think the Cubs have a shot at the pennant this year?"

"Ah, you seem to have lost your train of thought. After what they did last year, they're going to need to convince me."

We commiserated about last year's playoffs. The '84 Cubs had made it into their first postseason game since the World Series in 1945. They played the Padres, who were in their first series since the team's inception in '69. The Cubs, highly favored, won the first game 13-0. They won the second 4-2. They just needed to win one more game out of the next three to make it back to the series. After losing the next two games, Cubs fans were wondering if the curse of the goat was rearing its ugly head. But no National League team had ever recovered from being down two to nothing, so we were optimistic. That optimism proved valid as Leon Durham hit a two-run homer in the first. But it fizzled in the seventh as an easy grounder to first went under Durham's glove, scoring the tying run. Two batters later a ball bounced over Sandberg's head. We all knew the goat was alive and well.

"Do you believe in curses, Sister?"

She laughed. "What I believe doesn't matter. It only matters what others believe."

I thought that was wise, then realized she hadn't answered my question. Then I realized she hadn't directly answered any of my other questions either.

"You have me at a disadvantage," she said. "I don't know your name."

"My apologies, Sister. I'm Spencer Manning."

She nodded. "A pleasure to meet you, Spencer. What can I do for you?"

"I was talking with Benny, who told me you'd be the one to talk to. I'm a private investigator. I'm looking into the murder of a young man on Madison Avenue this morning."

She sighed and shook her head. "Yes… Reynolds."

"You know his name?"

"I make a point of it. That's at least a little bit of respect I can give them. They're not just statistics. How are you involved?"

I told her about the drugs and Mrs. Margot and asked about her relationship with Benny.

"We do what we can for the neighborhood. She runs the program here at the church. I talk with the kids and the families and help wherever I can."

She got up and moved to my pew. I slid over.

"The church already had a neighborhood program for the kids, but it wasn't very popular. With the help of the police and Benny, it expanded."

"Benny says your role is getting the kids on the street to come in here."

"Yes. But there are many who don't. But whether they do or not, I help where I can."

"Benny also wasn't real clear about where you came from."

She tilted her head back and smiled. "She's not sure at all."

"And that doesn't seem to bother her," I said.

Her head cocked to the side, and she raised her eyebrows. "Should it?"

I laughed. "No, I guess not. But given what I do, I can't help my curiosity. How did you end up here?"

She showed the slightest of cherubic smiles and said, "The Lord works in mysterious ways, Spencer."

I knew I wasn't going to get any more than that. I also knew it didn't matter. So I went back to the case.

"And what do you know about the Prophets?"

She shrugged. "Not much more than you, probably."

"Have you ever met any of them?"

"Several, including Renald Williams. We try to keep a conversation going and get them involved somehow. Renald has spent time talking to me about violence. He says he is just a simple business-man, and violence is bad for business."

I had never had the occasion to meet Renald, the leader of the Prophets.

"Pardon me for being cynical, but keeping the neighborhood safe so he can run his drug business doesn't exactly seem to have the right ring to it."

She nodded slowly. "I know. But I do what I can. Mr. Williams brings food to our food kitchen. He doesn't send it… he brings it himself."

I pursed my lips and shook my head. "Sounds like you're mak-ing a saint out of this guy. Capone gave turkeys to the neighborhood at Christmas."

"Would I like things to be perfect? Sure. But I take help where I can get it… without making judgment. A lot of these kids only get one meal a day, Spencer. There are so many battles. Winning some, or even one, is a good thing. If we can keep the people safe and fed, then we can get a better handle on the drugs."

"And how's that going?"

"Actually, we were seeing some progress last year… that is until his brother was convicted of murder. The violence escalated quite a bit after that."

"I know. A friend of mine was the witness." I told her about Stosh.

A man in street clothes came in through a door behind the choir area and began turning on lights. I glanced at my watch. It was a little before six.

"There's a choir rehearsal tonight at seven thirty," she said, anticipating my question.

"Are you hungry? I'm buying."

"I am. That would be lovely. There's a diner in the next block. The food is simple, but it's homemade and tasty."

We made our way out of the church, and I pushed open the door. As we walked down the steps she glanced at the homeless man on the parapet. He was still asleep. When we were two houses away, I asked about the man.

"He's a neighborhood fixture."

"What do you know about him?"

She shrugged. "Not much. He just appeared a few weeks ago. He's there every day… gone after dark. People leave money."

"You talk to him?"

"I approached him once, and he gave no indication that he cared I was there. I blessed him and walked away." She paused to wave and say hello to some kids. "I leave him food."

"Strange."

"Maybe where you come from."

I got her point.

We walked a block to Time To Eat, and she recommended the beef stew. We were the only ones there. I wondered how they stayed in business. After we ordered, she asked, "Do you think the Prophets are involved?"

"Well, it would be hard to think that they're not. And their raised fist was painted on the wall where Reynolds was found."

"I know. It's an easy conclusion to jump to. But…"

"Agreed."

She scooped up a spoonful of stew. "The name similarity is odd."

"It is… Reynolds and Renald. I wonder if it's some kind of message from above," I said with a smile.

"One never knows, Spencer. The Lord works in mysterious ways."

That was the second time she had said that. I finished my stew and my coffee and said, "Not so mysterious are the ways of the gangs."

She frowned. "No, unfortunately they can usually be counted on."

"But you keep trying to change that."

"I do."

"May I ask why?"

She shrugged. "I'm all some of these people have. I help them pick up the pieces. I sit with them and hold their hands, give them some hope, pray with them."

"It must be difficult. And who helps you?" As soon as I said it, I realized what a silly question it was.

She just smiled… the kind of smile a kid gets when he should have known better.

The waitress stopped and asked if we wanted more coffee. We did.

"Back to my jumping to conclusions," I said. "This all started with Reynolds selling drugs on Madison Avenue. Do you have any thoughts as to what he'd be doing down here?"

"I don't get much time to think, Spencer. Most of my time is spent holding someone's hand and dealing with the sadness."

"Well, you don't need to hold my hand, and you know more about this than I do. I'd appreciate your thoughts."

She finished her coffee, put down the cup, and looked up at me. "We get a lot of people, kids and adults, coming here. But they're buying, not selling. I'd only be guessing at why he was down here. But once he was, I'm certain the Prophets weren't happy about it. They're very protective of their turf. Competition is frowned upon."

"To the point of killing someone?"

"I'm guessing they would warn him first," she said, "and then if he didn't listen... Can I have your guess as to why he was there?"

"My guess is he wouldn't listen. He struck me as pretty cocky and arrogant. Rich kid from Kenilworth." I shrugged. "There are several possibilities, but another guess is it was some kind of initiation... rich kids needing to prove something or be a part of something. One odd thing is that he probably wasn't down there selling drugs the night he was killed. It had been a few weeks since his arrest. His mother says he was out with friends and was supposed to be home by eleven. When midnight came she called the police."

"So maybe it's not related to the drugs," she said.

"That would be a big maybe. He was killed where he had been arrested. It sent a message."

"Do they know when he was killed?"

"Not yet. He left his home about eight thirty."

I paid, and we walked back to the church in a light drizzle. I pulled open the heavy wooden door, and we sat on the aisle in a middle pew.

"So how can I help?" she asked.

I handed her my card. "If you hear anything on the street, I'd appreciate a call."

"Okay, I'll see what I can find out. It's all such a shame."

"It is. Especially since Reynolds was in the process of making a deal with the FBI. He may have gotten off without any jail time."

"A deal? Do you know what kind of a deal?"

The front doors opened, and three women walked in. They talked briefly with Sister Katherine and headed for the choir area.

"I don't. But the FBI is looking for bigger fish than a kid from the suburbs."

"Yes, of course. So there are two motives for the gang doing away with Reynolds."

"Yes, if they knew about the deal."

"There's not a lot they don't know about, Spencer. Do you know who was working the case?"

"An agent Thward."

Her eyes narrowed, and she looked a little less cherubic. She nodded. "I was afraid of that."

That surprised me. "You're not a fan of his?"

"Let's just say Agent Thward does everything he can to help Agent Thward. If someone on the streets benefits from something he does it's only a coincidence."

"I've heard that."

"You haven't met him?"

"No. But I plan to."

Her eyebrows went up. "Let me know how that works out," she said with a knowing smile.

I laughed. "I'll do that."

Three more people came in and she said, "We'd better leave the choir to their practice, Spencer. It's been a pleasure meeting you. I'll see what I can find out. But I wouldn't be too hopeful. The people here don't know much about rich kids from Kenilworth."

"No, I would think not. It was a pleasure meeting you also, Sister. Thanks for doing what you do."

"Oh, I'm not the one to thank."

I smiled. "How do I find you?"

"Benny and I have breakfast almost every morning at eight at the diner."

I shook her hand and walked slowly up the aisle, wondering if it was possible to fall in love with a nun. I decided that depended on whether or not you knew she was a nun. Sister Katherine lacked the usual clues. When I got halfway to the back I turned and looked, but she was gone.

***

The rain had picked up, and the man on the parapet was gone. I was looking forward to getting home. It had been a long, sad day.

But I needed to talk to Ben, my favorite retired State attorney, so on the way home I called and invited him to dinner on me, Saturday at seven. He was leery about what I wanted but was not one to turn down a free dinner. I then called Carol to see when I had an appointment with Thward. His office hadn't returned her call. She said she'd call back on Monday. Given what I had learned about Thward, I hadn't really expected to hear from him.

# Chapter 9

It was still raining early Saturday morning, but had stopped by the time I left for lunch at Stosh's, leaving a gray sky and that smell of rain in the air. The forecast was for more rain and strong storms later in the day.

The front door was open, and I let myself in. After he'd been shot, we'd had a talk about opening the door before looking, but I guess that didn't apply to just leaving it open. Stosh had his head in the refrigerator when I walked into the kitchen. He stood up, and I set a six of Schlitz on the counter.

"Hope you're hungry, kid," he said.

"I am, but the first thing you'd better hope is that it was me who walked in the door. We had a talk about that."

He stood up with his hands full of mustard and mayo jars. "Yeah, yeah, what are the odds? I've already beat the one in a million. And besides, I knew you were coming."

He handed me two bottles of Schlitz. "Open these, will ya?"

I pulled the opener off of its cabinet hook and popped the tops. "How long have you been a policeman?"

He didn't answer.

"If my memory serves me correctly someone was shot in this neighborhood last year. And I think he was a cop."

"My mother, God rest her soul, must have been unlucky enough to have been reincarnated as you. Pastrami, roast beef, ham. Spring training game on at two. Life is good. Let's eat."

I made a pastrami on rye and followed him into the living room. "You talk to Bast?" he asked.

"Yeah, very cooperative. He took me to the alley where they found Reynolds."

He ate. I ate and talked.

"Do you know a Benny Landez?"

"I've heard a lot. Met her briefly at a couple of functions. She's got a tough job."

"Agreed. But she seems to have help from above."

He gave me an odd look and then nodded. "Oh, you mean the nun. Sister…"

"Katherine," I said. "Not exactly your typical looking nun."

Stosh stopped his sandwich in mid-bite and stared at me.

"She's every fifth-grade boy's vision of first love."

"Good thing you're not a fifth-grade boy."

"Maybe not. She'd be easy to fall for."

He set his sandwich down. "Are you saying you're falling for a nun?"

I laughed. "There are worse things."

"Yeah, like falling for two nuns. Eat your sandwich. You talk to her?"

I nodded while chewing. "Yes. She's going to keep her eyes open."

"Listen, kid, it's a good thing what you're doing for the mother, but this one is going to be hard to solve. The kid got in over his head and stuck his nose in where he shouldn't. The gangs don't take well to competition, especially from the suburbs."

I finished the sandwich and got up to make another. "Get you anything?"

"Another Schlitz."

When I got back, I sat and asked, "You see the drug problem getting any better?"

He took a long drink and said, "Hard to be optimistic. We control what we can with the help of people in the community, like Sister Katherine. The gangs know where the lines are… like stay out of the schools. They cross the line we go after them… hard. But we just don't have enough manpower or money. The people who bank the money don't pay attention to what happens outside of their gates." He finished his ham sandwich. "It was the gangs, Spencer, but I know you're not going to let go of this. What's your plan?"

"I'll let go of it if it hits a wall. I promised I'd look into it, and I'm going to, but it may very well go nowhere. I'd like to see what Sister Katherine comes up with, and I'm going to put a tail on the senator's kid. I want to have a chat with him. He and Reynolds had some kind of connection."

"That connection may have been drugs, Spencer."

"May have. And now that you've opened the door, maybe the senator is it."

He shook his head. "Make sure you keep those thoughts to yourself. His lawyers are better than yours."

"Just thinking out loud."

"Try thinking silently. Let's play some gin."

I was up a buck eighty after an hour.

"What do you know about Thward?" I asked.

"Thinks a lot of himself." He fanned his cards and discarded a two.

"Bast says he gets results."

"I guess. Little fish. And he has thrown us under the bus several times to do it. He'll jeopardize a case to make a headline. But it's the big fish we're after, and he hasn't hooked any of those."

"So he doesn't always follow the rules?" I smiled a little. He just glared at me. "Doesn't make him all bad."

"Gin," he said. He usually beamed with gin. But he just wrote down my points. "Not a question of good or bad. It's a question of following the rules and being part of a team."

I didn't continue the argument.

"I'm thinking of having a chat with him."

He dealt and said, "That should be fun. Let me know how that works for you."

"From what I've been hearing, it won't work at all, but it's a rock I've got to turn over." I needed one card for gin. "This is all so sad. A kid who had everything going for him gets a funeral instead of a future."

"If you don't walk in front of buses you're not likely to get hit. And it's sadder for the kids he was selling drugs to."

I just sighed and drew. I remembered the first time Stosh said that to me about the bus. I was four. What I didn't remember is what I had done that made him say it. At the time I had no idea what he was talking about and just put it down to one of those things adults say that kids aren't meant to understand and shouldn't ask about. A few more years older, I figured it out by myself. And at some point I stopped walking in front of buses… most of the time.

I drew four times before I got my card and stuck him with four face cards. That brought my winnings to four bucks. "And there's a mother who has a big house on the lake but has lost her whole family. It's just plain sad."

He stacked the cards and said he had enough. "Kid, the sadness happens every day, mostly to people who don't have big houses on the lake. Some don't even have houses. In that neighborhood where your kid was selling drugs, most are good people just doing their best to raise kids in some really depressing conditions. They don't wish for fancy cars and big houses. They just want their kids to make it to their next birthday." He picked up the remote and turned on WGN for the Cubs spring training game.

"How do you live with it?" I asked.

"What do you mean?"

"How do you come home after a day's work and live with the sadness?"

He took a deep breath. "How many times do you remember your dad coming home and talking about it?"

I thought about it and said, "I don't."

"Right. If you're smart you leave work at work. If you bring it home, sooner or later you don't have a home to bring it to. Lots of divorces in this business. It's enough that the spouses have to worry about whether their husband or wife is even going to *come* home. They don't need to hear about the job."

I nodded and moved to the couch. As I stretched out I asked, "What do you hear from Rosie?"

"Nice try," he said. "I don't hear from Rosie. I won't hear from Rosie." He looked at me with a raised eyebrow. "You know, seems you think about her more when she's gone than when she's here."

"Do I have to pay for this therapy?"

He smiled. "The going rate is four bucks, kid."

By the third inning Stosh had fallen asleep, and I quietly let myself out.

I usually had dinner with Rosie on Saturday nights, but she wouldn't be back for a month. I was meeting Ben at McGoon's at seven.

# Chapter 10

A light drizzle started as I pulled into the parking lot. Ben was waiting for me at the bar with a bottle in his hand. Nathan showed us to a table next to the windows, and I ordered a Guinness.

"So, you want to tell me why you're bribing me up front, or do you want to draw it out for a while?" he asked.

"Bribe is such a nasty word." Jane brought my Guinness, and I raised my glass. He clinked it with his bottle.

"Yes, it is. What would you prefer? Coerce? Manipulate?"

"Yes, I'm threatening you with steak and beer. It could just be that I'm a nice guy making you an offer you can't refuse."

"I'll reserve judgement. What's up?"

"You heard about the kid from Kenilworth killed on the west side last night?"

He nodded as he ate a piece of bread.

"He was arrested for drug sales and possession a few weeks back, and the mother called me to see if I could help."

"Somebody you know?" he asked.

"Friend of a friend."

"I remember the case. Arrested on the west side. Drugs and rich kids make good headlines. And what did she want you to do? Seemed like there wasn't a question about guilt."

"No. They had him. But seems the feds were offering her kid a deal in return for information. She wanted me to make sure the kid was getting a fair shake."

"Not your usual line of work."

"No, but the friend connection made me sound like Superman. And the mother, Mrs. Margot, was pretty distraught. She had recently lost her husband and was losing her son."

"So you offered to look into it?"

"Yup."

"What was the deal?"

"I'm assuming it was less jail time for a name or two."

"Assuming?"

"Yeah. The kid wasn't talking. Pretty big dose of arrogance. So I had a chat with Detective Bast."

"Good man. But I'm guessing he didn't know what the deal was."

"Good guess."

"I'm also guessing Thward is involved in this."

"Yup. I met him at what was called a meeting but looked more like a cocktail party at Margot's house."

"What did you think of him?"

"Pretty self-centered. More of a politician than an agent."

Ben laughed. "I agree. He makes a dent in crime, but he's never made it past the street thugs. He'd love to get the top of the food chain… maybe this is his big chance."

"Maybe." I started on the last bite of steak and thought for a minute as I slowly swirled my Guinness. "Something's been bothering me."

Ben raised his eyebrows as he took a bite.

"All of the cars in Mrs. Margot's driveway were pretty high end except for my Mustang and a Ford Crown Vic with antennas, and I saw the police chief get into that. So one of the fancy cars must have been Thward's."

"Supposedly Thward's wife has money," Ben said. "He does this for fun."

"Hmm."

"What's that mean?"

"Just hmm. I'm not fond of him."

"Join the club. Nobody is. What's your take on Mrs. Margot?"

"Hard to tell. She is used to getting what she wants because money talks. When she saw I wasn't impressed she tried the sultry approach. When that didn't work she switched to the caring mother."

"Which one was real?" he asked.

"Who the hell knows? Maybe none. There's something odd about her. I certainly wouldn't trust her. But I'm pretty sure she'd throw someone under the bus if it served her purpose."

"Including her own kid?"

"Good question."

Jane stopped and asked if we wanted another beer. We both declined, and I asked for the check.

"So, PI, why have you popped for that steak dinner?"

"Would you like another tail job?" Ben had helped me with the case where Joey was framed and had offered his services if I needed him again.

"Is that all? I'd have done that *without* the steak!"

"I'll remember that next time."

"Who's the target?"

"Senator Nadem's kid, Mark."

His hands went up in the air. "You may have to say that again. I thought you said you wanted me to tail a senator's kid."

"Would another beer help?"

"I'm trying to figure out how I can give back the last one... *and* the steak! I was a prosecutor for nineteen years. I can damned well tell you what would happen if the senator gets ahold of that."

"Feel free to say no. I have other options."

"I'm not saying no... yet. Tell me about it."

I waved at Jane and held up two fingers. We were going to be a while.

"Friday started out with a phone call from Bast telling me Reynolds was found in an alley in his precinct. I drove to his office, and we had a chat. He told me about Benita Landez who runs a program for the neighborhood kids out of a church."

Ben nodded. "I know Benny."

"After that I drove up to Kenilworth and talked to Mrs. Margot. And after that I drove back to the west side to see Benita, who led me to the prettiest nun I've ever seen. At the end—"

"Wait, wait, wait. Back up to the part about the nun. I've seen a lot of nuns. Except for Julie Andrews, I wouldn't describe them as pretty."

"You would if you met this one... a nun with the face of an angel."

He looked at me with squinted eyes. "Has your head been turned by another pretty face?"

"What are you talking about? One can appreciate the aroma of a barbecue without eating the steak."

He laughed. "Yes, one can. But how's Kelly Green these days?"

"What does that mean?"

"That means one can, but you usually don't. Does she of angelic face have a name?"

"Katherine."

"That would be *Sister* Katherine, and other than smelling like steak, how is she involved in this?"

"She works the streets. Benita runs the program for the kids in the church, and Katherine recruits the kids and evidently helps in any way she can with the poor families."

"Sounds like an angel. I know Benny, but I wonder why I never heard of Sister Katherine."

"Evidently no one else had either. She just showed up one day and started working miracles. Benny said Father Brown probably knows more, but she didn't seem too interested in finding out."

Jane arrived with our beer.

We poured, and Ben raised his glass. "Here's to Sister Katherine." We each took a long drink. "So, why am I following the kid? Looks like a gang hit."

"It does. But I had Paul tailing Reynolds, and the only time he left the house was to meet Mark Nadem. They sat outside a coffee shop in Glencoe and had a drink. That makes him a piece of the puzzle. After a half hour Reynolds returned home. Mark drove off in his father's Maserati. Dad must have been out of town."

"A piece of the puzzle whose father happens to be one of the most powerful men in Congress. I wonder if his father knows he drives the Maserati."

"While the cat's in DC the mice will play."

The wind had picked up and was pelting rain that sounded like tiny pebbles against the window.

Ben took a drink and set down his glass. "Hard not to call this a gang killing and close the file."

I nodded. "I agree. But that's the easy road."

"Who else?"

"No clue. But I've been told several times that there are lots of people with fancy suits and big bank accounts tied to drug money who have an interest in not being too tough on crime."

"Yup. There are some politicians and rich people on the north shore who fit that category."

I took a deep breath and talked as I let it out. "And Senator Nadem is both. You ever have a case that led in that direction?"

"To the senator?"

"To anyone."

Thunder rumbled not too far away. "There were vague mentions but nothing concrete. Those people are protected better than the president."

"Maybe the kid was involved because his father was," I said.

"Or maybe the mother got involved after the breadwinner died."

"And if a politician is involved, maybe part of his protection is someone in law enforcement... like maybe a chief of police."

Ben laughed and finished his beer. "So your list of suspects includes a senator, a chief of police, and the mother of a kid with a bullet in his head."

I didn't answer because no answer was needed. It was obvious how silly that sounded.

"Who you got on your side?" he asked.

"Could be the same people you just mentioned... plus Detective Bast and Thward, as much as I hate to include him on the good side."

"How about Benny and the nun?"

I shook my head. "Hard not to trust a nun."

"Who can you definitely say you trust?"

"Well, Bast seems okay, and Mrs.—"

"Seems doesn't count. Who can you *definitely* say is not involved? People you know you can trust to be what they seem... always."

I thought about his point for a minute and then said, "Stosh and Rosie and Aunt Rose... and you."

"Exactly. Short list. And no one on that list is involved in this."

"So I can't trust anybody."

"Always a good plan. Who does your gut say you can trust?"

"Bast and Benny and Sister Katherine, and a little less... Thward."

"Ah... because they're supposed to be the good guys. The next time we get together I'll tell you about the good guys I've prosecuted."

"So I have a list of suspects."

"Yup. Maybe one of them pulled the trigger, or hired someone to. And maybe they're all involved. Maybe you've got an Orient Express thing going on."

I gave him a dirty look and sighed. "And maybe it was the gang."

"You mean the gang that was upset that some rich kid was stepping on their turf? The gang that would kill someone because they didn't like their hat? That gang? The one with motive and opportunity? The one you can count on to be exactly what they seem to be?"

That didn't need an answer. It was the obvious answer. Why complicate things?

"What does Stosh have to say about it?" he asked.

"Gang. But he's humoring me for the moment."

"Just be real careful about making accusations. When do you want me to start on the kid?"

"In the morning. I'll call Paul, and the two of you can figure out a schedule."

The rain had let up, and we decided to call it a night.

When I got home I called Paul and left a message for him to call me in the morning.

# Chapter 11

I was half awake when I heard the paper hit the driveway and glanced at the clock… a few minutes past six. I spent the next half hour getting out of bed. I pulled on a sweatshirt, started the coffee, and while thinking about breakfast went out to get the paper. I had worked out a deal with the paper girl, and she got the paper far enough up the driveway that I didn't have to walk far off the porch to get it. The sky was still gray, but there were breaks in the clouds. By the time I got back to the kitchen I had decided on scrambled eggs and bacon. I set the paper on the table, put a skillet over low heat, and started on breakfast.

The eggs and bacon and coffee were done at the same time, and I sat down. I started with orange juice, and as I was drinking I turned the paper over. The paper was upside down, but the headline was big enough to read without turning it around: "SENATOR'S SON MURDERED." I didn't have to read the story to know who they were talking about. I ate while I read.

The body of Mark Nadem had been found in his car around two a.m. Sunday morning in the beach parking lot in Winnetka. I had been to that spot many times to watch a red full moon rise out of the lake. It was peaceful with a sweeping view of the lake. But there were three bullet holes in his chest that added a sinister twist. A .22 semi-automatic Ruger had been found on the ground next to the car. One shot from a .22 probably wouldn't kill someone, but three would have much better odds. And a .22 was the preferred weapon of the Prophets. They were accurate, and ammunition was cheap. But if he was shot in his car, accuracy wasn't a problem. There was a lot of information about the crime scene and what the police were doing, but nothing more of value. I was reading it again when the phone rang.

"You seen the paper?" Stosh asked.

"Looking at it now."

"If you're planning on staying with this, and I assume you are, you need to carry a gun... always. I mean a gun you can carry easily, that will hold more than six rounds... so not your Magnum."

"I've been thinking about getting something that's easier to carry. You have a suggestion?"

"There's a company out of Brazil that just started doing business in the US. Taurus. They have a relationship that shares technology with Smith and Wesson. I've heard good things."

"I have to give the whole thing some thought. I very well may not continue. But if I do I'll be careful."

"If you do, talk to me."

"You know any more than what's in the paper?"

"Nope. Given who it is, not much is going to be on the grapevine. The feds will be all over this."

"Yeah. You still think it's the gang?"

"Hard not to, kid. They thought Reynolds was going to talk. If they thought that, they'd be watching him, and he meets with Mark Nadem. So now both of them are weak links in the chain. This is how they solve their problems."

"Nice and neat," I said with some sarcasm.

"Sometimes it is. I don't refuse gifts."

"Let's hope the bow doesn't come undone."

"Yup. But one good thing," he said.

"What's that?"

"Not my jurisdiction."

"Nope. This isn't going to be pretty."

"It never is, kid."

\*\*\*

I kept the receiver at my ear, pushed down the button and dialed Ben.

He answered with, "Morning, boss."

"How did you know it was me?"

"Doesn't take a genius after reading that headline. I guess I'm out of a job."

"I guess you are."

"Are *you*?" he asked.

I had wondered that myself. The original problem hadn't gone away, it just became more complicated.

"Not sure, Ben. I need to give it some thought."

"Mark was a suspect. If he didn't kill Reynolds your list is shorter."

"And if he did, it would be good to know."

"And both could be the gang. Maybe both were going to talk. I'd sure like to know what the rest of that chat was about when they met."

"That'd help. A lot of unknowns."

"One thing I do know," I said. "This is going to be a mess with the feds all over this. I'm already being ignored by Thward."

"And then there's the media circus," he said.

"Yup. Going to be hard to do my job with a whole circus watching."

"Let me know if you need me."

"Will do."

I hung up and took my coffee out to the back deck, slid a chair into the sun, and sat with my feet up on the bench. A cool, gentle breeze was at my back as I watched the sun climb higher over the trees to the east. There was a hint of a sour smell from the decaying leaves I had spread in the garden as a winter blanket. I always looked forward to the time when that sour smell was replaced by the sweet smell of new growth that spring brought. Crocuses were starting to show their heads. A vee of geese came over the roofs on their way back north.

Because of the money my folks had left, I was lucky to be in a position where I could take cases based on whether I felt like it or not. I took few and turned down many. I had taken this one as a favor to the friend who recommended me to Mrs. Margot and because I chose to believe Mrs. Margot cared about her son. That was still a factor. But that was now offset by the federal and media attention this case would get that would make things a lot harder. And after sitting for a half hour I had decided that the attention outweighed the positives and that some time up in Door County was a great option. I would quit the case... again.

As I was swinging my feet off the bench the phone rang. It was Paul. I told him it was a false alarm and wished him a peaceful Sunday.

# Chapter 12

Wednesday morning I was at my desk in the office working on notes for the case. I had called Mrs. Margot on Monday and told her there was nothing more I could do. She tried to talk me into staying with it to no avail. I wished her well and thought about heading for Door County. Watson was lying in the sun in front of the windows. It was tough being a detective's sidekick. The phone rang at a little after ten, and I heard Carol answer and then tuned her out. Most calls were deflected by her. But thirty seconds later the light on line one started flashing, and a few seconds later she leaned into my doorway. I had told her it was perfectly okay to holler from her desk, but she insisted that wasn't professional. I had offered to get phones with an intercom, but she said she liked the exercise.

"Spencer, there's a woman from Mr. Malbry's office on the phone. He'd like to speak to you."

"Thanks, Carol." That piqued my curiosity. Why would Mr. Malbry, who had made it clear that he didn't need or want my help, be calling me?

I picked up the receiver and pushed the line one button. "Manning."

A calm, steady voice said, "Mr. Manning, please hold for Mr. Malbry."

I was about to give up holding when he came on the line.

"Mr. Manning, Mr. Malbry."

"What can I do for you?" I said in my most unfriendly tone. I knew there was nothing I could do for him that he wanted to admit to.

"Mrs. Margot would like me to hire you."

I took a deep breath. "Yes, I know. But I told her Monday that, with the murder of Mark Nadem, I wasn't going to be of any help with her son and no longer wanted to be involved."

"Yes, I'm aware of that. But that isn't what she wants to hire you for."

I paused and tried to think what the catch was. He told me.

"Mrs. Margot was brought in for questioning in the murder of Mark Nadem. She wants you involved."

That stopped me cold.

"Mr. Manning?"

"Yes, sorry. The murder of Mark Nadem?"

"Yes, the gun found next to the body is registered to Mr. Margot. Mrs. Margot's prints are on it. I assured her we could take care of it, but she wants you."

I tried not to let my smile make it through the phone. That must have been the hardest thing Malbry ever had to say. I decided not to rub it in. "What can you tell me?"

"Not much. She was brought in an hour ago by Kenilworth police. The wheels on this will turn pretty quickly, what with the senator involved."

"I bet." The legal system was as bogged down as a fly swimming in molasses and needed reform for the sake of the accused who sometimes sat in jail for many months waiting for a hearing and even longer for a trial. Innocent lives had been ruined by the lack of quick turning wheels. But when the wheels turned quickly because someone with power and pull was turning the crank, certain things, like facts, tended to get overlooked.

"Why was she brought in rather than questioning her at her house? Didn't you tell her?"

"I didn't get the chance. Two detectives showed up at her door and told her they needed to question her in the murder of Mark Nadem. They told her Chief Sawyer wanted to question her at the station."

"She didn't call you?"

"She did. But I wasn't in. By the time my secretary found me, she was at the station."

"Sounds like they screwed up. Did she answer any questions before you got there?"

"No. And I raised hell with the detective."

"Did he care?"

"Didn't seem to. People tend to get cocky with a senator and feds involved."

"Seems easy to explain that a gun she owns would have her prints on it."

"It does, and I have made that point, but there seems to be something they're not saying."

I thought about that for a few seconds. "What does she want from me?"

"To find out who's behind all this."

"Is that all?"

"That's all."

Carol came in and sat in the chair across from my desk. She looked like a kid at her birthday party waiting to open presents. I squinted at her and went back to listening to Malbry.

"...so this is how it will work. We'll put you on retainer at our standard fee, and you'll report directly to me, keeping me informed of your progress. Mrs. Stadler will send you our contract."

I rolled my eyes at Carol.

"I'll take the case, Malbry, but that's not how it's going to work. There's only one person I work for, and that's me. There's also only one person I report to, and that's my client. Mrs. Margot can share information with you... or not, as she chooses. Where is she now?"

"We're still at the station. How soon can you get here?"

"Half hour."

I hung up and looked at Carol. "Okay, what are you bursting at the seams with?"

"Well, I just heard on the radio that Mrs. Margot was brought in for questioning about the murder of Mark Nadem, but I'm guessing you just found that out."

"Yeah."

"What would they want with her?"

I told her about the gun.

"I just work for a detective, but if I have a gun at my house it seems to me pretty normal that my prints would be on it."

"But not normal that it's laying by a body."

"No… What did Malbry want?"

"He wants me to take the case. Or rather, she wants me to take the case. I imagine that's the last thing Malbry wants."

"She's obviously saying she's innocent," said Carol.

"Well, I haven't heard her say anything yet, but that would be a good assumption. But as far as I know she hasn't been accused of anything."

"Do you think she's innocent?"

I laughed. "What I think doesn't matter, Carol. You may just as well ask Watson what *he* thinks. What do you think?"

"As your office manager, or as a mother?"

I smiled at the distinction and held out my hand. "Give me both."

"As office manager for a private detective I'd normally say I want to know more facts before I take a guess, and then I guess I wouldn't be taking a guess because we only deal with facts and see where they lead."

"Normally?" I said.

"Yes, but I don't work for a normal detective. You don't always need facts to do what you do."

I smiled.

"But as a mother, I can see where maybe she is guilty. She has had so much sadness. Her son arrested and then murdered… I can't imagine. If it were my son, I'd want to strike out at someone, and if I thought I knew who did it…"

"Sadness and anger and revenge all wrapped up in one woman. Not companions that make for rational behavior."

Watson wandered in the door, wondering where Carol had gone, and laid down next to her chair. She reached down and petted his head.

"So you're going to take it?"

"Well, seeing as how I've spent the last two weeks trying not to take her case and have already quit twice, and have told Aunt Rose I'd be coming up north soon, the obvious answer would be no. The same reasons for not getting involved are still there… a lot of cops and feds, a big deal politician, and a lawyer who wants me to disappear. None of whom I want to have to deal with."

"Is there a but?"

I took a deep breath. "I'll think about it some more and have a chat with her before I say no."

She smiled. "Would you like me to call Aunt Rose and tell her your trip is postponed?"

"Ah, you have added prescience to your many talents."

The smile turned into a laugh. "I know you, Spencer Manning. You're a sucker for the underdog… kids, women, dogs, even a crime boss."

I returned her laugh. "That's the mother speaking. The detective needs to have a chat with her. I'll be back later this afternoon."

"Okay, I'll wait until then to call Rose."

"You do that."

She got up and walked out, followed by Watson who didn't seem to know who paid for his food.

# Chapter 13

On the way to Kenilworth I tuned in to WBBM, the local news station. I didn't have to wait long for the story. They didn't have anything more than I did, but they stretched it to ten minutes.

To say that the Kenilworth police station was fancier than Stosh's precinct building would be an understatement. I had driven past but never been inside. It was a one-story, cream-colored, brick building off of Sheridan Road with an entrance framed in white marble. Visitor parking was around the side. The lot was full of TV trucks and fancy cars.

I parked in the last row and took the concrete sidewalk that ran along the side of the building. The sidewalk turned into a stone path as it curved around the front into a landscaped garden that featured a flagpole, several large boulders, and a bench with a plate that told me the garden was maintained by the Kenilworth Garden Club. Like all the homes along Sheridan Road, the front of the building was a showplace. But those who dared to run afoul of the law in Kenilworth didn't get to use the stone path.

An officer near the front glass doors asked what my business was. When I told him I was there to see Mr. Malbry, a stony attitude turned polite, and he held the door for me. I guessed the reporters didn't get to use the stone path either.

I stopped at the desk and was told by a very formal sergeant that Mr. Malbry was with a client and that she would let him know I was there, and I could have a seat. She said "Mr. Malbry" with a tone that bordered on reverence. I sat on the other end of a couch from a woman dressed in a gray business suit who was busy minding her own business reading a magazine. She didn't even glance at me. After scanning the room, which could have been a small foyer of a hotel, I picked up the magazine that was on top of a fanned pile... *Better Homes and Gardens*.

By my watch it was twenty-three minutes before an officer opened the door to the right of the desk and told me Mr. Malbry would see me.

\*\*\*

The interview room made Stosh's interview room look like a third world country. Soft fluorescent lighting, off-white walls with a few modern art paintings and a photo of the mayor, and a large, oblong, metal-rimmed glass-topped table made me feel like I was in a hotel rather than a police station. But I also figured this wasn't the only interview room. People who didn't contribute to the chief's campaign never saw this place.

Malbry's three-piece suit and stately bearing matched the ambience. Mrs. Margot's did not. She looked haggard, like she was on her third day with no sleep. She sat in one of the matching cushioned chairs and looked up at me with desperation, eyes a bit blackened from running makeup.

"Manning," said Malbry with the same disdain you might show a dog that had just peed on the carpet... again. I looked him over, trying to find something to look down at him about, but there was nothing. Everything from his fingernails to his posture was perfect.

I nodded at him and sat across from Mrs. Margot. I had no idea what to say to her. She started.

"Thanks for coming, Spencer. I don't know... I don't even believe this is happening."

That it was happening was obvious. Why it was happening was something I had been wondering. They wouldn't have brought in a prominent citizen of Kenilworth without some very good evidence and several conversations between people way above my pay grade.

I looked at Malbry. "Have you learned anything else?"

He looked at her and then back at me with a hard stare. "The murder weapon, with Mrs. Margot's prints on it, was found next to the body. That's all they've told me so far."

"Did they have an arrest warrant?"

"No."

"Then why—?"

"Because they misled her."

I turned to Mrs. Margot. "Why did you go with them, Jeanne?"

She shook her head. "They told me Chief Sawyer wanted to talk to me. I've given him a lot of money, so I thought that would be okay."

"Did they tell you you didn't have to go with them?"

"No."

I looked at Malbry. "Sounds like grounds for a lawsuit."

"We're already working on it, but they also didn't tell her she *had* to go with them. They were purposefully vague."

Jeanne started to cry. "I don't want a lawsuit. I just want this to end."

Neither Malbry or I responded to that. I was sure he didn't agree with her.

"So why are we still sitting here?" I asked.

"Waiting for Sawyer to finish with his media show. I'd like to hear what he has to say."

Jeanne's mascara was running. I got a box of Kleenex from a side table and set it in front of her. She wiped her eyes and slowly shook her head.

"First my son… and now this. I don't know how…"

"Now there, Jeanne," said Malbry. "I'll get this straightened out. We have an excellent team working on this already."

That didn't seem to give her much solace. And I got the feeling Malbry wasn't including me on his team. That was okay with me.

Malbry turned to me. "Mrs. Margot wants you involved. But with all the attention this is getting and all the agencies that will be involved, it's important we keep everything centralized."

That was fancy talk for *he wanted to be the big shot*.

He continued. "I have to insist that you work for me. You can do whatever it is you do, but you file reports with me and submit bills to me and will be paid by me, and I'll be the media contact. Is that clear?"

"Perfectly. Couldn't be clearer."

"Good, then I'll get a contract to you this afternoon, and—"

I would have laughed, but I remembered Mrs. Margot was at the table. I just shook my head instead.

"There will be no contracts. Mrs. Margot needs a good lawyer. I assume you are that. I'll let you take the lead on this and pay my bills, but I don't sign contracts. And if you want to be the media lap-dog be my guest. I don't find talking to the media to be productive. If there's anything you need to know I'll call. I have an excellent office manager who keeps excellent records, and if you need something for court they're all yours."

He took a deep breath. He was in a tough spot. His client wanted me, but he certainly didn't. His attempt to control me hadn't worked, but I thought I had thrown him enough bones to let him save face.

"Your reports will include all of your activities?"

I slowly shook my head. "No." If my reports included everything I did, I would have spent most of my time in jail. "They'll include the facts."

He reluctantly agreed.

All this wasn't helping Mrs. Margot. She was wringing her hands in her lap. "When can I get out of here?"

"We're working on that. Hopefully Sawyer will be here before lunch. If not, we're leaving."

"Back to the murder weapon, if I may," I said. "Can you explain your prints?"

Mrs. Margot looked up at me, but she just looked lost. She opened her mouth, but no words came out.

Malbry relaxed in his chair, reached out and touched her hand, and said, "The gun belonged to Mr. Margot. It was in a case in his study. The night—"

"I'll tell him," she said. She leaned forward with her arms on the table and clasped her hands. "The last night…" Her lips were trembling, and she started to cry. She took a piece of Kleenex and dabbed at her eyes.

"You don't have to, Jeanne," Malbry said quietly. I was surprised by his concern.

She nodded, blew her nose, and sat up straight taking a deep breath.

"The last night I saw Reynolds, I stopped him as he was going out of the house. I asked where he was going. He just said out. I kept after him, and when he turned at the door I saw a bulge under his jacket at his belt. I asked what it was. He told me it was none of my business. I ran at him and grabbed at it and knew it was the gun. His jacket wasn't zipped so I was able to grab it and pull it out of his pants. We fought over it, but he was stronger than me, and he ended up with it." She cried again and pulled more Kleenex. "I begged him not to take the gun, but…"

Malbry reached out to her again. "That's enough, Jeanne."

She gave me a pleading look and then looked down at her hands.

Malbry straightened in his chair and asked if I had any questions.

"Plenty."

He nodded. "For myself or Mrs. Margot?"

I looked at her. She was still looking down. "Not at the moment."

"Call my office if you do."

Somewhere along the way he had lost the attitude.

I assured her that I would do my best, and she gave me that pleading look again.

***

An hour later we all left the station after a chat with Chief Sawyer. He had nothing more than her prints on the gun, and after her explanation he apologized profusely. But he did add one more bit of information. There were two sets of prints found on the gun. The other had not been identified.

The morning did have one positive outcome. For the first time, I was glad Jeanne had Malbry. The Kenilworth police department wouldn't be so glad.

As I walked to the car, I thought about what had happened in that room and wondered which was the real Mrs. Margot. She had changed several times when she was trying to get me to look into Reynolds' drug charges. I had walked out of her house not knowing what was real and what was an act. The thought had crossed my mind that maybe it all was an act, that she was a chameleon, capable of changing and using whatever tactic worked best to get what she wanted.

By the time I got to the Mustang, I had decided that I had no idea if her tears were real or an act. And I had no idea if she was capable of murder. She must have known her son was going to see Mark Nadem. And there was one thing I did know... revenge could be a cruel mistress.

*** 

I stopped at the deli and picked up sandwiches for Carol and me. As I came in the back door, Watson, who was curled up next to Carol's chair, looked up at me and wagged his tail twice. Progress. As we ate, I told Carol about Mrs. Margot.

"She's upset, but she's also a good actress. She could just be upset because she was sitting in a police station."

"What's your gut telling you, Spencer? Do you think she did it?"

I finished the first half of my pastrami sandwich. "That's a great question. My gut is telling me that I should be wary. I don't trust her... not a good relationship to have with a client. But I'm keeping an open mind." I started on the other half. "Still nothing from Thward's office?"

"No, and I have called several times."

"Call several more times… every hour. Be the squeaky wheel. The man's a public servant… he needs to serve the public."

"Will do."

I rubbed Watson behind his ears, and that got a few more wags.

# Chapter 14

S tosh and I had missed a few Wednesday night gin games over the last few years but not many. He was in the kitchen when I got there.

"It's not Aunt Rose's, but there's cherry pie on the counter," he said.

I cut a piece, and we sat at the card table in the living room.

With a mouthful of pie, he said, "So, knowing you, I assume you're back working for Margot."

I finished my mouthful. "No, I am not," I said decisively.

His fork stopped halfway to his mouth. "I must have heard you wrong. Please repeat that."

I put down my fork. "No, I am not working for Margot."

"Well, I am pleasantly surprised. You made a good decision to walk away from that case... twice... for good reasons. I figured a murder suspicion would lure you back in. But with all the agencies that are going to be involved in this it's a good case to stay away from."

I leaned forward and folded my hands on the table. "I didn't say that."

His fork stopped again. "You didn't say what?"

"That I was staying away from the case."

He squinted his eyes and gave me his best disgusted look. "No you didn't... you said you weren't working for Margot. So who are you working for?"

"It's a bit confusing. Technically I'm working for Malbry. He wanted me to sign his contract, but I refused."

"Oh crap! I thought you didn't like the man."

"I don't, but I'm trying to like *her*, and she's the one in trouble."

He shook his head. "You were in and out and back in and back out again, and now you're back in. The same reasons that you left are still there... but much worse. It was bad enough with just Thward, but there are going to be Washington types tripping all over themselves. You have no idea what you've gotten yourself into."

"I've ignored those people before, Stosh. What I've gotten myself into is helping a mother who has lost everything."

He put down his fork and leaned back in the chair. "Perfectly good pie shot to hell. Okay, so what have you got?"

"Same as always at the beginning of a case... not much. But there's no shortage of suspects. I had a talk with Ben about who I can and can't trust. I think the list of suspects is the same as the people I can't trust."

"Who would that be?" He started back in on his pie. Evidently it wasn't completely shot to hell.

"Well, if Mark was involved in the drug business, Mrs. Margot had every reason to want him dead. She knew Reynolds was seeing Mark, and if she thought he was going to see him that night, she might put two and two together. And if Mark was involved in the drug business maybe his father was too."

He looked at me with both eyebrows raised.

"Rich *and* a ranking politician," he said.

"I'm not saying that's the way this is... just wondering about the mess that would be."

"Wouldn't be the first time." He sighed and set down the fork. The pie was gone. "Or the last. This job would be a lot easier if the guys who were supposed to be the good guys weren't sometimes the bad guys."

"Yeah, you need a scorecard."

He got up from the table and got the cards out of a drawer in the side table. "Who else?"

"Unfortunately, cops can be bad guys too. There are several here I don't know. No reason to mistrust Bast or his team, but I'm not closing any doors. And I don't care what anybody says, I'm not putting a nun on my list."

"You're letting a cherubic face sway your thinking."

"No, I'm—"

He held his hand up. "The reason we solve crimes is that the average criminal is dumber than a rock. But the smart ones… they'll reel you in and keep you hooked until, when it serves their purpose, they stick a knife in you. You never see it coming."

"No doubt, but you haven't met—"

"I don't have to. And your gut is probably right, but in this business it can get you killed. What better cover to work drugs than to be the nun who is trying to clean it up? You said she's always on the street. She knows the neighborhood and the people and who's doing what when."

"Yeah, well…"

"Well nothing. All I'm saying is keep your eyes open and a leash on your emotions. Many a pretty face has been attached to a purse with a knife in it."

He handed me the deck, and I shuffled and dealt.

As he fanned his cards, he said, "But the most likely answer is the gang. Rich kids from the suburbs cutting in on their action. They needed to send a message."

"The message was sent with Reynolds."

He shrugged and discarded a three. "Or maybe the gang hired the kids to expand business into the burbs. Maybe Thward put pressure on the senator's kid, and the gang thought he was going to talk too."

"Lots that doesn't make any sense," I said.

"Welcome to my world. Always a lot of pieces. It'll make sense when you fit the pieces together. Gin." He laid down his cards. "And then there's the puzzle that never gets put together."

"Yeah, the gang is good at covering its tracks."

He shuffled.

"Why would they bring her in just because her prints are on the gun?" I asked.

"To calm the waters."

"Pardon?"

"They did need to talk to her. And there's a lot of pressure from above to get this solved, so they needed to make it public... let everyone know they were doing something."

"Pretty cruel to put her through that. She just lost her son."

He shook his head. "Nobody said this game was polite."

"One thing odd about the prints," I said. "There were two sets found... hers and an unknown, which I assume is Reynolds'."

"Ah, yes. Why are her prints on file?" He picked a card.

"Exactly."

"Might be good to find out. So what's your plan?"

"I'm trying to get an appointment with Thward."

He laughed. "Good luck with that."

"He's not returning calls."

"What else?"

"I need to buy a nun breakfast."

# Chapter 15

S ister Katherine had said that she and Benny had breakfast every morning at Time To Eat, so I left the house hungry and headed south. Thursday morning traffic on the Kennedy was worse than usual. I made up some time on Ogden, and the side street had no traffic, but I was ten minutes late. I pulled into a spot five buildings west of the diner. A woman across the street was sweeping dust off of the cement steps in front of her three-flat and onto the sidewalk leading through dirt and weeds to the front walk. Two windows were boarded up. A black cat was stretched out on her window ledge. The air was humid and smelled of wet dirt.

Three boys were sitting on the stoop of the building I was parked in front of. I had no idea how old they were… somewhere between twelve and twenty. They were wearing the same shirts and caps and passing around a cigarette. I wondered if that was how they'd spend their day, sitting and waiting for something to happen, something they could tell their grandkids. With drugs and guns and unemployment, all too often it did happen. Their main decision in life was which gang to join. And I could see the reason why from the blank looks on their faces. The gang offered something the system didn't… something to belong to, a reason to get up in the morning. These kids weren't the problem, but without them and others like them the problem wouldn't exist. They didn't seem to notice me, but they did notice my Mustang. I wondered if I was tempting fate. I also wondered if the cat had more on its mind than the boys did.

Benny and Sister Katherine were offering an alternative, but there were a lot more kids in the gangs than in that church basement.

I had decided that if I was going to go looking for trouble I'd better be ready if I found it. So, despite my aversion to carrying a gun, my new Taurus with its flat profile was in a shoulder holster under my jacket. In my wallet was a card that said I could do that. It was one of many cards that defined my existence.

I walked east and passed a grocery store and a barbershop with the red-white-and-blue-striped pole on the wall next to the door. The door of the grocery was propped open. There were two signs in the barbershop window. One said "Closed," the other "Two Chairs No Waiting." It was an old shop. The barber I went to had five chairs, and I usually had to wait.

Coming toward me from the east was a grizzled old man pushing a cart and ringing a bell. Judging by the sign on the side of the cart, sharpening knives was his specialty, but wares of various sorts hung from the sides of the cart. I wondered if he ever sold any. A dog barked from somewhere down the street to the west.

Benny was sitting by herself in one of the middle booths, engrossed in a sheaf of papers.

"Is this seat taken?" I asked.

She looked up and smiled. "Mr. Manning. What a nice surprise." She held out her hand. "Please sit."

I slid in opposite her.

"What brings you to our neck of the woods?"

"I heard this was a hot spot for breakfast," I said with a smile.

She frowned, looked up and down the aisle, and then looked back at me with an impish grin.

"You and I seem to be the only ones who know about it."

"We'll keep it our secret," I said. "The service will be great."

She nodded and sipped her coffee. The waitress came over with a pot and poured me a cup. She handed me a menu.

"Would you two like to order?"

"Give us another five minutes, Carmen. Thanks."

Carmen was short and plump and had a smile that made me forget about the street outside.

"You come here a lot," I said.

"Almost every day."

"Does it get busier?"

"Not much. But they do a better lunch business." Her eyes glazed over as she stared out the window. "This isn't a neighborhood where people eat out much… or at all. But it used to be. This place has been in Carmen's family for forty years. When they started, this was a different neighborhood. Now people can hardly afford their apartments. Several generations live in the same rooms."

I let that thought sit and then said, "I was actually hoping to see Sister Katherine."

She took another sip and said, "Me too."

"Do you know where she is?"

She shook her head. "She's hard to keep track of. She's here most days for breakfast, and we use this as our meeting time. But she's a bit like the wind. If she's not here, something came up with one of the kids or one of the families. If there's nothing critical, I'll see her here tomorrow. If there is, she'll stop by the church."

Carmen walked around the counter and back to our booth.

"Ready?"

"Sure," said Benny. "The usual please, Carmen."

"I'll have the Double Special, please, over easy." Two eggs, two strips of bacon and two pancakes.

"Toast?"

"Wheat, please." I handed her the menus.

"Coming right up."

I glanced at my watch. Eight fifteen.

She sipped her coffee. "What did you want to see Katie about?"

"I've been doing my best to get away from this drug case… and then Reynolds' murder." I started on my coffee. "But it keeps pulling me back in. I assume you heard about the senator's son being killed and Mrs. Margot being questioned about it."

"Of course… about all the news is talking about."

"I met with her and her lawyer yesterday, and she wants me to help, against the advice of her high-priced lawyer."

"Not fond of you is he?"

"To say the least."

She smiled. "I'm going to assume if you agreed to look into it, a part of you thinks she's innocent."

"Good assumption. But don't ask me how big that part is."

She looked past me as the door opened. It wasn't Katie. But the customers had doubled. They grew again a minute later when two policemen came in and waved to Benny.

"And how do you think Katie can help?"

I took a deep breath and shook my head. "I have no idea. But this is where it all started. And if I had stayed on the drug charge I would have been talking to Sister Katherine."

She nodded. "And you're figuring the two murders are related."

"Hard not to think that."

Carmen arrived with the food. I was hungry.

After a few bites of her omelette, Benny asked, "You going to talk to Bast?"

"I wanted to talk to Sister first, but as long as I'm here I might as well stop by. I'm also still trying to get an appointment with Thward."

She laughed. "Good luck. That's one arrogant son of a bitch."

"So I've heard, but I have a very persistent office manager. I'm hoping whoever answers the phone in his office will get tired of her."

"Probably will, but that doesn't mean Thward will care."

"How do I get ahold of Sister Katherine?"

"This is your best bet, if you can manage two days in a row."

I laughed. "Two days in a row of not having to eat my own cooking? I think I can manage."

We chatted about the weather and the Cubs, finished our coffee, and went to work. Outside the diner, the neighborhood had come to life, but it was far from bustling. The knife sharpener's cart was parked three buildings down from the diner. Hopefully he had found a customer. The boys were still there, and so was my Mustang. I nodded at them as I opened the door. Two of them nodded back.

***

A s long as I was in the neighborhood, I decided to have a chat with Bast. Traffic had picked up, but the short drive to the fourth precinct station only took ten minutes. I told the desk sergeant who I wanted to see, and he tilted his head toward the stairs. Bast wasn't at his desk, but a detective in the hall said he had gone to the head and would be right back. I sat on a wooden chair and thought about Reynolds while I waited. My thoughts meant nothing.

He came up on me from behind. "Manning, what brings you back to paradise?"

"I was in the neighborhood... thought I'd see if you had anything new."

"In the neighborhood? You lost?"

I laughed. "Met somebody for breakfast at Time to Eat. Thought I'd see if you had anything new on Reynolds."

He sat and shook his head. "Nope. Not going to either. The feds took everything from me after the senator's kid was killed and the gun was IDed. They're swarming on this like flies on a dumpster."

"So I heard."

He looked puzzled. "Why are you asking? I thought you quit."

"Yeah, I've been trying, but I'm back in. Mrs. Margot wants my help."

"Ah, I see."

"But her lawyer doesn't. He doesn't think much of me."

"And you so likable," he said. "If her lawyer comes from the same congressional district as her that's understandable."

"How much time you think they'll put in on Reynolds?"

"Well, none on the drug charge. Why pursue a case where the defendant is dead?"

I nodded. "How about his murder?"

He shrugged. "Not nearly as much as the senator's kid. Unless of course they overlap."

"And don't you think they do?"

He shrugged again. "Maybe... maybe not."

"Don't you want to know?"

There was a rap on the door.

"Detective, Mrs. Lazon and Michael are here."

"Thanks, Becky. Tell her I'll come and get her in a few minutes." He turned back to me with a sigh. "There's a lot I'd like to know." He thumbed through the pile of folders on his desk, pulled one out, and held it up. "Michael Lazon. Theft. He's one of Benny's kids. Part of the deal is he meets with me once a week. Mom insists on coming, and I've got no problem with that. There aren't many parents involved around here." He held up the rest of the pile. "Michael is one of the easy ones. The rest of these... well, there's just not enough time or personnel. So, sure I'd like to know, but I can't afford the luxury of looking into a crime that no longer means anything."

I sat forward in the chair and said, "I think it might mean something. That's what started all this. And then there's the murder."

"That the feds have taken over."

"Do you have any information on the drug case?" I asked.

"Just what you already know."

"No interviews?"

He shook his head. "Wasn't much time between that and the murder, and it was just another case on the pile."

It looked like Reynolds Margot would just be a folder in a drawer. "Okay, thanks. If you happen to run across anything would you let me know?"

"Of course." He got up, shook my hand, and walked me out to the bench in the hall where Michael and his mother were waiting.

"See you, Detective."

"Yup. Good luck, Manning."

\*\*\*

As I was pulling out of the parking lot, my car phone rang. I pulled into a spot and picked it up.

"Spencer, it's Carol."

"Yes, it is. How's Watson?"

"I'm fine, thanks for asking."

I laughed. "What's up?"

"The squeaky wheel finally got some grease. Agent Thward will give you fifteen minutes of his time at eleven this morning. Can you make it?"

"Sure. Nice job!"

"Do you need the address?"

"Nope. Federal building downtown, right?"

"Right."

"Thanks, kiddo. I'll stop for lunch on the way back."

"Okay. Good luck."

"Should be interesting. Adios."

As I was waiting to pull into traffic the phone rang again.

"Me again, Spencer."

"You miss me?"

"Like a dog misses fleas. You got another request for a meeting."

"I'm a popular guy. Who?"

"Larry Maggio would like to see you. He specified after lunch."

A squad car pulled up behind me. I waved him around.

"What would you like me to tell him? How long do you think your appointment with Thward will be?"

I laughed again. "Less than fifteen minutes. He's just seeing me to stop the wheel from squeaking."

"So what time?"

"He's not far from the federal building. Tell him one. I'll get lunch down there. I'll make it up to you."

"From the FBI to the Mafia. You run in strange circles."

"As long as I keep running, my dear."

"I'm looking forward to hearing about it."

"Lunch tomorrow. Thanks, Carol."

I pulled out of the lot and headed downtown.

# Chapter 16

As soon as I opened the door to Thward's office I picked up the smell of cigarette smoke. A middle-aged woman wearing a blue blouse looked up at me from behind a wooden desk with a typewriter on a side extension to her left. She wasn't smoking. The nameplate on the front of her desk identified her as Mrs. Mitchell. There was a couch on the wall to my left and cushioned chairs against the wall to my right. Three doors behind her led to offices, one of which had the window blinds closed. I was ten minutes early.

"Good morning," she said. "May I help you?"

I gave her my best smile. She deserved nothing less after answering all of Carol's calls. "Good morning. Spencer Manning. I have an appointment."

"Certainly, Mr. Manning. I'll let Agent Thward know you're here."

She pressed a button on the intercom. "Agent Thward, Mr. Manning is here."

There was a ten second pause.

"Mrs. Mitchell. The appointment is for eleven. Perhaps you should have one of your children teach you how to tell time."

She closed her eyes for a few seconds and took a deep breath. "I'm sorry, Mr. Manning, Agent Thward is busy at the moment. Please have a seat. He'll be with you in—"

"Ten minutes," I said with the same smile.

"Well, yes."

She gave me a look that thanked me for not saying more, but there was plenty more I wanted to say.

I watched the clock on the wall. At exactly eleven her intercom buzzed, and Thward told her she could show me in. She stood and opened the door for me. I winked at her as I walked by and found the source of the smoke. It hung in the air of his office. I didn't know if taking short, shallow breaths would help any, but that was my plan. I did have to admit that, his personality aside, he had created an atmosphere no one in their right mind would want to be in.

Thward's view from the eighth floor was nice, but not as nice as Maggio's. There were lots of buildings between him and the lake.

Thward didn't stand and didn't offer to shake hands. I sat in front of his desk. I thought I should at least introduce myself.

"I'm—"

"I know who you are. Aside from the fact that you have a persistent secretary, why am I giving you time?"

"Well, in the interest of finding out—"

"I also know *about* you, Manning. And I know you like to poke your nose in where it doesn't belong. Maybe that's all right with the Chicago police, but this is a federal agency, and we don't need whatever help you think you can be."

"Poking my nose in, as you so quaintly put it, has worked out rather well in the past in several cases."

He just stared at me and picked up the cigarette that was burning in an ashtray. "Why are you here?"

I shrugged and with a smile said, "Justice?"

He laughed. "That's a good one. Good luck with that. If you don't have a better answer, you know where the door is."

I did, and I was anxious to use it.

"I started working on the drug case against Reynolds Margot."

"Oh yes, I do remember you at the little soiree Mrs. Margot threw. Sweet-talked her into writing a big check, I'm guessing."

"Keep guessing. I heard you offered him a deal. What was it?"

"You'll have to ask her, if she's not in jail. Seems like the apple didn't fall far from the tree."

I ignored that. "She didn't seem to know."

He sat silently for about twenty seconds. While he was thinking I looked closely at his face. I didn't know why I hadn't noticed before. He was bigger than me... could probably do okay in a brawl unless it was with guys who knew their way around brawls. But his eyes were beady and intense... too small for his face... the kind you see on little creatures that have to be looking for bigger creatures that want to eat them.

He stopped thinking and said, "That case is closed, which leads me back to my original question. Why are you here?"

"Mrs. Margot has asked for my help with her current situation, and since this all started with a drug arrest, I thought finding more about that would be helpful."

"Did you now?" He put out the short stub of the cigarette and lit another. "Okay, I'll be helpful. I'll give you one question. Then your time is up."

"Did you find any reason why Reynolds Margot was on the west side of Chicago?"

"No. You can see yourself out."

"Do you have a guess why?"

"Did I not make myself clear?"

I was pretty sure we weren't going to have a friendly conversation, but it was worth a shot. And I still wanted to know about the deal he had offered to Reynolds. But somehow I got the feeling he wasn't going to tell me, so I didn't ask. I left.

And I was certainly glad to be getting out of there. As I closed his door, I took a deep breath. It was still far from clean air, but it was a great improvement.

Mrs. Mitchell looked at me with pity. "I apologize for Agent Thward, Mr. Manning. I'm sorry you had to endure that."

"Not nearly as sorry as I am for you, Mrs. Mitchell. I get to leave."

She looked sad and nodded. I nodded back. As I was reaching for the door her phone rang. I had one foot in the hall when I heard my name.

"It's for you, Mr. Manning... your secretary."

I took the phone. "Carol? Is everything all right?"

"Sure. Been calling your car phone."

"What's up?"

"Maggio's secretary called. He has to reschedule. Wants to know if you can make Monday same time."

"I can, but I'm not at his beck and call. Please call back and tell him I can't make it until Thursday. Have him schedule a time."

"My, you must have appointments that aren't on the schedule. How am I supposed to arrange your calendar if you keep me in the dark?"

"You done?"

"Yes. Are you coming back this afternoon?"

"Yes. About forty-five minutes, I'll pick up lunch."

"Sounds good. See you."

I thanked Mrs. Mitchell and headed out.

# Chapter 17

I got outside and took another deep breath. I'd never take those breaths for granted again. When I got to the car, I called Ben and got his message machine.

"Hey, Ben, Spencer. I'd like to pick your brain. I need information on a couple of people. If you're available, I'm buying McGoon's. If I don't hear from you I'll see you at seven."

\*\*\*

By six I hadn't heard from Ben, so I headed for McGoon's. I was a half hour early, so I spent it in the bar with a Guinness and conversation about nothing in particular with Jack. There was only one other person at the bar, and his glass was full. He was busily working with a pencil and a pad of paper. Jack had told me Mondays and Thursdays were the slowest days of the week. People were recovering from the weekend and getting ready for the next one. He was glad to see me... he could only polish the bar so many times.

After ten minutes, he reached under the bar and brought out three darts and set them in front of me.

"What's this?"

"New idea from the boss." He pointed to the board on the wall behind the bar. "Three tosses for a buck. Bull's-eye wins a free beer."

"What's the first ring win?"

"Nada."

"Wow. That's certainly leaning in the house's favor."

"Yup. The boss wasn't born yesterday."

"What happens to the dollars?"

"Boss splits with the barkeep."

"Not a bad deal. How long you been doing this?"

"Just started Monday."

"How many takers?"

"A lot."

"How many Bull's-eyes?"

"One."

I laughed and reached into my pocket. No cigar, but I did hit the board with all three.

Jack retrieved the darts. "You're zeroing in on it. You're bound to win this time. Reach back in your pocket and treat the little lady to a free beer."

I looked around and laughed. "When you're done being a side-show hustler, I'd like my barkeep back."

He smiled and said, "Gotta do something to make the hours go by on a night like this."

A couple walked in and sat at a table.

"Keep your wrist warm. I'll be back."

But before he got back, Ben arrived. I told him about the darts. He said he had better ways of throwing away money.

I swung off the stool, and Ben announced that, since I was buying, he had skipped lunch so he'd have room for the twenty ounce steak.

Nathan seated us in our usual booth in the back corner where we had a small measure of privacy.

We both ordered steak and a stuffed mushroom appetizer, and Jane returned in a few minutes with a Guinness for Ben and another for me. She hadn't asked if I wanted another.

"So, to what do I owe this largesse?" Ben asked after taking a long drink.

"I need to pick your brain about a couple of people." Ben had been in the state's attorney's office for eighteen years and had seen all there was to see. His sudden decision to retire a few years back at the age of forty-two had taken them by surprise. There was something that had prompted that decision. I had been working on a case to clear a Charles Lamb. Ben was the prosecutor for the state. I found proof that cleared Charles and was headed to the courtroom, but I got there too late. Charles had been found guilty, and as he was being escorted out of the courthouse, he threw himself through a fifth-floor window. Ben was devastated. He had told me life was too short, and he needed to start enjoying it and could afford to do so. But he had many friends still in the office, and there wasn't much he didn't know about. And after all those years he knew where all the bodies were buried and had a lot of favors he could call in. He had called in a few for me.

Jane arrived with the appetizer. As Ben cut into a mushroom, he said, "I assume this has to do with the Margot case that you're not working on."

I took a deep breath and a bite of mushroom. "Well, I've been trying to not work on it, but I haven't been very successful. Mrs. Margot keeps dragging me back in."

"Good-looking rich widow. No surprise there. How hard did she have to drag?"

"Pretty hard. All along the way this wasn't something she needed me for. They had the kid dead to rights on the drug charge."

"And were working on a plea deal."

I nodded. Ben did keep his finger in the pot. "Right. So it should have ended with an easy court appearance. No reason for the kid to die."

"No reason we know of. So if it was so easy why did she hire you?"

I slowly shook my head. "She needed a friend for moral support. She just wanted to know her son was getting a fair shake."

"And was he?"

"I don't know. I never found out what the deal was. The kid wasn't cooperative and neither was the lawyer. Do you know Malbry?"

He laughed. "Sure. The go-to man for the big money on the north shore. Fancy suits and cars."

"He certainly has more than his share of arrogance. In a very short meeting, he made it clear I was not needed."

"I'm surprised you even got to meet with him."

"I wouldn't have, but the money in Mrs. Margot's checkbook bought me twenty minutes. She insisted."

He smiled as best he could with the last of the mushrooms in his mouth and then said, "I would have loved to have sat in the corner for that."

"You go up against him in court?"

"Sure."

"Win?"

"Won a few, lost a few. Mostly it was settled before we walked in the room, and the appearance was just a formality. He was good at plea bargains. And with a system bogged down in red tape and a long backlog, we were pretty willing to agree to anything reasonable. Is it him you want to know about?"

"No, I don't care about him. I—"

Dinner arrived.

Ben cut into his steak, took a bite, and sighed. "I've been salivating about this moment all day. So who *do* you care about?"

"I've had several meetings with a Detective Bast on the west side and a rather strange meeting this morning with Agent Thward of the FBI."

Ben nodded as he chewed. After a drink he said, "I'd rather not know one of those."

"Not hard to figure which one."

"So what do you want to know?"

"What has your experience been? How were they at their jobs? What kind of men are they? Dedicated? By the book? Cut corners? Whatever you've got."

It really was a slow night. There were only two other couples in the dining area, and Nathan had kept them far away from us.

Ben's steak was about a third gone. I reached into my pocket and placed a ten-dollar bill next to his plate.

"What's that for?"

"Ten says you won't finish."

"The hell I won't! Especially now. I'm looking at a new set of clubs."

I laughed. He had no need for my ten-spot. He eyed the rest of the steak with a gleam in his eye and talked in between bites.

"Bast is as good as they get. By the book right down the line. He'd get along well with Stosh. I don't think I ever lost a case he was involved in. He's been offered promotions but thinks he can make a difference on the west side... and he does. It's still a mess, but it's a lot less messy because of him."

"And Thward?" I cut into my last two bites.

"Aside from one arrogant bastard, he gets his share of convictions. But they're all plea deals for guys pretty far down the ladder. He's never brought us anyone anywhere near the top of the food chain."

"Why do you think that is?"

"My guess? Nobody likes him. He pisses off everybody he works with... to the point where they'd rather not share information. Nobody asks for his help, and nobody helps him if they can get around it."

"Seems like that would make someone worthless. Why does he still have a job?"

"Been doing it a long time. Hard to get rid of government employees. He keeps his nose clean, and he does take people off the street."

"What about their lifestyles?"

"Don't know. There are very few cops I got involved with outside the courtroom. Why do you ask?"

Jane asked if she could take my plate and if I wanted another beer. I said she could and I didn't. She glanced at Ben and smiled. "Think he'll finish that?"

I smiled back and pointed. "There's ten dollars says he won't. You want in?"

She laughed. "No thanks. I like to hold onto my tips."

As she walked away, Ben asked, "So why do you ask?"

"Because I've got a lot of people involved in this and nothing pointing at any of them. And maybe Thward never gets any big fish because those fish keep him happy."

"Maybe."

"There are bad cops, you know."

"I know," he said. "And nothing worse than someone who's supposed to be a good guy turning up bad. But it's rare."

"Thankfully. But it's a heck of a temptation."

"Bast too?"

"You did tell me not to trust anyone."

"While that makes for a pretty depressing life, it's a good strategy until you get proof otherwise." He slowly took a large bite and showed signs of slowing down. "But you have the advantage of having some people you can trust."

"I do, and that keeps me going." We both knew he was on that list.

"What other suspects?" he asked. "Your client is a possible for the murder... good motive, and it was her gun."

"Yes, but not conclusive, and they haven't arrested her. But I'm looking at the drug arrest. That's where all this started. I think it's all tied together. If I can figure that out, the rest of the pieces will fall into place."

"You think she was involved with that?"

"I have no idea. And there's the senator's kid, and while we're at it, the senator."

Ben almost choked on his steak. "That's a pretty big net you've got."

"And Chief Sawyer in Kenilworth."

He actually stopped eating. "Spencer, I—"

I held up my hand. "I know. But I was invited to a meeting a few weeks ago that included Thward, her lawyer Malbry, and Chief Sawyer. It was more like a social event than a get-together about a kid with an arrest file. I'd be willing to bet more than ten bucks Mrs. Margot wrote a big check to Chief Sawyer's campaign fund."

"So he's on your list."

I nodded. "You know anything about him?"

He cut another piece. He was going to make it. "Nope. Nothing negative. He's your typical chief showing up at all the events and keeping as much swept under the rug as possible. No city is free of crime, but in Kenilworth you usually don't hear about it. Bad for reelection."

"Think Thward could be dirty?"

He shrugged as he chewed the last piece, pushed his plate away, and wiped his mouth. "Anybody could be dirty. It's always on the back burner."

"Well—"

He held up his hand. "Okay, almost anybody. Stosh and Rosie excepted. But you never know what effect circumstances will have on someone's life. Look at Stosh's medical bills with Francine's cancer. Dirty money could start looking pretty good."

I sighed. "Yeah, but not Stosh."

He raised his glass. "Not Stosh."

We both finished our beer.

"I don't want to see one of the good guys go bad, but if it was Thward I wouldn't be too upset."

Ben laughed. "You'd have to stand in line. Who else?" He stabbed the last piece of steak, put it in his mouth with his right hand, picked up the ten with his left, and thanked me while he chewed.

"Well, there's the kids' advocate, Benita, and the nun, Sister—"

"Whoa cowboy. Cross Benny off your list. A nun? Are you smoking something?"

"You're vouching for her?"

"We go way back. You got Stosh... I got Benny."

"Okay, I'll make her a very distant maybe."

"Whatever. Back to the nun. Sister Katherine, if I remember correctly. You suspect a nun?"

Jane asked if we wanted another beer. We declined, and I asked for the check.

"Works with Benny… mostly on the street. Supposedly knows everyone in the neighborhood."

"And that somehow makes her a suspect?"

"No. What makes her a suspect is that I don't know her, and she isn't Stosh. And she seems to just have appeared out of thin air and started helping."

He laughed. "Sounds more angelic than suspect."

"And there's Mrs. Margot. She switches characters like a great actress. I feel sorry for her, but I don't trust her. She knows more than she's saying."

"Maybe they all do."

"Yup. That's what makes this job so much fun."

Jane brought the check.

"So what's on your agenda?" Ben asked.

"I want to talk to Sister. She and Benny have breakfast almost every morning at a little diner on the west side not far from the church where Benny runs her program. I went this morning, but Sister didn't show. I'll try again tomorrow. And I'd like to talk to the priest at the church."

"You suspect him too?"

"No, but I'd like to see what he knows about Sister Katherine. I'd feel better about her if I knew the history. You don't just show up and start nunning."

"Nunning?"

"You got a better word?"

"Probably, but I like nunning."

I put four twenties on top of the check and said, "And then there's the senator."

"You don't trust politicians?"

"I'd rather deal with a thief than a politician. You can count on them to be exactly what they appear to be. How many politicians do you think are clean?"

Ben laughed. "They don't have to be clean. They just have to appear to be."

"Yeah, well, his son is dead and was involved with Reynolds. Who knows?"

He pushed back his chair and stood. "I'm pretty sure *you* will by the end of this."

"One can always hope."

"Thanks for the steak, Spence."

"My pleasure. Thanks for the chat."

"Let me know how things go."

"Will do."

# Chapter 18

**M**y favorite part of the day has always been just before dawn, sitting on the deck, listening to the birds, and watching the black night slip into the subtle colors of dawn. Friday was no different.

I made coffee and sat on the deck thinking about how something that started with a simple drug arrest had turned into two dead kids. I knew bad things could snowball when someone stepped off the path of legality, but there was something about this that I was missing. Those kids had walked into something that was much bigger than them. I just had to find out what that was.

Just past five thirty I noticed a bit of brightening, but the sky was cloudy, and it didn't get much brighter. It wasn't supposed to rain, but there was little hope for a sunny day.

\*\*\*

**I** parked right in front of Time To Eat a little before eight. I looked down the street and saw the same teens on the same stoop. Another day of waiting had begun. Benny and Sister Katherine were sitting at a table next to the windows. There were three other customers in the diner.

"Good morning, Benny… Sister Katherine."

"Good morning, Spencer," they said in unison.

There were three glasses of water on the table and a pot of coffee and three mugs.

As I was about to ask if they had ordered, Carmen arrived with a tray and breakfast, including the Double Special for me with wheat toast, the same as I had ordered yesterday. I gave them both my best skeptical look. Benny just smiled. Sister poured coffee.

As I took a cup from her I said, "I can't help wondering how my food arrived without me ordering, one minute after I got here."

Benny smiled some more, and Sister said, "The Lord works in mysterious ways." She passed a cup to Benny.

"So does Sister Katherine," Benny said.

"And how did you know I'd be here?" I asked. "I mean, I did say I'd come two days in a row, but something might have happened to change my plans."

"I knew," said Sister Katherine.

I nodded slowly, gave her my best skeptical look, and started in on my eggs.

We chatted about nothing important for a few minutes, and then Sister said, "Benny told me what you've been doing. I may have something for you."

"I could use something."

"Well, it's not much, but I have a man who says he saw someone in the alley the night Reynolds was killed."

I changed my look from skeptical to interested. "That's not something… that's a lot. Tell me."

"He says he saw a half-track in the alley. Two men lifted something out and carried it into the alley."

I stopped chewing. "Pardon? A half-track? Like an army half-track?"

Sister smiled. Benny had a bit of a smirk.

"Well, of course not, but… yes."

I finished chewing. "Care to explain?"

As we ate, she told me a sad story about a man named Rafael Melendez. But the only name he responded to was *Corporal* Melendez. Rafael had served in the army in World War II and fought in the Battle of the Bulge. He was a foot soldier, and his duty was as an overnight front-line lookout. He spent the night-time hours watching for German soldiers, for any movement or lights that might mean trouble was coming. And his last position was in a farmhouse. He was one of the lucky ones who made it home, but he didn't make it back in one piece. His mind was still in a farmhouse in France. That was how Rafael dealt with the horrors of war. Some escaped with alcohol, others with drugs. I had been lucky. I hadn't seen any horrors. I was stationed in Germany with the military police. The worst I saw was soldiers who had too much to drink.

Rafael now lived with his sister, Maria, in an apartment building across from the alley where Reynolds was found. Maria, with the help of a government stipend, took care of him.

I finished the last of my eggs and asked, "What was he doing up in the middle of the night?"

"He's still in that farmhouse, Spencer. He takes up his position at the window every night and watches… all night long. He goes to bed after breakfast and tells his sister the horizon is clear."

I just shook my head in amazement. "How sad. Was it a body they carried into the alley?"

She shook her head. "He didn't say."

"Did you ask him?"

Her reaction was odd. She scrunched up her face and said, "You don't really ask him things. He just tells you what he thinks is important."

"Did he say anything else about that night?"

Benny said, "One odd thing. He said he saw a tracer."

"A tracer."

"Yup."

Sister said, "I didn't know what he was talking about. Benny told me it is a round of ammunition with a chemical that burns and leaves a visible track of its path."

I nodded. "But that would require a round to have been fired. Were there any reports of gunshots?"

Benny replied. "I checked. There weren't. And there are nights when there are."

"Coulda used a silencer. I gotta tell you, Sister, I was pretty excited when you said you had a witness. But this guy isn't even *on* the credibility scale. Seems like a good chance he's making it all up."

"Except for the fact that a kid died in the alley that night."

"Yeah, except for that. But we don't even know if it was the same night."

"Yes, we do," Sister said.

"How?"

"Because Rafael keeps a log. His mind only does one thing, but it does that one thing very well."

"Did you ask what time it happened?"

"It's in his log. I don't remember the exact time, but I'm sure it's accurate… three something."

I asked if I could talk to him. She said I could, but I wouldn't get any more information. I said it couldn't hurt to try. And I wanted to meet Corporal Melendez.

I told them breakfast was my treat and offered to drive to the apartment building. It was about a mile away. Benny declined, saying she needed to open up the church basement. As we drove I asked Sister if he would be awake. She explained that he had a meal after the sun came up and spent time writing in his logbook. He slept from around ten until five or six while Maria worked. Our timing was perfect.

***

The stone apartment building had once been white. It was now the color of worn-in dirt. It could have used a good sandblasting, but it wasn't going to get one. It held memories of better days when the west side of Chicago offered something better. Rafael and Maria lived on the second of three floors. Sister Katherine led the way up stairs covered with worn carpet. The walls were gray stucco that had once probably been white. She stopped at the second door on the left from the top of the landing, a door with a cross hung in the center.

Sister's knock on the door was answered by a timid "Who's there?" Sister answered.

I heard a chain slide, and the door was opened by a thin, dark-haired woman who, despite being worn down by life, was obviously happy to see Sister Katherine. Subtracting a few years for what life had offered her, I guessed her to be in her sixties. She was equally happy to see me as she shook my hand and welcomed me into her home, offering no apology for its look of bare necessity. Rafael was sitting at a small, rickety table by the window, writing in a notebook. Next to the notebook was a pair of beat-up binoculars with one eye-piece missing. A pole lamp with a torn shade stood next to the table. The lamp was on. The northern exposure didn't let in much of the dull day.

It was a one-bedroom apartment with a kitchenette. Three bottles of pills stood next to the sink. Crocheted pillows on a worn couch, a few knickknacks on an end table that may have been handed down, and two pictures behind the couch added a touch of home to the dark room. One picture was of Jesus, and the other was of Maria and Rafael in his uniform standing next to a train. He looked happy and proud. Both of them had lost that look.

"We are sorry to bother you, Maria. I know you're getting ready for work. Mr. Manning is a private detective looking into the murder of the young man in the alley. I told him about what Rafael saw, and Mr. Manning would like to talk to him."

Maria looked sad and worried. "You can, but I'm afraid he doesn't talk much, Mr. Manning. He—"

"Please call me Spencer. Sister Katherine explained, and I fully realize the situation. I'm so sorry. I'd like to try."

She still looked worried.

"If he gets upset, I'll stop. I don't want to add to your troubles. I was in the army too. Maybe we can find something to talk about."

"Okay. Please pardon me. I need to get ready for work."

"Sure."

She walked to Rafael and kissed him on the forehead. He didn't react.

I walked over to him, stood on the opposite side of the table, and said in a firm voice, "Corporal, I'm Lieutenant Manning."

Before he even looked at me he was standing. He came to attention and held a salute.

I returned it and said, "As you were, Corporal. Be seated."

He sat and said, "I'm sorry, Lieutenant. I didn't hear you come in. It was a long night."

"I know it was, Corporal. Was there anything of concern?"

"No, sir. It was quiet."

"Good. Good job. I'd like to talk to you about what happened a few weeks ago, the night you saw the half-track and the tracer."

"Yes, sir. I have my log." He flipped through his notebook. "Here it is. What would you like to know? I did file a report."

I nodded. "I know. I read it. Very thorough. I just have a few questions."

"Yes, sir." He sat rigidly in the chair.

"You can relax, Corporal. You had a long night."

"Thank you, sir."

I glanced at his notes. "You wrote that you saw a half-track. Did it have any markings? A plate on the back or front?"

"None that I could make out. It was very dark. No moon that night. I'm sorry."

"No problem, Corporal. I understand."

Sister Katherine walked over to the window and looked out on the gray day. Even on a sunny day this room would still be dark. It faced north and never got any direct sunlight.

"There were two men?"

"Yes. And they lifted something out and carried it away from the vehicle."

"You couldn't see what it was?"

"No, sir."

"Your log says they got there at 3:10 and left at 3:25. Could you see what they were doing for fifteen minutes?"

"No, sir. I couldn't see them… the half-track was blocking."

I nodded. "You saw a tracer. Did you hear a shot?"

"No."

"Did anyone else hear a shot?"

"No one else was here, sir."

"I see. And when they left, which way did they go?"

"They went east."

"Did you go down to the ground?"

"No, sir! My orders are to observe only."

I nodded. "Yes, Corporal. Very good. And have you seen any-thing since then that was suspicious?"

"No, sir. Nothing other than a few locals out early before sunup."

"Okay, Corporal… thanks. Good work."

Rafael went back to his logbook as Maria came out of the bed-room. She had changed from a simple house dress to a yellow one with flowers and a white blouse. Instead of pulled back in a ponytail, her hair was just touching her shoulders. A bit of makeup had given her a healthier look.

"Do you have a minute, Maria?" I asked.

"I have a few, but I can't miss the bus."

"If you do, I'll drive you. Did Rafael say anything to you the night he saw the half-track and tracer?"

She shook her head, and her eyes welled up.

"No, he didn't. But you have to understand, Mr. Manning. He doesn't see things or hear things like the rest of us. He's in his own world most of the time. And that world is back in that farmhouse in France."

I nodded. "I understand. I'm so sorry."

She wiped her eyes with her fingers. "But he's happy. He doesn't have a care in the world. The only thing he cares about is standing his nightly duty."

Sister Katherine had walked to Maria and put an arm around her shoulder.

"Well, thanks for taking care of him, Maria. Just one more ques-tion. This happened a little after three. Do you recall hearing any-thing that could have been a gunshot?"

"No. After Sister Katherine told me what had happened I tried to remember. But there was nothing that woke me up."

"Okay… thanks, Maria." I handed her my card. "Call me if you think of anything."

She took it and nodded. "I have to go now."

"So do we," I said.

We all walked out together, and I thanked Maria for letting me talk to Rafael.

Maria walked to the corner as the bus was coming down the street.

Sister and I stood on the sidewalk at the bottom of the stairs.

"So, Spencer, did you get anything that helped?" she asked.

I sighed. "Not noticeably. But there are times when something that seems unimportant suddenly becomes meaningful. This job is mostly about digging and moving pieces around until they fit."

"Do they always fit?"

I laughed. "So far I've been lucky. But our friends in the police department have a lot of cases with missing pieces. What's on your agenda?"

"I have to go see Father Brown at the church. After that, back to doing what I do… just find where I'm needed."

"Would you like a lift? I'd like to chat for a few minutes if you have time."

"Sure. Thanks."

I held the door of my baby-blue Mustang and drove the ten blocks to the church.

# Chapter 19

I parked on the street and waited for Sister on a wooden bench in the fenced-in garden behind the church. The same man was asleep on the ledge at the side of the front stairs. A light breeze rustled tree leaves and made the spring day a little chilly. The bench sat on brick pavers and was surrounded by beds of multi-colored flowers. Mom would have loved it. Two maple trees would offer shade on a hot summer day. Twenty minutes later Sister joined me.

"That took a bit longer than I had thought. Sorry to keep you waiting, Spencer."

"No problem, Sister. This is a nice spot to spend some time. Who keeps up the flowers?"

"We call it the Ladies' Garden Club, but there are two men who help out too. I don't think they mind the name."

"My mother loved gardening. She would have liked this."

"Would have?"

I briefly told her the story of how I had lost my parents a few years back and my sister when we were kids.

"I'm so sorry, Spencer. That's so sad." She reached out and touched my arm.

"Thanks. But I had a lot of good years. They were great parents. That's one reason I find it so hard to understand families like the Margots who seem to have been so... I don't know how to describe it... disjointed? Unloving? They had everything, and yet they had nothing that mattered."

"That happens a lot, Spencer, especially when a lot of money is involved. The money becomes more important than the family."

"I guess."

We watched a robin fly in and land on a branch of the maple.

I continued. "Then I look at someone like Maria who gives her life to care for her brother and has so little. Yet there is a lot of love there. Do you know what her job is?"

"Yes, she's a secretary for one of the department stores downtown. They let her come in late so she can take care of Rafael."

"Who watches him during the day when she's gone?"

"No one." The bird flew off.

That seemed odd. "I would think he'd need twenty-four-hour care."

"That would be optimal. But there is no money for that. She has all she can do to pay the rent and buy his pills. And since he keeps watch all night he sleeps during the day while Maria is gone."

I wondered if the pills were worth it. "Isn't she afraid he'll wander out?"

"Not at all. He is very dedicated to his orders, which are to keep watch from that farmhouse. He wouldn't leave unless he was ordered to, and who is going to do that? And there are neighbors there during the day who know about the situation and are more than willing to help if need be."

We watched the breeze in the trees for a minute.

"Spencer, I don't see how anything Rafael said is going to help you."

I nodded. "Probably not, but he did see Reynolds being pulled out of a car and carried into the alley."

"Well, not quite. He saw a half-track. How do you think that'd stand up in court?"

"Not well, but I don't plan on seeing him in court." I turned to face her. "What we have to do is take his story and work backwards to reality."

She smiled. "Pardon?"

"His mind creates a new world, but it has its basis in our world. If a car hadn't pulled into that alley, he wouldn't have seen a half-track. He doesn't invent things... he just reworks them and makes them fit in the only world he knows."

"Makes some sense. How do you fit the tracer into your theory?"

A squirrel ran across the courtyard and disappeared into the bushes.

"He must have seen *something*."

"But it wasn't a bullet," she said.

"No, but he saw a flash of light. Maybe a match lighting a cigarette, or that match being tossed away."

"And he turned that into a tracer?"

I shrugged. "Why not?"

"Would a match have fingerprints on it?" she asked.

"No, but a cigarette butt might, along with saliva."

"Should we go back and look in the alley?"

I sighed. "If it was last night. But too much time has passed. And even if we found something, the police wouldn't waste time on it. I bet we'd find a handful of butts in that alley."

"So even if that's what he saw, it gets you nowhere."

I thought for a bit. "Maybe not."

She crossed her arms and asked, "What's that mean?"

"That means sometimes things have to roll around for a while before something useful pops out."

She laughed. "Thanks for clearing that up. I won't pretend I know what you're talking about."

I returned her laugh. "Don't worry. Most the time I don't either."

"Well, have faith that the Lord will provide."

I smiled. "You have more pull in that area than I. Sooner rather than later would be nice."

She laughed again. "That I have no control over."

I nodded and looked up at the gray sky.

"You look lost in thought," she said.

I took a deep breath and let out a sigh. "Just thinking about those two kids and drugs."

She raised her eyebrows. "It's a shame, but there are many others whose names never make the papers, Spencer."

I nodded again and shook my head. "I don't understand the drugs."

"What about it don't you understand? Why those kids got involved with it?"

"Lots, but no, that I can understand. It's all about money. Reynolds kept protesting that he didn't take the drugs. He wasn't a user. Somehow that made what he was doing okay. I get the money and power part of it. Crime I understand. What I can't understand is the addiction. I don't know what would make someone kill and steal to get that next score."

The squirrel ran back across the pavers.

"You're not addicted to anything?" she asked.

"Not *that* much. Nothing that I couldn't give up if I had to."

"Then you're a lucky man... far luckier than people who get hooked because of people like your Mr. Margot and the gangs. Most of them are hooked for life... or death."

"And that's what I don't understand. I know it happens, but I just can't imagine what it does to a person, how something can have that much of a hold on someone."

"I take it you've never tried drugs."

I laughed. "I don't even like taking aspirin."

She smiled that cherubic smile. "Do you drink?"

I turned and looked at her, knowing where that question was going.

"Not to the point of addiction. It's not a drug."

"I won't argue with you about that point. But there *are* people who are addicted who will do anything for that next drink. But it's worse with drugs. The first high is amazing. But after that it takes more to get that feeling back, and you never do, but you keep trying. And eventually it destroys you."

I agreed. "Yes, but alcohol doesn't seem as serious. It's not mind-altering."

She smiled again. "I won't argue that point either."

I returned her smile. "If you're not here for a good argument what are you here for?"

"Ah. That's something you'll have to figure out for yourself." The squirrel peeked out from under a bush. "If you do, let me know."

I sighed again. "I wish there was an easy answer."

The breeze picked up, and the squirrel disappeared.

"I don't have the answers, Spencer, but maybe I can help a bit."

I waited patiently and watched for the squirrel to reappear.

She sat up straight on the bench and took a deep breath. "There once was a teenage girl who was addicted to heroin. When asked why she did it, she answered that when she got high it was like touching the face of God."

I had been listening and looking at the bush. I turned slowly to her and opened my mouth, but no words came out. That was the most powerful statement I had ever heard. It needed no explanation, and I wondered about the girl.

"What happened to the girl?"

She cocked her head a bit to the right and said, "She found a better way of touching the face of God."

I was again speechless. I didn't have to ask. Her face was as peaceful as any I had ever seen, and her eyes were warm and welcoming. I had no doubt she brought that peace to the people in her neighborhood, and I considered taking her off my list. I had been fooled by a female's look before, but doubting her seemed sacrilegious. There was quiet power behind her look. She was convincing without any effort.

She raised her eyebrows and asked, "Does that help you, Spencer?"

"Not a lot. But the only drug stories I've heard have ended badly. Yours seems to have a happy ending."

"I don't know that you could call what I deal with every day happy, but I have found my place."

I wanted to ask what the path to that place had been, but realized it didn't matter.

There was a flash of lightning to the west but no thunder, and light raindrops foretold more to come. Neither of us made any effort to escape.

"You've heard nothing else on the street, Sister?"

"Not a thing, Spencer. These people keep to themselves. Surrounded by violence, a closed mouth is a survival mechanism. I'm sorry... I wish I could help."

"Maybe you have."

"How so?"

I laughed. "I have no idea. But I've found when I have nothing, if I start turning over stones people get nervous, and when people get nervous nothing turns into something."

Her look of peace changed to concern. "Be careful what stones you turn over. The gangs here don't get nervous... they strike and don't bother asking questions."

"I appreciate your concern. Are there other gangs besides the Prophets?"

"A few, and they cause more trouble."

"How so?"

"The Prophets are the big dog. The others are little dogs trying to look big. And they cause a lot of trouble trying... shootings, robberies. The Prophets are more a big business, and trouble is bad for business. They know where the line is."

"And you think a gang is behind this?"

She shrugged. "Who else?"

"A good question. If I find out I'll let you know." The rain picked up a bit. "Prophets?"

"That would be my guess. This seems to be about territory. And for the most part, the territory belongs to the Prophets." The squirrel ran across the stones again. "I need to get to work, Spencer. Thanks for breakfast."

"My pleasure, Sister. We may do it again."

She smiled. "I'll look forward to it. And if I hear anything I'll be in touch."

"Thanks."

She went in the side door as I walked out to the street. The homeless man was gone. I wondered where he went when it rained. I sat in the car for a minute before I turned the key. The sadness in this case kept adding up like pages in a book. Every time I turned one there was another. And it was getting me down. Then I thought of Sister Katherine, who dealt with this every day and looked at me with strength and peace. I wondered how she did it, but then realized she had been through worse... far worse. And she had survived. And the people in the neighborhood were better off for it.

***

The phone rang as I started the car. It was Carol.

"I've been calling every five minutes. Mrs. Margot wants to see you. She's quite upset."

I sighed. I still wasn't sure about Mrs. Margot, but I could imagine being upset after what she went through at the station.

"Thanks, I'll call her."

"And I have a suggestion."

"What?"

"Since you aren't carrying your portable phone around, start wearing your beeper again. I can beep you if there is something important, and you can call."

"Good idea. I'll get it when I get back."

"When will that be?"

"Sometime this afternoon. Depends on Mrs. Margot."

"Okay. I'll leave it on my desk if I'm gone."

"Thanks, Carol. See you sometime."

I flipped to Margot in my notebook and dialed. I wondered why she thought I was so valuable... all I had done for her so far was quit.

# Chapter 20

The maid let me in and showed me to the den. She said Mrs. Margot would be with me in a few minutes. I spent the time looking again at the wall of Mr. Margot's plaques and awards. In the middle of the wall, one caught my attention. It was next to Robert Margot's degree in Business Administration from Northwestern. It was a plaque naming him as president of Alpha Epsilon Pi fraternity in 1976. Northwestern is a big school, but I would think back-to-back presidents of the same fraternity would know each other. Bast had acted like the name Margot was just another name in a report.

I felt someone was watching me and slowly turned. There in the doorway was a small, white poodle. As I walked toward it, it turned and walked away.

I sensed more than heard Mrs. Margot come into the room.

"Hello, Spencer. Please have a seat."

She sat on the brown leather couch and held out her hand at her side. She looked worn and tired.

"How are you doing, Mrs. Margot?"

She slowly shook her head. "Jeanne... please." There was a pleading look in her eyes.

I nodded. "Jeanne. I'm sorry for what you're going through."

She cocked her head to the right. "Can I assume you wouldn't feel sorry if you thought I was guilty?"

I smiled. "I might feel sorry either way, but so far I'm on your side."

"Well that's a relief. Nice to know someone is. They told me not to leave town. Like a criminal! Why would I leave town?"

I thought of the way people who couldn't afford bond were treated in Cook county jail before getting a trial. And Mrs. Margot was complaining about being told not to leave town and suffering in her mansion on the lake. Maybe I didn't feel as sorry as I thought I had.

"Tell me again what happened."

"The police showed up at my door... two detectives. I don't remember their names. I thought it was about Reynolds, but he said he wanted to question me about Mark Nadem. He said he wanted me to come with him to the station... Chief Sawyer wanted to talk to me. I about collapsed. I called Malbry, but he wasn't in his office. His secretary said he was in court. I left a message about what was going on, and she said she'd get ahold of him. The detective said I could call again from the station."

"And when you got to the station?"

She took a deep breath. "I was treated like cattle. I was brought into a room and left with a female officer. I called Malbry again. His secretary said he was on the way to the station and not to say anything until he got there." Some of her worn and tired look was replaced with anger. Her hands balled into fists. "After all the money I've given Sawyer, this is how I'm treated."

When this was all over, if she wasn't guilty, I'd take her to county jail and show her how the other half is treated. If she was guilty she'd find out for herself.

The maid came in with a tray with coffee and biscuits.

"How do you like yours, Spencer?"

She had just assumed I wanted some. "Black, please." The maid poured. I thanked her.

Mrs. Margot took a sip of coffee and offered a biscuit. I declined.

The dog came in and sat in front of her.

"What happened when Malbry got there?" I asked.

"He looked angry. He said I didn't have to go with them, and he was sorry he wasn't available."

I nodded. "Is the poodle a new addition?"

She smiled. "Yes. My therapist said I needed some company to deal with the loss of..." Her eyes teared up. She waved her hand as an apology, and I told her it was okay. I knew what she was going through, except for the murder suspect part.

She wiped her eyes and asked, "Can you help me, Spencer?"

"I'll try. Tell me about the gun."

"It was in that wooden case on the credenza," she said as she pointed. "I would take it out and just look at it once in a while. One night I opened the case, and it was gone."

"Reynolds took it?"

"He must have. The only other person in the house was the maid." She was staring blindly out the windows. "There were nights he would be gone most of the night. I'd hear his car come in after three or four. I asked him where he went, but he gave me vague answers... out with the guys. I told him I wanted him home by a decent hour, and he'd just laugh. Told me I was old-fashioned. I never was able to tell him what to do. I shouldn't have let him..."

She started to sob. I put my hand on her shoulder and let her get it out.

"You only can do what you think is right. Probably nothing you would have done would have mattered." I didn't really believe that, but I thought it would make her feel better. She could do with less guilt.

"Did the gun show up?"

"Yes. When I got up in the morning the first thing I did was look. It was in the case."

"Had it been fired?"

She shook her head. "No. It didn't smell."

"Could he have shot it and cleaned it?"

"Cleaning anything would be beneath Reynolds."

I didn't doubt that. "Did you ask him about it?"

The poodle jumped up on her lap. She held it like it was her child. Maybe it was.

"I did. He said the guys were going shooting. But when I told him it hadn't been shot he said they changed their minds."

"When was that?"

"It was about a week before he was arrested."

"What happened to the gun?"

"I took it and told him not to take it again. He said he wouldn't." She was unconsciously petting the dog. "But the night that he was…" She started to cry.

"When we were at the police station you said you fought over the gun that night."

She nodded.

"So your prints were on it."

She nodded again and sniffed. "I should have gotten rid of it a long time ago. But I just can't get rid of anything of my husband's." She looked vacant and lost. She shook her head and looked up at me. "He might still be alive."

I assumed she was talking about Reynolds, but it was her gun that had killed Mark.

"It's easy to second guess," I said. "I don't think it would have mattered. Did you mention the gun to the police?"

"No. I couldn't imagine why they didn't have it. It wasn't in the case. Reynolds must have taken it, but it wasn't on the list of his possessions."

I could, and I didn't like where my imagination was going.

"So when did you next hear about the gun?"

"When the police took me to the station and my lawyer told me the police had the gun. It was used to kill Mark, and my prints were on it."

"And your prints were on it because you fought over it."

"Yes."

"And Reynolds' because he took it. But he certainly didn't kill Mark." There were few things certain in life, but one surely was that you can't kill someone if you're dead.

"No, he certainly didn't."

"So if Reynolds had the gun the night he was killed, what happened to it after that?"

She shrugged. I wasn't expecting an answer. But she gave me a dejected look and said, "Maybe you can find out."

"Maybe I can. The gun was registered to your husband, right?"

"Yes. I'd been meaning to change the paperwork, but I never got around to it."

The dog lifted its head and rearranged itself.

"Do you know Senator Nadem?"

"We donated sizable amounts to his campaign over the years, and we've been to the same parties."

"Have you talked to him since all this happened?"

She shook her head.

"Do you think he'd talk to me if I mention your name?"

"I have no idea, Spencer. I think he's blaming me."

"Maybe. One more question, Jeanne. The police were able to match your prints. Why are your prints on file?"

"When I got out of college I got a job with the Evanston police. I had a degree in psychology, specializing in stress, and they were starting a program of clinical help for officers involved in traumatic cases."

I had a feeling I knew where the degree was from, but I asked anyway. Northwestern.

"Okay, Jeanne. I'll be in touch." I stood up. "I'll let myself out."

She barely nodded.

I took two steps and then turned and asked, "Did you know Detective Bast before Reynolds was arrested?"

Her head jerked slightly toward me, and her eyes widened for a split second. After a deep breath she said, "Of course not. Why would you ask that?"

"No particular reason. Just wondering. Goodbye."

The maid appeared out of nowhere and showed me to the door. I asked what her name was. It was Maddy. I held out my hand and said, "Nice to meet you, Maddy."

She smiled. "You also, sir."

I smiled back. "Spencer."

She was still smiling. "Spencer, sir."

I was glad to get out of that house. As I pulled out of the long drive I thought about what Jeanne was dealing with. Her son had been arrested and then killed, and she was suspected in a murder. And there was something going on with Bast. Maybe that was none of my business. And maybe it was. I did know one thing for sure. I was looking forward to a Saturday gin game with Stosh.

# Chapter 21

I was up with the birds Saturday morning. The sky was clear, and the air was a bit humid. I watched the sky brighten and read the paper on the deck. The sports page offered the most hope. The year 1985 was forecast to be the Cubs' year. They had added players at key positions over the winter, had plugged the holes that made for the disaster of 1984, and were making plans for the first World Series on the north side since 1945, which they had lost.

A little after seven I made scrambled eggs, bacon, and toast and settled back in on the deck. Mom's perennials were making another yearly appearance. I wondered about the vagaries of life that had taken away my family and thought I needed to spend some time with Aunt Rose. That always helped.

\*\*\*

Our Saturday gin date didn't vary. The rut we were in was comfortable. I always felt at home when I turned onto Stosh's street lined with brick homes in a middle-class neighborhood of hard-working people. The yards and the houses were well-kept, and neighbors knew each other. The dreariness of Friday had given way to bright sunshine. When I showed up at a few minutes past twelve the table was set up in the living room with a deck of cards in the middle and the scorepad at one of the corners. A selection of deli meats and bread was laid out on the kitchen counter, and the Schlitz was in the fridge. I pulled out two slices of dark rye, loaded on corned beef, and covered that with Thousand Island dressing. We ate at the card table.

"So, kid, what's the status of the Margot case? You quit yet?" He laughed.

"Not yet, but I've thought about it."

"You should," he said with a mouthful of roast beef. "You're in the middle of a circus. Bunch of egos running around in clown outfits. Murder of a senator's kid… everybody wants credit for solving that one."

"I'm getting that impression."

"Bast has to deal with it… you don't."

"Might end up that way, but Mrs. Margot appears to be caught in the middle of this mess, and she has had enough on her plate. Her son was no prize, but he was her son."

He nodded and took a long drink from the bottle.

"So you think she's innocent?"

"Of murder… yes. But when I asked her if she knew Bast before Reynolds was arrested she reacted with a shock before saying she didn't and asking why I asked."

"Why *did* you ask?"

I told him about the fraternity plaques.

"Could have just been a guy thing. Lots they don't share with their wives."

"And maybe things get shared that the husbands don't know about."

"Hanky-panky?" he asked with sarcastic disbelief.

I started on the second half of my sandwich. "I know, hard to believe *that* could happen. But there was something that startled her. Sure like to know what it is."

"Why were her prints on file?"

"She's got a degree in psychology, something to do with stress, and got a job working for the Evanston police with officers who had been in stressful situations."

"Yeah, I remember something about that." He took another drink. "Pretty ironic given all the stress in her life."

I agreed and ate the last of my sandwich. "I'm gonna make another sandwich. You want anything?"

He tipped up his bottle, finished it, and handed it to me as he said, "It's a lot easier to solve other people's problems."

I took the bottle and my plate and headed for the kitchen.

When I got back he had turned on the TV. Spring training on WGN.

"What do you know about the gun?" he asked.

"The kid was making trips to the west side to sell drugs. He probably took the gun with him... for protection is my guess."

"Probably made him feel like a big shot, but firing it is something else altogether."

"Yeah. Who knows? Another guess is whoever killed him took the gun."

"A good guess. Now all you have to do is find whoever."

"That's all." I took the cards out of the box. "The gun is used to kill Nadem, and the only prints on it are Reynolds' and Jeanne's. She—"

"Jeanne?" he said with a smile.

"She's asked me several times to call her Jeanne. I'm getting used to it."

"How much?"

I just glared at him. "Kenilworth brought her in for questioning because her prints were on the gun. She wasn't too happy—"

"She agreed to that?"

I started shuffling and told him how it had happened.

"Lawyer?" he asked.

"Called him, but he wasn't in. He read the riot act when he got to the station."

"Not fond of lawyers, but that wasn't by the book on the part of Kenilworth. Whatever she said will be disallowed if it comes to that."

"She didn't say anything, but not a gold star for the police. I wonder why they bent that procedure."

He took the last bite of his sandwich and washed it down. "Pressure. They're getting squeezed from all sides to solve the murder."

"Murders."

He sighed. "Yeah, well, only one matters to the people running the circus."

I shook my head. "So they pull in a woman who just lost her son based on prints that have every reason to be on that gun?"

"They're grasping at straws. Now they can say they did something. And at the moment it's more than everyone else is doing."

"You don't think they're doing anything?"

He laughed. "Oh, they're doing plenty. They just don't have anything."

"How do you know?"

He laughed again. "I guarantee you, when they have something it'll be all over the news."

I agreed.

"Got a plan?" he asked.

"Need to start shaking some trees."

"Which ones?"

"No idea. I'm hoping for some guidance from above."

"Pardon?"

"Sister Katherine says the Lord will provide."

He smiled. "He just might, but sometimes the Lord needs a bit of help."

"While I'm waiting I'll have a chat with the senator."

He laughed again... harder. "Oh you will, will you?"

"Doesn't hurt to try."

"Feds and a senator... let me know how all that goes."

"I'm gonna open some doors and see who walks in."

"Said the spider to the fly. Now deal, before you shuffle the spots off the cards."

***

**T**he Cubs beat the Mets, and I won three bucks from Stosh. I went to bed early with Chandler's *The Big Sleep* and tried to think of a way to bluff my way into a meeting with a senator. Two hours later I closed the book and hoped a plan would come to me in a vision.

# Chapter 22

I got to the office Monday morning a little after ten. Carol had pulled out my beeper and set it on my desk along with a note saying she'd be back around ten thirty... something at Billy's school. Watson opened one eye and looked at me to make sure I belonged there and went back to sleep. I added some notes to the Margot file for Carol to type and heard the front door being unlocked a little after eleven.

"That you, my girl Friday?"

"Someone else have a key?" She walked into my office and sat on one of the wooden armchairs.

"Nope. What was going on at school?"

"A play about George Washington. Billy was a tree... a talking tree that gave advice to George."

I laughed. "Didn't read about that in the history books. How'd he do?"

"The audience loved him."

"He'll be a star someday. Thanks for the beeper."

"Sure. If I don't reach you on the phone I'll send a message. Anything new on Margot?"

"Nope, unless you count a lot of negative vibes from Bast and Stosh. The general consensus is I won't get much cooperation from the feds or the senator."

"I wouldn't think so. How are you going to stir *this* pot?"

Watson wandered in and lay down next to Carol. Man's best friend.

"Been trying to think of a way to talk to Senator Nadem."

"I could try the same tactic I used on Thward… just keep calling for an appointment."

I laughed. "I have a feeling his secretary wall is stronger than Thward's. But wouldn't hurt to try calling. He has an office in Glencoe. Would you see if you can work your magic?"

"Sure." Watson followed her out without as much as a glance back at me.

I was working on the notes when she came back in.

"A very pleasant and proper Miss O'Keefe informed me that the senator was not taking appointments because of a family tragedy. But he reads all of his mail, and I was welcome to put my concerns in a letter."

"Sure he does, and pigs can fly." I sighed. "Thanks for trying."

"But she did share some information about his schedule. He's attending a ceremony tomorrow for the dedication of the Am Shalom Temple in Glencoe."

"Hmmm. I read about that in the paper this morning. I've driven by… it's a beautiful building on the lakefront."

"I hear wheels turning."

"Slowly. Thanks, Carol. I'll have these notes ready for you in a few minutes."

"Do you want me to try calling again?"

"No, I think I'll take a drive up there and see if I can work my charm in person."

"Which version of your charm are you planning on using?"

I laughed. "I'll play it by ear."

She gave me a sly smile. "Maybe you should take Watson with you."

"You think he'd come?"

"Only if there's food involved."

"One of these days I'll have to have a chat with him about who *buys* that food."

"You do that. When are you going?"

"No time like the present."

"Good luck. Call if you need anything… like a lawyer or a bail bond."

"Or a new office manager."

She waved on her way out of my office.

\*\*\*

Traffic was light, and it only took a half hour to get to Glencoe. Nadem's office was on a corner lot on the edge of the downtown area. It was a two-story, stone building with his name prominently displayed on the large glass windows. A red Maserati was parked right in front. He was in. I parked two spots away and walked in. The only person in the outer office was a nicely dressed woman who looked to be about thirty, seated behind a large white desk. She was on the phone with a headset, working hard at earning a living. Three nails on her left hand had already been done. They were a light shade of blue to match her sweater and the sapphire collar pin on her white blouse. I stood by the door and watched and listened. She was very politely telling someone about how busy the senator was and that they should write a letter. When she disconnected I walked slowly to her desk. She kept working on her nails.

With a rehearsed smile she said, "Good morning… how can I help you?" She struck me as the kind who'd dot her i's with little hearts.

I smiled back. Mine was rehearsed too. "Good morning. I'd like to see the senator."

She gave me a look that mothers sadly give to children who aren't going to be able to go to the circus and then went back to her nails. Two left. "I'm afraid Senator Nadem isn't in."

"His car says he's in."

She didn't hesitate for a second. "The senator is often driven to an engagement."

"When will he back?"

"He has a full schedule today. Perhaps not until this evening."

There was a hallway behind her, and I could see three closed doors. There was a muffled voice coming from behind one of those doors.

"Seems like someone is back there," I said, nodding to the hallway.

She wasn't flustered a bit. "Several people are on the senator's staff, but I don't see where that's any of your business, Mister..."

"Manning, Spencer."

"And what is it you want, Mr. Manning?"

"It's personal."

"Well, if you would like to send a letter requesting an appointment and stating your personal issue, we will review your request." All of that without looking up once from her hands.

I glanced at the nameplate on her desk and the ring on her finger.

"Thank you, Mrs. Stadler. I may do that." I smiled... she didn't. I said goodbye and wished her a nice day. She just nodded. I made her day nicer already... I left, but I didn't go far.

I wanted to see who the voice belonged to, so I sat in my Mustang, rolled the window down, and figured whoever it was would be going out for lunch. It was another hour until noon, and I had nothing else to do.

***

The hour went by slowly. No one had come or gone. I was getting hungry and decided I'd give it until twelve thirty. At ten after, the door opened, and Senator Nadem walked out, alone. I was surprised he had no security. I got out of my car and caught him just as he was opening his door.

"Good afternoon, Senator," I said with a smile.

He smiled back... that typical greet-a-voter smile. One hand was still on his door handle.

"My name is Spencer Manning. I'm a private investigator working for Mrs. Margot, and I'm wondering if I can have a few minutes of your time."

The smile disappeared, and he let go of the door. "I'm just heading to a meeting, but I'm sure I have nothing to tell you, Mr. Manning."

He didn't ask who Mrs. Margot was.

"You never know. And I may be able to help you."

"And how do you figure that?"

"I'm sorry about your son. I think it's possible that his death and that of Reynolds Margot are related."

He banged his hip into the car door and slammed it shut. "And accosting me in the street and adding to what me and my family are going through is your way of showing how sorry you are?"

"I do apologize, Senator. But I did try to call, and I was in your office an hour ago and was told you weren't in."

"You have a lot of nerve, Manning. What is it you're trying to do?"

"Find the truth."

"Perhaps you haven't read the papers, but there is an army of federal agents and police looking for the same thing."

"Maybe they're not looking in the right places."

His face was turning red. He gave me a hard stare and said, "I'd be careful if I were you. You might be sorry you stuck your nose in where it doesn't belong."

I smiled. "Oh, I'm sorry already."

"Sorry for what?"

"For voting for you. That sounds like a threat."

He slowly shook his head. "Not a threat... just advice. Advice a wise man would follow."

"Great. I'll see if I can find a wise man to follow it."

"You're going to walk away right now or I'm calling the police. You won't know what hit you. Don't be stupid."

"Never been big on innuendo, Senator. If by stupid you mean not following your orders, that's never worked out well with me."

"Well maybe you should learn."

I shrugged. "Old dog, new tricks, Senator."

I was done being a smartass... I walked away. He pulled out before me, squealing his tires as he drove off.

I sat in the car for a few minutes wondering where that got me and decided it hadn't gotten me anywhere for the moment. But that tree had been shaken, and in the past things happened when I shook the trees.

I started the car and picked up my phone and dialed Ben. He answered on the third ring.

"Just caught me, Spencer. Lunch and a round of golf. I've only got a minute. What's up?"

I asked if he wanted to join me for a temple dedication. He was thrilled, as long as it included lunch on me. It was a good thing he'd work for food… I couldn't afford his rates. I told him about my problem of getting some time with the senator, and he asked what I had up my sleeve. I had no idea. He said he might have an idea, but it might cost me another lunch.

"What do you have in mind?"

"Politics is a dirty game. If there's dirt on somebody, somebody else is usually going to find it. And where money and power are involved there's a lot of dirt. Money changes hands, and the dirt is swept under the rug."

"So?"

"So, after eighteen years in the state's attorney's office I know where a lot of those rugs are."

"Are you telling me you've got something on the senator?"

"I'm not telling anything, but I'll make some calls."

I thanked him and wished him a good game. He laughed and said a good game was when he came home with all his clubs.

# Chapter 23

Tuesday was a beautiful sunny day. Not a cloud in the sky... a perfect spring day. The ceremony was scheduled for ten. I picked up Ben at nine, and we took the Edens Expressway north to Lake Street.

"You ever wonder why the Edens doesn't have any billboards?" I asked.

"Nope."

I pulled around a semi. The Mustang easily pulled away from the truck.

"You never noticed?"

"Nope. But now that I've noticed, it seems odd."

"Not odd if you know why," I said.

"And you know why?"

"I do."

"You going to tell me?"

"If you ask." I pretended to concentrate on driving so he wouldn't see how much fun I was having playing with him.

"Jesus. Okay. Why?"

"Because there's a law against it," I said, glancing at him.

His jaw dropped, and his eyes widened. "A law against it? Okay, cut the clowning. What's the real reason?"

I nodded. "That *is* the real reason. The Garden Club of America was on a campaign to beautify our highways back in the early seventies. That led to the Highway Advertising Control Act in 1971.

Most of the Edens runs through residential areas or forest preserves where billboards aren't allowed. But even in the commercial areas there are local laws against them."

"That's amazing. You're pretty smart."

I laughed. "It has nothing to do with smart. It has to do with only talking about things I know."

"A rare quality."

"Here's a bit more. It was named after William Edens, a banker who was an early advocate of paved roads. He sponsored the first highway bond issue in Illinois in 1918."

"A treasure trove of information."

I turned off the Edens onto Lake Street and headed over to Sheridan Road to take the leisurely drive through the richest congressional district in the country. We gawked at the mansions with tennis courts and gatehouses bigger than my house. The cheap houses were on the west side of the road. The real money had beachfront and a view of the lake.

"So did you make your calls?" I asked.

"Yup. One paid off."

I pointed at a huge glass structure that looked more like an office building and shook my head. "Which one?"

"The one that's meeting us for lunch. Her name is Halley Rundel. Seems she and the senator had an affair five years ago that lasted a couple of years."

I sighed. "That's become the norm, especially up there in money land. How's that going to help me?"

"There's a bit more to it."

"Did his wife find out?"

"Yes. But they kissed and made up."

"Okay. Back to how's that going to help."

"He evidently got Halley hooked on heroin."

"Nice. But the stories of drug addicts don't usually hold up too well."

"She went into rehab and is off the stuff."

"Good, but—"

"But the story continues."

"Did he pay for the rehab?"

"He did, for a while."

"Fine upstanding citizen. A while?"

"After a few months the senator told her he couldn't keep paying for the rehab. Evidently the missus found out about it and had a fit."

"Imagine that," I said. "Don't blame her. But I wonder why he listened to her."

"Well, here's why. I looked into our dear senator. He married money. He makes a good living, but not enough to support that lifestyle. The house, the cars, the trust funds... all hers. Her daddy was in the steel business."

"Ah, nice way to make a living. Good old Daddy. End result is Halley is left with some bills."

"And she isn't happy about it."

"Nope. And she's willing to talk to you. But perhaps we won't need that."

"How so?"

"I'm thinking just mentioning her name might make the senator more cooperative," Ben said.

"Or more angry. Our last meeting didn't end well. Where are we meeting her?"

"I wasn't sure how long this would go, so I told her twelve thirty. There's a diner called The Hideaway a little north of here on 41. Looks like a dump, but they've got great burgers."

"How did you find that?"

"I get around."

"You do, but not usually to places that look like dumps."

I turned off of Sheridan onto South Street and headed west a few blocks to Green Bay Road where I turned right. After a few more blocks I turned onto Lincoln, made a right on Vernon and in less than a block turned into the entrance to Temple Am Shalom. I pulled into the first spot off the street. The lot was about half full. We left the windows down and walked toward the chairs set up in ten rows in front of the temple. In front of the large glass doors was a platform with a podium and five chairs. Senator Nadem was second from the left. Two very stern looking men in black suits stood on either side of the platform. I had a feeling I wouldn't get too close to the senator.

A man whom I assumed was the rabbi was speaking. I didn't recognize any of the others. We sat in the last row as the rabbi thanked everyone for coming and introduced the guests. Aside from the senator, there were the mayor of Glencoe and two officials of the temple. He said he'd keep his comments short, and Ben rolled his eyes. He'd heard that promise before. But, with only a few comments about the wonderful opportunity for worship, the rabbi did just that. He was overjoyed to dedicate the new Temple Am Shalom, the new home of the first Hebrew congregation on the north side of Chicago, founded in 1867. He then introduced Senator Nadem.

The senator was dressed in a gray suit with a light-blue tie that fit him perfectly and looked expensive. His tie was probably worth more than my two suits. In his job it was all about image. But I smiled as I thought he came in second place in the fashion show to Larry Maggio, my friendly crime boss, whom I had never seen in anything but a three-piece suit. There was a pecking order, and Maggio was on top.

Nadem smiled wide at the crowd... with a lot of perfect teeth but completely devoid of warmth and feeling. They were taught that in Politics 101. A lot of wavy brown hair, not one hair out of place. His teeth couldn't have been any whiter. I waited for them to glisten in the sun, but they let me down. I watched the crowd more than listened, but his main theme was religious freedom and the diversity of faiths in his district. The spin was that he was somehow taking credit for that. As he spoke he scanned the crowd. I was sure the scan found me. I lost interest in what he was saying and looked at the temple.

The white building sparkled in the morning sun, but it didn't look like any temple or church I had ever seen. The sides looked like the bows of boats standing on end side by side. Each bow was a window with the peak at the top. The roof sections matched the boats and reminded me of a nun's coronet except that instead of the wings sweeping out to the sides the sweep was up to the middle, perhaps reaching toward heaven. A light breeze off the lake gently rustled the leaves and made sitting in the sun comfortable.

When everyone had given a speech, the rabbi again thanked everyone for coming, welcomed all faiths to services, and invited everyone to stay for refreshments inside the temple where there would be a receiving line.

"We staying?" Ben asked.

"Yeah. I'd like to hit the receiving line."

"You planning on saying something to Nadem?"

"I'll play it by ear, but probably not. I just want to remind him that I'm not going away. Maybe something will fall out of that tree if I keep shaking it."

"And maybe you'll end up on the wrong side of the bars."

I smiled. "That's what friends are for."

"Ah, I knew there was a reason you kept buying me food. But if I'm in the middle of a good round you're going to have to wait."

I laughed. "You coming?"

"Sure. Don't want to miss any fireworks."

The ceremony had only lasted forty-five minutes, so we had plenty of time. We waited for the line to form and stood at the end. I figured that was my best chance to say something if I had the chance.

The senator was smiling at a voter when he noticed me. The look of anger on his face made me feel honored that he remembered me. When I got up to him, I smiled and said, "Holly Rundel sends her regards."

He was standing next to the rabbi, so he couldn't tactfully say what he probably wanted to. But I had a good guess what it would have been. The two black suits were a yard behind him. I smiled and said something to them about it being a nice day for a dedication. They didn't smile back, and they didn't say a word. But they stepped up, almost touching his shoulders.

I smiled some more. "It's all right boys... I don't bite."

I moved on and had a few nice words with the rabbi. We didn't stay for the refreshments.

"Well that wasn't as fun as it could have been," Ben said as we walked to the car.

"But it was productive."

"How so?"

"You saw the look on his face. I got under his skin. And he knows I know something he'd rather not have known. Now he'll be wondering where I'll show up next. And I got to play with a couple Secret Service goons."

"Where will you show up next?"

I shrugged and got in the car. "No clue. I'm playing all this by ear."

"I'll stick with golf. I may be a bit aberrant, but at least I know where the path is."

We were the first ones out of the parking lot. As I turned back onto Lincoln, Ben said, "Since we have some time, you wanna take a look at a Frank Lloyd Wright house?"

"Sure. Where?"

"It's almost due east of here on Sheridan. So go back to where we turned off and head north. We're looking for 850, but it should be pretty obvious."

It was. Sitting on a rise next to a ravine on the west side of Sheridan was one of Wright's prairie style homes. A lot of glass gave a nice view of Lake Michigan. The single-story home was sided in brown board and batten that fit in with the trees and shrubbery on a good-sized lot. I pulled onto the shoulder across the street.

"That's what I'd expect from Wright," I said. "Very picturesque and typical."

"Yup. Pretty similar to his houses in Oak Park. But the outside covers up a lot of problems."

"Such as?"

"He designed for style and to fit into the environment. Function took a back seat. Such as his homes are known for leaky roofs. Whoever buys one does a lot of remodeling on the inside."

"I'll stick with my humble abode," I said.

"Me too, but it would be fun to spend a weekend. Can't beat the view."

"I'm good with taking a tour. And did someone mention cheeseburgers?"

As I pulled into the drive and turned around, Ben asked if I knew who invented Lincoln Logs.

"Lincoln?"

"Uh, no. Frank's son John."

"Really?"

"Really. They worked together and were working on the Imperial Hotel in Tokyo when an argument over salary ended with father firing son. John needed something else to do and started making wooden toy buildings. He used the interlocking timber design his father used to earthquake-proof the hotel and thought the toy cabin looked like the childhood home of Abraham Lincoln."

"How much of that did you make up?"

"Not a bit. Don't be so cynical."

I laughed. "Thanks for the history lesson."

***

D espite the detour, we got to The Hideaway a little before noon and got a booth. From the outside it bordered on seedy. But there were eight Harleys parked in front. Guys who rode Harleys knew where the good burgers were. The inside décor was that of a typical diner with a guy with big shoulders in a T-shirt behind the counter with arms that looked like they could lift a horse. Ben pointed to him, and he returned a two-fingered salute and waved us to a booth. A waitress who appeared to be in her seventies, with tattoos on both arms, brought menus. She wasn't exactly typical. Neither was the lack of cigarette smoke. We told her we were waiting for someone and ordered beer. There wasn't much of a selection... Pabst, Miller, and Hamms. Stosh wouldn't have been happy. We both ordered PBR.

I mentioned the smoke and the salute.

"He owns the joint. His wife died of lung cancer a couple years ago. He thinks it's related and did something about it. He has a T-shirt that says 'The surgeon general is an idiot.'"

"Pretty forward thinking for a biker diner. I'm surprised he didn't worry about losing customers."

"He didn't have to. Every biker that comes in here was at her funeral."

"And how would you know that?"

"I was there too. There was a little problem with drugs a few years ago. He and the state came to an agreement that included his help with something only he was qualified to help with, and we developed a friendship of sorts."

"And I'm guessing the qualified help wasn't exactly by the book."

"Depends on whose book."

At twenty after, Halley walked in. I knew it was her. She didn't have any tattoos.

# Chapter 24

**W**hat she did have was a look of late twenties innocence—long hair that was a lot more blonde than God had ever intended, very blue eyes that also argued with God's plan, and hardly any makeup. Her skin was puzzling… she was almost white, which didn't fit with the hair and eyes. I would have figured her for a tanning booth.

I stood up and waved, and she walked over and slid in next to Ben. All of her motions were choppy. He gave me a smug look and then made introductions. The waitress showed up a minute later and asked Halley what she wanted to drink. When she asked for tea the waitress just stared at her. She switched to water. With a look of disbelief at me, the waitress walked away shaking her head.

"Not a tea type of place," I said.

She laughed nervously. We talked about the weather until the waitress brought the water and took orders for three cheeseburgers.

"Ben told me some of your story, Miss Rundel. Why don't you tell me about you and the senator. How did you meet?" I figured that was a good ice breaker, but I already knew. The same way almost everyone meets… proximity. Same place at the same time, and one thing leads to another. Late night at the campaign office. But I wondered what they had in common. Proximity isn't much of a basis for a long-term relationship.

She started talking… and tapping her nicely manicured nails softly on the Formica tabletop.

"I was helping with his campaign six years ago, just out of college. I thought he was the best, out to save the world and so energetic. Everyone loved him." She took a few sips. "I guess I did too... after a while."

I gave her some space, and she stared at her glass and touched the left corner of her mouth with her tongue. Then she took a deep breath.

"We ended up working late one night, and everyone else had left. He asked if I wanted a drink, and I didn't want to refuse him, so I said yes. He offered Scotch or wine. I took the wine, and I guess I had too much. But we were working, and I just lost track as he kept refilling my glass. One thing led to another, and..."

I gave her a few seconds while she thought about the "and."

"How long did it last?"

She shrugged. "A little more than a year."

The burgers arrived. I figured she wasn't too hungry. I wasn't too hungry myself. Ben asked me to pass the ketchup.

"Was it supposed to last forever?" I asked.

She nodded. "He said he was leaving his wife."

"But there were problems," I said. "There was the son, and the house, and the things he had to work out for the divorce."

She just stared at her food. I wasn't telling her anything new.

Ben slid the ketchup back, and I added some to my plate for the fries. I offered it to Halley, and she shook her head.

I smiled at her and said, "I hear the burgers here are special. A girl's gotta eat."

I got a little smile, and she said, "Maybe I will have the ketchup."

I passed it.

I knew the story. It hadn't changed since the beginning of time. But she needed to tell it. And I figured if she told it maybe there'd be something I could use. But at the moment I wasn't sure what I'd use it for, whatever it turned out to be.

I took a bite and after a few chews asked, "Then what?"

"After a few months of hearing about his problems, I told him we needed to break it off. He said he loved me, and he just needed a little more time. When I refused he said I needed something to calm me down… make me think better, he said."

"What was that?"

"Marijuana. He said it would help me realize what I really wanted." She took a bite. "I told him I didn't do drugs. He said it wasn't a drug."

"So you did?"

She put the burger down as her eyes filled with tears. "I couldn't say no to him. I wanted to believe he was going to leave his wife." She sat up straight, took a deep breath, and dried her eyes with the napkin.

I let her be. Ben kept eating, looking like he wasn't interested in the conversation. But I knew he'd be able to repeat every word later.

She took another bite and chewed slowly.

"The only problem was there was something besides marijuana in the marijuana. He grew elephant ears, and I felt like my words weren't coming out of my mouth. I was afraid, but he told me it would be all right. He said that as he was unbuttoning my blouse." She looked up at me. "When I met him that night I had planned on breaking it off, but I couldn't control what was happening. I wasn't a part of it. It was just happening."

"Where did you two meet up, Halley?" Ben asked.

"He has an apartment a few blocks down from his office. He uses it for out-of-town guests, and…"

There was the *and* again.

Ben was done eating. I was getting there. Halley was nibbling. He gestured at the waitress, and she brought two more beers and refilled Halley's water.

"Did you do the marijuana again?" I asked.

She looked lost. "Yes. He… I knew it was wrong, but he… I just couldn't say no."

"It's okay, Halley. What happened?"

She looked down. "I got hooked… on heroin." She pushed some fries around with her fork. "It got so bad. I was arrested one night in Winnetka. I don't know how I got there. I was supposed to meet him at the apartment, but he didn't come. I started without him and then left. I ended up in Winnetka with some heroin in my purse."

Her eyes welled up again. "I was so stupid."

"He took advantage of you. It wasn't your fault."

She looked forlorn. "That's nice of you to say, but sure it was. I should never have started any of that."

"So what happened with the arrest?"

"I called his office the next morning. He bailed me out. I told him I had enough and that I was going to rehab and that he was paying for it... or else I'd tell everything to the cops."

Ben looked at me, and I knew he was thinking she was lucky to be alive.

"Looks like rehab worked," I said.

"It did. I'm trying to get on with my life."

"But what went wrong?"

"His wife found out. Somehow she saw the checks to the center. She told him she wasn't financing a drug addict. I'm sure she didn't know the whole story."

"I'm not so sure. Did you consider going to the police?"

"A friend told me I should, so I went to his office and told him I would do that if he didn't pay."

"What did he say?"

"He told me if I ever came to his office or threatened him again I'd be arrested. He told me no one was going to take the word of a druggie over him."

"Arrested for what?"

"He didn't say. But he knew people... I figured he could make things happen."

"Did he use the heroin too?"

She shook her head. "No. He did do the marijuana, but he never touched the heroin."

I took a long pull on the beer. "I'm so sorry all that happened, Halley. And I'd love to be able to make him pay. But I don't see anything here that is going to help me."

She stared out the window for a good minute. There was a decision she was trying to make.

"I have something." She was still staring out the window. "I know where he got his drugs."

That got my attention. The bottle was halfway to my lips. I put it down. Since the beginning of this case the list of suspects had kept growing, including a nun. And I figured suspecting a nun didn't improve my chances of getting into heaven. But none of those suspects had led me to anything that helped... until now... until Halley uttered that short sentence.

I watched my hand turning the bottle in a circle and then glanced at Ben. He was looking at me with full attention. He could have asked the question just as well as I, but it was my ball and my game. And I knew he was thinking the same thing. When someone wants revenge they are willing to make things up to get it. Ben had been in the courtroom for twenty-some years, and his take on this would be something I'd listen to. I was glad he was there.

"How do you know, Halley?"

"Because one night I followed him. We met at the apartment, and he wanted sex. I needed... something else before that was going to happen. He said he was all out but could get some in an hour. He left, and I followed."

"You didn't think he might see you?" I asked.

She shrugged. "I didn't care. I just wanted a hit."

"Why did you follow him?"

She paused long enough for me to pretend I was casually taking a drink of beer. There was nothing casual about it. I was fully aware.

"He knew I needed the stuff, and knew he'd get sex every time. We met often enough that those times took care of me. But I hated him and wanted to stop the sex. I thought if I could find out where to get it, I could say no."

The waitress came and asked if Halley was through. She had only eaten half her burger, but she was done. The waitress asked if she wanted a box. She didn't. The waitress stacked the plates and asked if there'd be anything else. I told her no, and as she walked away, I turned back to Halley.

"And where did he lead you?"

"An apartment above a Chinese restaurant in Highwood. There was a door with stairs next to the restaurant. He went up the stairs."

"Was there more than one apartment?"

"I don't think so. I parked and opened the door. The stairs led up to a landing at the top, and then there was a turn to the right."

"Do you remember the address?"

Her hands were clenched on the table in front of her. She was staring at them. "Yes… 211 Park. There was a mailbox just inside the door, but there was no name on it."

"Then what did you do?"

She shrugged. "I left and was at the apartment when he got back with the stuff."

"You didn't say anything?"

"No. I needed it."

"And he didn't know you followed him?"

She shook her head. "If he did, he didn't say anything."

We were all quiet until Ben asked, "Why are you telling us this, Halley?"

She didn't hesitate. "Because he wasn't very nice to me."

I would have put it a bit stronger. "No he wasn't. I know it wasn't easy telling us. Thanks."

She shrugged again. "What are you going to do? Can you get him?"

"We need to talk about it, Halley. It gets pretty cloudy where the law is concerned. And if it comes to it, you may need to file a complaint. And that may be something you may not want to do. But we'll talk about it. I'd sure like to pin *something* on him."

She just stared at me with a blank look and no hope.

I reached across the table and covered her hands with mine. "I'm sorry you had to go through all that. But I'm glad you are okay now. That wasn't an easy thing to do."

I started to take my hand away, but she looked up at me with moist eyes and held onto it.

After a few seconds I pulled it away and handed her my card. "If you can think of anything else, call me."

She glanced at the card and then nodded.

The waitress came back with the bill, and I left a twenty and a ten on the table. Probably her best tip of the day.

After a wave to the boss, Ben held the door for both of us, and we walked to our cars. Her Chevy was parked two spots away from my Mustang. I leaned on the door frame after she opened it and thanked her again.

She turned and looked up at me with parted lips and said, "You're tall, Spencer."

I nodded with a smile. "My parents planned it that way."

Her lips parted a bit more. "You could kiss me."

There wasn't anything natural about the way she said it. It sounded like she was reading from a script. I nodded and said, "Yes, I could. But I'm not going to."

She looked defeated, and I wondered how many times she had been turned down before.

"You don't think I'm pretty."

I pursed my lips and breathed in and out through my nose. "You are attractive. But I have someone who has all my attention, and I'd like to keep it that way. You'll find someone too."

She turned slowly and got in the car. I walked to mine, where Ben was leaning on the roof watching me. The sun was bright, but I felt like the world was pretty gray.

# Chapter 25

started the car and asked Ben if he had another hour. He didn't have to ask why.

"Sure. It'll only take us twenty minutes to get up to Highwood."

I headed back toward Green Bay Road.

"Do you think she's credible?" I asked.

"If she was on the stand I think the jury would believe her."

"Do you believe her?"

"Ah, different question. And I'm not sure I have an answer. It never mattered what I believed… just what the jury believed. If I could make them believe the sun rose in the west I had done my job, and all was well with the world. The fact that I knew it rose in the east didn't matter. I got used to not having an opinion."

"Well, that's a pretty lame answer."

"It's all I got. But if you want a gut opinion, I'd say I believe her."

"There's money involved. Bills weren't paid."

"Yeah, that does tend to make black look white. But I don't think she's looking for money. I think she just wants to see him get what's coming to him."

"And what is that?" I asked as I turned north onto Green Bay.

"Another good question. There's lots of things, but nothing that stands out with probable cause for an arrest. You'd like to get him, wouldn't you?"

"Yup."

"Why?"

"Because he's a bastard and a pompous ass."

He laughed. "If you try to take care of all the pompous asses in the world you won't have time to eat. You have any idea how many pompous asses I've had to deal with? Hundreds. Some of them I put behind bars, and some of them I worked for. Most of them made me wonder how they managed to get their shoes tied in the morning."

"So if he is beyond the long arm of the law, we get him the round-about way."

"Aren't you a little busy with something else at the moment?"

"Isn't going too well. And I've thought from the beginning that there are several loose threads that could be tied together here. It all started with drugs. And now the first lead I get is about drugs."

"Cause and effect don't always go together."

"No, but I've never believed in coincidences."

"How about Clausewitz?" Ben asked.

"Pardon?"

"There's just as good a chance that Nadem has nothing to do with Margot. And there's a good chance you're charging in on your white steed again rescuing the damsel in distress."

"So what does that have to do with Clausewitz?"

"You know what Clausewitz said."

"Yeah, war is an extension of politics."

"That too. But *don't fight a war on more than one front* is what I had in mind."

"What if the fronts merge?"

"Then charge ahead. But don't see things that aren't there just because you want that to happen."

"I should have brought my boots with me... getting pretty deep in here."

"Just saying."

The windows were down, and we were both quiet, listening to the wind.

As we passed the sign for Highwood, Ben asked if I knew where I was going.

"Not exactly, but we'll find it. There's a pretty small downtown strip along Greenbay Road. The restaurant must be on a side street. I don't remember seeing it on Greenbay. But I've been to the bowling alley, Minstrel's Alley."

"Odd name for a bowling alley."

I stopped at a red light as we pulled into town. "It was the first bowling alley in Lake County, but the reason I went was that local musicians would just show up and play. There was great music every night."

The light turned. "Look for Park," he said.

It was the second street to the right. There was a drugstore on the corner. The Chinese restaurant was down half a block on the south side. I passed it, turned around in an alley, and parallel parked two doors down from the restaurant on the north side of Park in front of an Italian restaurant called Mama's.

"I'm gonna go take a look," I said. "Stay here and keep your eyes open. Honk if there's company."

An elderly couple walked past the restaurant as I got out. Other than them the street was empty. A sign in the restaurant window said they opened at four. Adjacent to the restaurant door was a wooden door with a small pane of glass at the top and the numbers 211 above it. I opened the door slowly.

It was exactly as Halley had said, except she hadn't mentioned the grungy part. There was a single mailbox on the right recessed into the wall with no name on it. The small window above the door let in just enough light to see the stairs. There was no carpet on the stairs. I stood and let my eyes adapt a bit to the dark and saw a switch next to the mailbox that I assumed was for a light. But I didn't want to possibly alert someone in the apartment by turning it on. I listened for a minute and heard no sounds except for a car driving by. The stairs led straight up to a small landing. I climbed halfway up to where I could see around the corner. There was a little alcove on the right with another wooden door about five feet away. The only advantage to climbing the stairs farther would have been if the door was unlocked. I wasn't going to break in.

There were several disadvantages. Without carpet on the stairs it would have been hard to climb all the way without making some noise. If someone was home I didn't want to announce myself. And with only one exit, and that at the bottom of the stairs, I would be trapped if I was at the top and someone came in the front door. I didn't even want to meet the mailman. I would have liked to put an ear to the apartment door, but I decided against it.

The street was still empty when I walked back across.

I got in the car and described the inside to Ben.

"Couldn't ask for a better spot for an ambush," he said.

I started the car and pulled out the phone.

"Stakeout?" asked Ben.

"Yup."

"I'm in if you don't get it covered."

I nodded.

Three would be optimal, but I knew they'd all take twelve hour shifts if I asked. Double time after eight hours was enough incentive. My first call was to the pool hall where Ralph spent all of his free time. Outside the city they were called billiard parlors. Ralph was there, and I told the man who answered it was important. If I didn't say that, Ralph would finish a game if he was in the middle of one. I had once had to wait fifteen minutes.

"Hey, Spencer," he said with anticipation of a paycheck. "What's up?"

"Simple surveillance up in Highwood, but I need you now."

"How long?"

I explained the situation. "Until this guy shows. If he doesn't, two days."

"Who else?"

"Don't know yet, but I'd like to get three so you can take eight hour shifts."

"At double pay I'll stay up all night if you strike out."

"Okay, thanks. Stop by the office, and pick up a portable phone from Carol."

I gave him the address and told him we were parked in front of Mama's.

The second call was to Paul. He was in. Third call was to Rebecca. I got her answering machine and left a message for her to call me. Those three were the ones on my A list. I had others, but the quality dropped. But this was an easy job, so I read off another number.

"Before you go to the B list, I'd like to get in on this," Ben said. He knew about my lists. I accepted. He had been involved in cases before where I needed surveillance, and he wouldn't take money. And since this was coming out of my pocket, I didn't mind saving a few dollars. But I'd owe him a few dinners.

By three fifteen Ralph and Paul had arrived and were sitting in the back seat, and we worked out the plan. Other than the mailman at a little after two, no one had shown up at 211 Park. Ralph and Paul flipped a coin. Ralph would take the first shift until midnight, and Paul would relieve him. Ben would take over at eight. They would hand off the phone and call me if anyone showed up. It would be an easy job. Mama's opened for lunch at eleven and closed at ten at night. I had introduced myself to the manager and explained the situation. She was hesitant until I took out two fifties. And two doors from Mama's was a twenty-four-hour laundromat.

I figured it was likely someone would show around dinnertime, so Ben and I stayed until seven. We got a table next to Mama's window, and I bought dinner. Still no one across the street. At seven I walked across the street and into the Chinese restaurant. I asked for the owner and said I was trying to get ahold of the fellow next door and asked if he had seen him. He said the guy came in for take-out a couple times a week. Good customer. He gave me a description. Thin, about five and a half feet tall, long black hair sometimes in a pony tail, and a straight scar on his left cheek. I asked if he ever saw anyone else going in or out. He hadn't, except for the mailman. Said he minded his own business.

As we pulled out of town, Ben asked, "What happens after two days?"

"I'll climb the stairs."

# Chapter 26

I pulled into Stosh's drive Wednesday at six for our regular gin night. Before I shut off the engine I called Ben. No one had come to 211. Even the mailman had passed it by Wednesday afternoon.

I let myself in the front door.

"Hi, kid," Stosh said as I walked into the kitchen. "It was a tough day, so we're staying in. I got soup and sandwiches at the deli."

"Fine by me."

We took our food and beer into the living room. He took the recliner, and I sat on the couch.

"So what was so tough about your day?" I asked.

"It started last night. I didn't get home till eleven. A bunch of robberies over on Lawrence around three. Eight stores got hit at the same time. Same general description from all of them. A guy about five eight, slim, black pants and sweatshirt and full-face ski mask. One of the stores had a camera, and it showed exactly that."

"Same guy?"

He shook his head, finished a bite, and washed it down with Schlitz. "All of the robberies were within five minutes of each other. Eight different guys all dressed alike."

"What'd they get?"

"Anywhere between fifty and three hundred dollars. Total of seven sixty."

"Not much of a haul for all that effort."

"No. Doesn't make any sense. One guy robbing one or two plac-es I can see. But split eight ways?"

I picked up the second half of my roast beef sandwich. "Maybe it was practice."

He ate and looked at me sideways with raised eyebrows.

"Don't look at me like that. Maybe there is something else planned, and they needed to know how the police would react in such a scenario."

"Scenario, eh? Who you been hanging around with? You've been watching too much television. The whole neighborhood's full of little ma and pop stores."

"Maybe not that neighborhood." I finished a big bite and the rest of the beer. "Or maybe it was a diversion. No other reports?"

"Nope. Just the eight."

"Well, that's what I'm going with... a diversion for something bigger, like a bank or a jeweler. They wanted to know how you'd respond. And they hit at a shift change."

"I'm glad you've got it all worked out. Three officers called in sick this morning, so I jumped in a car. Nonstop all day."

"You know, some guys actually work *every* day."

I got a look.

"Speaking of not working, how's your case going?" he asked.

"Aside from pissing off several people, there's not much."

"Who you pissing off now?"

"Well, there was Thward, and I've got a senator not too happy with me." I told him about my visit to his office and the temple dedication.

"When you need someone to bail you out, don't call me. You want another beer?"

"Sure."

He took the bottles and plates into the kitchen and returned with two more.

"But I found a lead." I told him about Halley and the surveil-lance at 211.

"I don't have friends in Highwood. Watch your butt." He took a long drink and then shook his head. "And I voted for that bastard."

"Me too."

"Be careful, Spencer. People don't get to be senators without a whole lotta clout and friends in the right places. That buys them a lot of power that out-rules little things like laws."

"Noted. Cards?"

"If you don't mind, I gotta pass tonight. I'm beat. I'm gonna turn in early."

"No problem. We'll pick it up on Saturday."

"So, the suspected drug dealer is your only lead?"

"Pretty much."

"*Pretty* much?"

"It's not really a lead, but I've got an idea."

"Which is?"

"Which is not something I want to share at the moment. It's not the best idea I've ever had."

He laughed. "Most of your past ideas weren't exactly by the book. But somehow things worked out."

"Yeah, well this time nothing is working out. I'm still waiting for the Lord to provide."

"Ah, your silent partner. Speaking of which, you seen the nun lately?"

"Nope. But another breakfast isn't a bad idea."

"Watch yourself, kid. She's married."

We chatted for another twenty minutes while I finished my beer, and I left him to his beauty sleep.

# Chapter 27

I got up at five thirty Thursday morning and took a cup of coffee out onto the deck. The sky was overcast, and there was a smell of rain in the air. The sky had lightened a bit, but that was it. The radio was playing in the kitchen. The Cubs had defeated the Giants in a split-squad preseason game the day before, 10-6… lots of pitchers' duels in the preseason. I had considered going south for breakfast but decided that time on the deck listening to the birds was a better idea. But I did want to check in with Sister Katherine and decided on Friday.

When the drizzle started I went back in and listened to the silence. After three years, that was something I hadn't gotten used to. It had become a part of the house, just like the pictures on the wall. I could almost reach out and touch it. Both Stosh and Rosie had told me to sell the house and get my own place, but I couldn't bring myself to do that. There were memories I didn't want to let go of. Maybe someday. I walked through the kitchen into the living room and sat down next to the snack table that held the chess board. Dad and I had always had a running game. This one was frozen in time. He was ahead by a knight and two pawns, but I had a strategy to expose his castled king. Rosie had suggested I have someone finish the game with me. Maybe that was a good idea, but not yet.

I decided to get some house chores done and go to the office late-morning. I thought that plan would be changed when the phone rang a little after nine. I figured 211 had finally come home. But it was Carol, telling me Larry Maggio wanted to meet with me at two. I laughed.

"What's so funny?" she asked.

"In the past I've refused to drink with him because it was before noon."

"I've never known you to drink before noon, so that wasn't a sacrifice."

"Well, it was a little one… it was Glenfiddich."

There was a bit of a pause on her end.

"Glen what?"

I laughed again. "It's a single malt Scotch whiskey. Hard to find anything better."

"I'll take your word for that. So is two good?"

"It is… thanks. I was going to come in, but now I'll just head downtown."

"Well then, I'll ask you now. I'm wondering if we can get a computer."

Now there was a pause on *my* end.

"A computer. The IBM isn't good enough?" I had read some articles about computers. Seemed like a good step forward, but some said they needed to get some bugs fixed before they really caught on. Some said they never would. But some had said that to Ford.

"IBM is leading the way. Even they think the Selectric isn't good enough."

"Why don't you look into to it and get some prices. We'll chat next time I'm in. I'm all for improving the lives of my personnel."

"Which would be me."

"Exactly. You're so good, sometimes I think I have a staff of three."

"Whew. That reminds me… Watson needs to go out. Have fun with Maggio."

I put a few things away and wondered what the Chicago crime boss wanted this time. Our relationship in the past had ranged from my being kidnapped to his helping me solve a case. It was hard to

know what to expect. I didn't like the coincidence of the timing.
Drugs were certainly a big part of his business.

***

T raffic was light, and I got to his high-rise building fifteen minutes early, so I walked down the block thinking and wondering if
there was something I had missed. If this was about my case, there
was something that interested Larry Maggio. And if there was, I
should already have seen the connection. After all, I was the detective. But walking didn't help. I couldn't see it. Just as I got back to
his building it started to drizzle. I walked to the elevators, waited for
a door to open, and punched twenty-two. It let me off in front of the
glass wall that was Maggio's office.

The same friendly receptionist was at the front desk. She told me
Mr. Maggio was ready for me, and I could go in.

Two men were in the office. Larry Maggio was sitting behind
his desk and stood when I walked in. The other man, younger than
Maggio, stayed sitting. As usual, Maggio's three-piece suit was perfect. This was the third time I had seen him, and it had been gray
every time. But the ties had changed. The first time it was navy, the
second a pale blue, and this time red. The other man wore tan slacks,
a dark-brown dress shirt, and a sport coat. I was glad I was wearing
my best pair of jeans.

As Maggio offered his hand the man stood up and took a step
toward me. Maggio introduced us.

"Spencer Manning… Renald Williams."

I tried not to look surprised, but I was sure I failed. I don't know
what I expected the head of the Prophets to look like, but it wasn't
your average Joe you'd see on the street. There should have been
some sinister aspect, but there wasn't.

"Try not to look too surprised, Spencer. Have a seat." He pointed
to the chair at the opposite corner of his desk from Williams.

"Can't blame me for that. I would have thought you two were
rivals. Sitting peacefully in the same room seems odd."

Instead of replying, he took a bottle of Glenfiddich 15 from the bar shelf behind his desk and half-filled the three glasses on the credenza under the shelf. He handed one to each of us and raised his. I took a sip and held the glass in both hands. There was a crystal ash tray on his glass-topped desk, but neither of them was smoking.

Maggio sat and said, "We're both businessmen, Spencer. As such, we are smart enough to do what is good for business."

"I'm not saying that's not a good business policy, but most businessmen don't sit down and drink with their rivals. And pardon my saying, but your employees aren't exactly going to be winning awards for employee of the month."

We all nursed our drinks. "Sometimes they do sit down..." Maggio said, "...if it serves both of their purposes."

"And there's something here that serves your purposes?" I asked.

"There is," Maggio said.

I glanced at Williams. He hadn't said a word.

He set his glass down on the table next to his chair and said, "We have our businesses, Mr. Manning. Some of those businesses overlap, and we have worked that out with as little... shall we say friction, as possible. When something interferes with business, we find it best to talk about it and try and find a solution."

I just stared at him, hoping he would say something that would be more in keeping with a conversation with a crime boss and a gang leader. He didn't.

I shook my head. The tension in the room was heavy. "I feel like we're calmly talking about spending on the company parties cutting into the profits. But you wouldn't have me here to talk about that. So why am I here? ...I ask myself. The answer has to be Reynolds Margot." I took another sip. "But darned if I know why. There's nothing you need *me* for. And you're certainly not going to help *me* with anything."

Williams started to talk, but Maggio interrupted him. He added whiskey to his glass and offered more to Williams and me. We both declined.

He capped the bottle and said, "Mr. Williams contacted me because your name has come up in prior conversations. He knew I knew you and asked if I would arrange a meeting."

"My name came up?" I said.

"Yes, you have been of service to me in the past, service that worked out well for both of us."

That was true. In a case a few years back, I had discovered who was framing his book maker, Joey the Juicer, someone I had developed a working relationship with as he had helped me on another case. It's not only politics that makes strange bedfellows.

"So, I arranged this meeting," Maggio continued. "Mr. Williams can take it from here."

Williams emptied his glass and set it on the table.

"Mr. Manning, I think this meeting can be mutually beneficial. I will be honest with you, and perhaps you can provide me some assistance."

I suppressed a laugh. "I don't mean to be antagonistic, but given what you do for a living, the word honesty doesn't have a lot of value. And I'm wondering why you need Mr. Maggio as an intermediary and why we're meeting in his office."

He held his hands out, palms up in front of him, and shook his head slowly, as if the answers were obvious.

"As Mr. Maggio has already said, he knows you... I don't. If I had called your office would you have agreed to a meeting? And as to why we're here, my whereabouts tend to be somewhat fluid. This is a good neutral ground. To your point, what I do for a living is provide a service. Drugs have existed in society for a long time. If it wasn't me it would be someone else. And perhaps someone else not as friendly."

I knew he was right about the someone else, but I said, "We could argue about that all afternoon and get nowhere. My whereabouts are not fluid. If you want to meet in the future, it can be at my office."

"I'll keep that in mind."

I finished my drink and set down the glass. "So, what is it that you think could be mutually beneficial?"

"Are you making any progress with your investigation into Mr. Margot's death?"

"If by death you mean murder, I don't see where that's any of your business."

"No, of course not. What I hear is that you have many suspects, including me, and nothing that points to any of them."

I didn't ask how he knew that… he wouldn't have answered.

"If that is true, how is it you think you can help?" I asked.

"You can rule out me."

This time I didn't surpress my laugh. "Pardon me, but I'm just supposed to take your word for that? I know full well that you didn't pull the trigger and you have an air-tight alibi. But nothing happens in the Prophets without your knowing about it. And your raised fist was painted on the wall in the alley."

He shrugged. "Anyone can tag a wall. What better way to point the cops in the wrong direction? I'm not that stupid."

I had taken that into consideration. I knew he wasn't so stupid as to leave his calling card behind.

"I agree. But perhaps you don't have as much control over your… followers as you would like."

"My… *followers* are followers because they follow orders. Nothing goes on that I don't know about."

I paused a few seconds before I said, "Like your brother?"

He just stared at me.

"I'll keep looking into everyone on my list until I make the decision, based on evidence, that someone should be removed from that list," I said.

"Of course you will. Good to be thorough. Good luck with some of those names." He showed a little smirk.

I took a deep breath. "So that's how you think you can help me. How do you think I can help you?"

He smiled. "I'm getting pressure from the police. Pressure for something I had no hand in. You're working with Detective Bast. Once you take me off your list, I'm hoping you share that with him. The… *pressure* is bad for business."

I laughed again. "I'm all out of sympathy. Whatever I do will be because it is the right thing to do based on where the evidence leads. If it puts you in jail, it puts you in jail. If it exonerates you and puts someone else in jail, so be it."

He nodded. "Yes, Mr. Maggio assured me you're fair. I respect that."

How nice. "Are we done here?"

"I've said what I wanted to say," Williams said.

I thanked Maggio for the drink and stood up.

"Oh, by the way," Williams said, "how's Sister Katherine? I haven't seen her in a couple weeks."

I didn't know how to take that. It could have been a veiled threat. But after what Sister said about Williams, it didn't feel like one. But it was out of character for a gang leader.

"Hardest working person I know. I've got a lot of respect for her."

"As do I," Williams said. "She cares about those people and puts her time where her heart is."

The feel of this meeting was odd. The tension was still there, but concern and caring from this guy was out of character with what he did. I would rather just think of him as a bastard who belonged behind bars. And he did. But I didn't want my viewpoint conflicted by a caring side. And I had to remember that Sister accepted him for what he was and took what he had to give.

"I'd hate to see her get hurt," I said.

He gave me a hard stare. "Whoever hurt that lady would have to answer to me. Not one of my *followers*... me personally."

I believed him. I turned to Maggio and said goodbye.

He smiled. "I'm glad you could make it after noon, Spencer."

I nodded without smiling back. I turned to my left and nodded to Williams.

"Manning," he said.

The secretary wished me a good day, and I stepped across the hall to the elevator. I looked back at the office and wondered about an idea. By the time I got to the lobby I had made a decision. I sat in a red leather chair thinking about Sister Katherine and what she had said about Williams and what he had said about her.

*** 

I watched people come and go for twenty minutes before Williams walked out of the center elevator. He walked confidently across the tile in front of the elevators and had taken about ten steps before he saw me. He looked a bit surprised and walked over to where I was sitting. My stomach turned at the thought of what I was about to do. But instead of thinking about him I thought about Sister Katherine and her philosophy about Renald Williams. She spent her whole life just trying to do something about the little things she could help with. She accepted what he was and took what he had to offer. I wasn't sure I could do the same. And even if I could, I wasn't sure he'd agree.

He nodded and said, "Manning. Waiting for someone?"

He looked a bit surprised when I said, "You."

If it were anyone else I'd have suggested coffee. But just because I wanted to use him didn't mean I had to socialize with him. I invited him to sit in the chair next to me. What I had to say needed to be private, and what could be more private than a lobby where people were coming and going and not paying any attention to anyone else. This was an office building… no one used the lobby for meetings. There were other chairs and couches. Our two were the only ones being used.

He sat, patiently waiting for me to tell him why I wanted him. I was surprised he was so good at it. He probably wasn't used to being patient.

"I was surprised by your… um, feelings about Sister Katherine," I said.

He gave me a tiny smile and a furrowed brow. "Not incapable of respect, Manning. I don't meet many people as dedicated to what they do as she is. She's an exceptional person."

If we were having coffee I would have asked why a person dedicated to what she was dedicated to, which was dealing with the trouble he caused, wouldn't lead him to change his ways. But that wouldn't have been a successful conversation. My parents hadn't raised an idiot.

"Yes, she is," I replied. I watched the parade walking by for a minute and then turned back to him. He was still waiting patiently.

"You also said you weren't involved in the murder."

He nodded.

"Let's say I believe you."

He didn't respond. Normally I would have thought someone like him wouldn't care whether I believed him or not. But he had arranged a meeting to tell me just that. While sitting in the lobby, I had thought about why he would do that. I hadn't thought of a reason that made any sense.

I took a deep breath and said it. "Since I believe you, I could use your help."

I spent five minutes telling him what I wanted and the next twenty talking about how to do it. He didn't hesitate at all before agreeing, and he made some suggestions I hadn't thought of. It depended on timing. At some point I would need to contact him. He gave me a number where someone could reach him within minutes. I added my pager number and gave him my card with all my contact information.

He stood up, nodded, and said, "Manning."

I nodded from the chair and said, "Williams."

I watched him walk away and thought about Sister Katherine. She had been right about two things. The Lord had provided. It wasn't dished out on a silver platter, but He had provided. And the second was that the Lord certainly does work in mysterious ways. I sat in the chair for ten minutes, wondering about what I had just done and remembering what Dad had told me more than once… those who make deals with the devil play by the devil's rules.

# Chapter 28

I called Ben from the car. Today the postman had stopped, but he was the only one. I told him I'd meet him for dinner around six and then I'd check out the apartment. But first I needed to have a chat with my sidekick, Watson.

He was lying on his bed on the side of Carol's desk. He stared at me when I came in the back door. I thought I saw his tail move, but I may have imagined it. I knew it worked… he used it plenty when he saw Billy.

"Hi, Spencer. You making any progress?" Carol asked.

"Nobody has shown up at the apartment. I'm going to check it out tonight."

"You think that's a good idea?" she asked as she handed me the mail. I had told her several times to handle everything, but she didn't want to be responsible for something that didn't matter to her but might matter to me. So I took the mail. There wasn't a single thing that didn't end up in the garbage.

"Good is subjective. I usually don't stop to wonder if something is a good idea or not… I just do what seems like the next thing to do. So far, so good."

She smiled. "So far, so lucky."

"I'll take all I can get."

"If you have a minute, I have some information on computers."

"I do, but you're the office manager. If you think it's a good idea, then go ahead and get one."

"Good is subjective."

"I've heard that. In this case, you're the subject. If you think it will help, by all means get whatever you think is best."

"Could be over a thousand dollars."

"It's a write-off. Get it."

"But—"

"But nothing. You run the office because you do a good job of it, and I don't want to. Let me know how it works out."

I glanced at Watson. He was asleep, or pretending to be. Either way, I was on my own. I made a few notes in the Margot notebook and headed north.

*** 

Ben was sitting at a table by the window at Mama's when I got there, nursing a Peroni. It had been raining off and on all day, but only a drizzle. That changed as I turned onto Park, and I had to run from the car to the restaurant. I hung my jacket on the back of a chair where it dripped onto the floor.

Ben smiled and said, "About time you got some exercise."

"You mean like you who has been sitting here all day?"

"Hey, I more than make up for it chasing that little white ball."

A waiter came and asked what I preferred to drink. What I preferred and the Coke I ordered had to do with working or not. There obviously were times when I drank while working. I hadn't turned down Maggio's Scotch. But I wasn't planning on breaking into someone's apartment at the time. I *am* capable of forethought.

He brought the Coke and asked Ben if he wanted another. Ben declined. We asked for a minute to look at the menu.

"So just the mailman?"

He nodded. "Just the mailman. I wonder if your man has moved on."

"I wonder. And if he did, I wonder why."

Ben finished the last of his beer. "Mind if I offer a suggestion?" he asked.

"Of course not."

"If it were me, I wouldn't…"

The waiter was back.

"What have you had?" I asked Ben.

"Spaghetti for lunch. Thought I'd try the lasagna."

I closed my menu. "Two lasagnas with meat sauce, please."

"Yes, sir." He picked up the menus and bowed slightly.

I smiled at Ben. "Did he bow at lunch, too, or do they just get formal for dinner?"

"He wasn't here at lunch. But no bow."

"So, let me guess. You wouldn't let yourself into someone else's place of residence."

"It's a habit you get into while working as a prosecuting attorney for the state."

"Yeah, every job has its drawbacks. If it makes you feel any better, I'm not too thrilled about it myself."

"Then…"

I sighed deeply. "It's come in handy in the past. Not exactly dealing with your high-class upstanding citizens."

"You are forewarned."

"I am."

We watched the apartment and chatted over some good Italian food. I told the waiter to give my regards to Mama. He told us not to tell anyone, but there wasn't a Mama. The owner was a Greek who liked Italian food. You can't count on anything these days.

I had hoped that by some miracle our man would show up during dinner, but he didn't. I'd much prefer having a chat with whomever answered the door. Not much else happened either. Only two cars drove by in the last hour. But Highwood wasn't a destination… it was just the town you had to go through to get somewhere else. And there was only one other couple in the restaurant. I wondered how they stayed in business.

At a little after seven we made plans. Ben took up watch in my Mustang and would honk three times if anyone showed up. That would give me a chance to be outside the door knocking if someone came in the front door.

The rain had stopped. Street lights were on, shimmering in puddles on the street. The wind was coming in off the lake, bringing with it a slight fishy smell. I crossed to 211 and quickly went inside. I stood for a few minutes and, hearing nothing, carefully climbed the stairs. I got to within about ten steps of the top when I smelled it. I had smelled it before... it wasn't a smell I would ever forget.

I headed back down the stairs, this time not worrying about being quiet.

Ben rolled down the window as I approached my car, a confused look on his face.

"I'll be right back. Gotta make a phone call."

"There's a phone in your car."

"Yes, there is. But I don't have the number for the police department. Be easier to call from Mama's." I started to walk away and then turned. "I wonder if they even *have* a police department." When I got back I explained.

\*\*\*

Ben asked if I wanted him along when the police came. I told him that the things I tended to say were usually best said without witnesses. I thanked him and told him I knew help was nearby. A patrol car pulled up five minutes after I made the call. His lights were going, and he left them on when he got out of the car. I figured he didn't get much chance to run the lights.

I had told the woman who answered that there was a foul odor coming from an apartment at 211 Park. She asked what it was from, and I told her I didn't know, but that I'd meet the officer in front. A slightly overweight man, a head shorter than me, who looked to be at least fifty, got out and pulled on a ball cap. I walked across the street and met him. There was a stain just above the "Laney" name tag on his white shirt.

"You the guy who called?" he asked.

"Yup." I moved back a step. He smelled like he hadn't showered in a while.

"What kinda foul odor?"

I stopped myself from saying it was like him except worse. "Like something died."

"What?"

"Be a good idea to look and find out."

"You got some ID?"

I pulled out my wallet and handed him my license. I couldn't help staring at his eyes. They were almost perfectly round, but they had no color and no sign of life. They needed a neon sign that flashed "Nobody Home."

"Private, huh. This odor have to do with business?"

I shook my head with a bit of exasperation. I was tired of his questions and just wanted to get the door open. "Depends on what's causing the odor."

"Hmmm. You carrying a gun?"

"Nope." I got a look of disbelief.

"PI working on a case and no gun?"

"My hero was Sheriff Taylor."

"Who?"

"Never mind." I nodded toward the door. "We're not going to get anywhere standing out here."

He gave me a look, turned, and headed for the door. I followed him in, and he flicked on the light.

Almost to the top he stopped. Without looking back at me, he said, "Something smells."

"Hence my call."

We continued to the landing and turned the corner. He glanced up at the bare bulb hanging from the ceiling and then took two steps to the door where he listened for a long minute. All was quiet. The smell was worse at the top. I wasn't looking forward to going inside.

Looking over his shoulder, he said, "I'm going to knock. You stand back, tough guy."

Tough guy? I held back the many comments that were on the tip of my tongue and felt sorry for the citizens of Highwood if they ever needed help.

He pulled his gun with his right hand and knocked with his left… three hard raps. There was no answer. I had no hope that there would be. He stood there for another minute and knocked again.

I had a feeling he had no idea what to do next, so I made a suggestion.

"Why don't you try the knob?"

He nodded slowly, like he was thinking about it. I wanted to tell him it wasn't breaking and entering if you were the police and had plenty of probable cause.

He tried it. It was locked.

He turned to me. "It's locked."

I nodded and waited for him to figure out his next move.

"Guess I could break it down… or call a locksmith."

"I guess you could." I could have had it open in thirty seconds, but I knew Ben wouldn't have agreed with my telling him that. I actually figured that out all by myself. And I knew there was no hurry. If there had been some reason, I would have put my shoulder into it and had it open in two seconds.

He keyed his radio and called the station. After a brief conversation he had it worked out that the fire department would come and deal with the door. When he didn't move I suggested we wait outside. I figured that even if I had to stand near him the smell would be better.

I waited for a car to pass and then walked over to my Mustang. I leaned against the car and filled Ben in while we waited.

# Chapter 29

A fire truck turned onto Park and stopped in front of 221 within five minutes. We had passed the fire station on the way into town, and it's a small town. Three men got out, and one had a chat with Laney. Ben stayed with the car. He figured I now owed him several beers and said he didn't want the smell to affect his tastebuds. So I crossed the street alone.

As I stepped onto the sidewalk, Laney said, "This is the guy who phoned it in. PI. Says he's on a case but doesn't know if this is part of it."

The firefighter looked at Laney and said, "You can turn your lights off. Everybody knows we're here."

Laney looked sheepish and headed for the patrol car.

I introduced myself to the firefighter. The other two were getting gear off of the truck. They came back with an axe, a large pry bar and what looked like it would do the job of a battering ram. They stepped toward the front door.

Laney joined us, turned to me, and said, "You wait out here, tough guy."

"I don't think so." I could hear Ben rolling his eyes.

He puffed out his chest for the firemen who were waiting with the door open and said, "This is a crime scene. You're waiting."

I laughed. "A crime scene? Guy goes away and forgets to have someone come in and feed his dog and the dog starves to death and you're calling that a crime scene?"

He half opened his mouth. I had confused him. He closed it and then said, "Your case is a dog?"

"Not saying what my case is. All I'm saying is I called this in, and I'm going up the stairs. And you're wasting everyone's time."

One of the firefighters spoke up. "He's right about that, Laney. Let's get this done so we can get back to status."

He gave in. "Okay, okay. But you're going in last."

He led the way and then stood aside. The pry bar did the trick. There was no dead bolt, and the latch gave with just a little pressure on the frame. The firefighter pushed the door open with his foot, and the smell got a lot worse. It certainly wasn't a dog.

We all covered our mouths and noses with our arms and walked into the room. Two of the firefighters backed out and said they'd put away the gear. The room was about as bare as a room could be. One wooden table and chair, a small metal cabinet, and a couch were all that was there. A small bedroom was off to the left. Laney and the firefighter headed into the bedroom, so I was the first to spot the shoe sticking out from behind the couch. I walked toward it. It was the kind of thing you knew you had to look at, but you didn't want to… hoped it wouldn't be what you thought, but knew it was. And then I looked.

He was lying on his back and had on jeans and a brown shirt. There were several clues that the medical examiner would be able to use to take a stab at the time of death. The body was starting to bloat, and bugs of some sort were crawling on his face. A dead body takes up a new rung on the food chain. There was a thin red ring around his neck. Not hard to guess what had killed him.

I called Laney and walked away from the couch. He and the firefighter walked back into the room, and I pointed to the couch.

"Holy Jesus!" said Laney.

The firefighter just shook his head. He'd probably seen worse at fire scenes. He was already out the door when Laney ordered everyone out with, "Okay, this is a crime scene. Nobody touch anything." I was right behind the firefighter. When Laney figured out he was all alone, he followed us down the stairs.

The firefighter held the door for me, and I walked back out where life was happening. It was a dark, cloudy night, and the drizzle had started again. And I had brought the smell with me. It was in my nose, and I'd probably have to burn my clothes. I walked over to the Mustang and filled Ben in.

"This is going to be a long night," he said.

I agreed.

***

A half hour later we were in the office of Chief Rayburn, a man with a full head of white hair and a slight look of discontent at being called in after hours. Laney had stayed at the scene, guarding the front door. Two other officers arrived before Ben and I left, and one of them told me they had called in a crime scene team from Highland Park, the village to the south. Laney had wanted to take me in. He probably had visions of bright lights and an attitude that he could only get away with because of the badge. But he was over-ruled by someone, and I was allowed to find the police station by myself.

The chief looked at me. "Manning. Any relation to Chief Manning?"

I nodded. "My father."

"My condolences, son. I had a lot of respect for him... a good man." He took a deep breath. "I hear we have a problem."

He didn't wait more than ten seconds before realizing I wasn't going to respond.

PI 101... don't offer information. I was sure Ben was proud of me. But I *was* wondering what he meant by *we*.

He then turned to Ben. "And you are?"

"Ben Tucker."

PI 102... just answer the question.

The chief nodded slowly and sat back in his swivel chair. "Okay, Ben Tucker. Why are you here?"

I started to answer, and the chief held his hand up.

"Ben looks like a big boy. Let's see if he can handle this one."

"Friend of Spencer. We had dinner at Mama's."

"Always appreciate a little business in town." He smiled and turned back to me. "And what brought you to knocking on the door of Mr. Swayne?"

A name for the body.

"A case I've been working."

He smiled. "This is going to take a while, boys, if I just get little answers every time I ask a question. Pretty soon you're going to want your lawyer."

I smiled back at him. "That won't be necessary. He's sitting right next to me."

He sighed and said, "Jesus. Care to tell me about the case?"

"Client privilege, Chief."

"Sure. Doesn't hurt to ask. Sometimes I get lucky if someone doesn't have their lawyer sitting next to them."

"Well, about that." I explained. "Ben came along because he's my friend—"

"And I was promised a beer," he said.

"Thanks, that helps a lot," I said.

He smiled. "Just trying to be truthful."

The chief wasn't smiling.

"Back to your case. I'm assuming we're both interested in trying to find the killer. Given that assumption, I'd appreciate whatever information you can share. For instance, why were you paying a visit to Swayne?"

I glanced at Ben, and he nodded.

The chief smiled and shook his head. "Like a ventriloquist act. You two should go on the road."

I gave him a look that wasn't a smile. "It was about drugs and was removed several layers from my client. It's like this... I started down a road looking for an answer to a problem. That road led to another where I made a turn, and somewhere down that street I turned into an alley. That alley led to another street where I found Mr. Swayne because someone in the alley had mentioned his name."

He set his elbows on his desk, folded his hands together, and rested his chin on his hands. Then he looked at me for a bit. He sighed again and rubbed his chin with his left hand. "So Mr. Swayne was supplying someone with drugs?"

I nodded. "So says someone."

"I hate to ask, but who is that someone?"

Ben shook his head.

"Never mind," the chief said. "I got the signal."

"First, it's hearsay. And second, one of those roads I turned off on has some implications that I'd really hate to get wrong."

An officer knocked on the door and came in when the chief beckoned.

"Coroner is on site, Chief, along with the team from Highland. Coroner says he'll have a better time when he gets to his lab tomorrow, but he's guessing sometime late Tuesday. Cause of death, pending anything further, is strangulation."

"Okay. Thanks, Jeffers."

The officer glanced at us and left.

The chief sighed again. "I've been at this for almost thirty-five years. It's our second homicide."

As I started to open my mouth he said, "I could do without it. If you find anything down those streets and alleys, I'd appreciate hearing about it."

"Sure. Whatever I can, Chief. And I'd like to know the time of death."

He nodded. "Call tomorrow afternoon. I'll leave word with dispatch to let you know."

"And anything else you come up with?" I asked.

"Oh sure... since you've shared so much with me."

I smiled. "We done?"

He shook his head. "I think we were done an hour ago." He looked at Ben. "On your way here you passed the Night Owl. Not a bad spot for a beer. Open until midnight."

"Thanks, Chief," Ben said.

\*\*\*

**W**e walked into the Night Owl a little before ten thirty and both ordered a Guinness. It was a slow night… only three other people there. There was a country band with a guitar, drums, and a singer telling us about love and lonely train whistles and prison. If they were playing for tips it was a slow night. We picked a booth away from the crowd and talked for ten minutes.

Ben took a draw on his beer and asked, "What's the chance of it being a coincidence that you mention Holly Rundel to the senator and you find Swayne dead two days later?"

"No chance at all."

"If it's not a coincidence, it happened pretty fast."

I set my glass down. "Yup, he lost no time thinking about it."

"I'd like to know Holly is okay."

"Me too." I finished my beer. "Finish up, and we'll call her from the car."

I left a ten on the table and another in the tip jar in front of the band and got a nod from the guitar player.

\*\*\*

**I** let out a sigh of relief when she answered. I told her about Swayne and my one-way chat with Nadem at the temple. She asked if I thought she was in danger. I said if something was going to happen it probably would have happened by now. I asked her if she had someone she could stay with who Nadem wouldn't know about. She did. I told her to get out as soon as possible and to check in with my office and leave a number where I could reach her. I told her not to go anywhere she usually went and asked where she worked. She was currently unemployed. I told her I was sorry, but that made her life easier at the moment. I also told her to make sure she wasn't followed and if she was, to call me on my car phone. She wasn't happy with me. I didn't blame her.

I pulled away from the curb and turned toward home.

"You think she's in danger?" Ben asked.

"I don't think so, but doesn't hurt to take precautions. If it *was* Nadem, he acted immediately. I'm betting Swayne was dead before he saw much of the afternoon. And if Nadem was going to kill her he would have had it done Tuesday. I'm thinking it would have been too close to home to kill someone I had just mentioned. Taking out the dealer was removed enough so as to not be tied directly to him."

"I hope you're right."

"Me too."

"What's next?" he asked.

"Breakfast with my favorite nun... if she shows up."

"I'll cross my fingers."

We didn't talk much the rest of the way home. I dropped him off and was asleep by midnight.

# Chapter 30

The sun was back Friday morning. I left at seven, fought the traffic into the city, and parked in front of Time To Eat at ten to eight. Sister Katherine and Benny were already in their booth. They both looked happy to see me and waved through the window.

"What brings you, Spencer?" Benny asked.

"Just catching up, and I need to have a chat with you, Sister."

"Chat away," she said with a smile.

Carmen arrived with coffee and asked if I wanted my usual. I did.

"Well, it's not quite that easy. I need to talk to you privately."

She cocked her head at me. "I assure you, anything you say to me Benny can hear too."

I nodded. "Yes, she can, but I don't think she'd want to."

"Well that's pretty cryptic," Sister said.

Benny just looked at me with a furrowed brow.

"It is. How about this? We all have breakfast. Then you and I, Sister, will go for a walk, and I'll tell you what I need. You can tell Benny or not as you decide."

"Deal," Sister Katherine said.

I sipped my coffee and asked, "Anything new on your end?"

Both shook their heads. Benny said, "Nothing concerning what you're looking into. Although there seems to be less drug activity on the streets."

"Well I guess that's a good thing."

"Yes, but it won't last," Benny said. "Anything on your end?"

Carmen brought their food and told me mine would be up in a few minutes.

I told them about the drug dealer but left out Senator Nadem.

Benny looked thoughtful and asked, "What's the connection to Reynolds?"

"I was afraid you'd ask that. I can't really say. A couple people removed from that case. They may be related, and they may not."

She nodded and took a bite of scrambled eggs.

Carmen came with my eggs, bacon, and pancakes.

"So, what's next, Spencer?" Benny asked.

I shrugged and finished a bite. "Just making the rounds. Next stop is Bast."

"Doubt if he'll have anything," she said. "Especially since the feds have taken over."

"Probably not," I said. "But I know some cops who wouldn't let them get in their way."

"Most wouldn't. But from what I hear, there's a lot of dead ends."

"And a lot of unanswered questions." I washed pancakes down with coffee and said, "Doesn't hurt to ask."

"No, it doesn't."

Benny and Sister had finished eating. Benny laid her napkin on the table and said, "Since I'm obviously not wanted, I'll leave you two to your secret meeting."

I started to apologize, and Benny said, "Just kidding. Let me know if I can help."

"Thanks," I said. "Appreciate it."

Sister Katherine watched Benny leave and then watched me finish my eggs. I pushed the plate to the edge of the table and told her about my meeting with Maggio and Williams. She was surprised.

"I didn't think those two would ever be in the same room," she said.

"Not something I would have expected either," I said. "I seem to be the common link." I told her about my idea and my conversation with Williams. I also told her that I couldn't do it without her help, and even then it was a shot in the dark. I wasn't in favor of shots in the dark, but at the moment I didn't have anything better. After twenty minutes of questions and making it very clear that she thought I was crazy, she agreed.

I offered her a ride back to the church, but she had business in the neighborhood. She did let me pay for breakfast.

***

I parked in the public lot at the station and was told that Detective Bast would be available in a few minutes. Ten minutes later the desk sergeant said Bast could see me and asked if I knew my way. I did.

I knocked on Bast's door frame, and he waved me in.

"Hey, Spencer. Have a seat."

I pulled a wooden chair up to his desk and sat.

"You tied any loose ends yet?" he asked.

"No. I keep finding more without tying the ones I got."

"I know the feeling."

An officer knocked on the door and held up a file folder.

"Leave it on the chair, Tom. Thanks."

He dropped the file and left. Bast said he had to hit the head and would be back in a few minutes.

When he got back I said, "I was hoping you'd have something."

"Nothing. The feds have asked for files and information, but if they have anything they're not sharing."

"So much for a team effort," I said.

"Par for the course."

"I did run into something yesterday that might interest you." I still didn't know who to trust, other than a drug dealer and a nun, and that wasn't a choice… I had to trust them if I was going to try my idea. But the murder in Highwood was on the news, so I had no trouble sharing that with Bast. What wasn't on the news was my name. Chief Rayburn was the only name mentioned besides the victim.

Bast leaned back in his chair and folded his arms on his chest. "What would that be?"

"You hear about the murder in Highwood?"

"Yup. Lots of excitement for that sleepy town."

I agreed. "Guess who called the police."

His eyes widened, and he looked surprised. "Really!"

I nodded.

"How did you get involved?"

"Just following a lead. Could have nothing to do with Reynolds, but there's a drug connection that's hard to ignore."

"Who is the connection?"

That I wasn't willing to share... yet. "Until I know it *is* a connection, I'm not saying."

"Seems like something I should know."

"If and when I connect the dots, I'll do that."

"Okay. Not like I don't have anything else to do. You—"

He was interrupted by another knock on the door. Another officer asked if he could see Bast in private. He left the room, and I again scanned his plaques on the wall.

Bast came back in holding a clear plastic bag with a white substance in it.

"Seems we have a problem, Spencer."

"We?"

He nodded. "Officer Magellis found this on the floor of your car tucked under the passenger seat. You know anything about it?"

"Like what?"

"Like what it is or what it was doing there." He sat behind his desk and laid the bag on the top in front of him.

I did have an answer, but I didn't like it. My guess was it was cocaine, and it was there to frame me.

"I have no idea about either of your questions."

"You didn't put it there?"

"Of course not."

"So someone else must have."

"Good guess. How did Magellis happen to find it under the seat of a parked car?"

"I asked him that. Seems like your car attracted some more attention, and he saw the bag."

"Well, it wasn't there when I pulled into your lot, so it was put there in the last twenty minutes. Someone walked onto a police lot and slid that under my seat."

"Looks that way. I told you you should lock your doors."

"Yeah, you're not the only one. Are there cameras?"

He shook his head. "Not in that lot."

"Great. So what now?"

He took in a deep breath and sighed. "This leaves me with no choice. I've got to hold you on suspicion until we get that analyzed. But you can sit here instead of in a cell."

"Thanks. And when will that be?"

"I'll fast track it. Couple hours at the most." He sat up straight in his chair. "I'm going to assume you're being set up. Could this have anything to do with the Margot case and the dealer you found dead last night?"

I shrugged. "Maybe. I don't have enough to know what has to do with what."

"Who led you to the dealer?"

I shook my head. "Can't say."

"If I knew, I could help. I have more resources than you."

I smiled. "Only because I haven't talked to my resources yet."

He smiled back. "Doesn't hurt to have more on your side."

"I know. Thanks. I'll share when I can."

"You want to make a phone call?"

"I do."

He turned his phone around, stood up, and said he'd be back in five minutes.

I called Ben, hoping he wasn't out playing golf. I didn't know if he was or not, but he didn't answer the phone. I left a message, sat back in the chair, and thought about being arrested because of a case I had been trying to quit for a month. Then I called Stosh and filled him in.

His reaction was, "Well, I guess that was inevitable. You go looking for trouble you're going to find it."

I didn't get a whole lot of comfort from that, but he said he'd work on it. I had no idea what that meant.

Bast was back a few minutes later. He didn't ask any questions. He shuffled papers, and I sat and thought.

***

**B**ast's phone rang an hour later, and he said, "Send him back." He hung up and looked at me. "Your lawyer is here. He's coming back."

I was standing by the window watching traffic when Ben walked in. Bast nodded to Ben and left again and closed the door. Ben looked at me and shook his head.

"For a guy who should be taking life easy, you sure know how to make it difficult."

I sat on the corner of Bast's desk. "Yeah, I could be taking out my frustrations by beating the hell out of a little white ball instead."

"Now, now, don't alienate your attorney. I was going to ask who you pissed off, but it seems obvious."

I had thought about that. "Maybe it does… maybe *too* obvious."

"What does that mean?" he asked. "This has to be Nadem. You pried into his affairs and didn't obey his warning to butt out. You show up at the temple, mention a name, and his drug dealer ends up dead. One day later, you're calling your attorney because you've been set up for drug possession. And you don't think it's Nadem?"

I moved to the chair… not the wooden one, Bast's chair with the cushion. "Not all by himself."

Ben threw his hands up. "Of course not all by himself! He's one of the most powerful senators in the country. He's got people in places you don't even know exist. He snaps his fingers, and people jump."

I wasn't going to argue that point. "Let's assume I'm going to be arrested. Shouldn't you be doing something about that?"

"First, yes, you probably are. They're not going to frame you with flour. Second, hard to do anything until it happens. Third, yes, I am. I've got people too. I can't head it off, but I can minimize your time behind bars."

I nodded my thanks.

Ben sat in the wooden chair. "Okay, let's look at this. Somebody had to know you were here to plant that in your car."

I nodded again.

"So someone was following you."

"Or knew I was going to be here, or knew I *was* here."

"Meaning?"

"Meaning I had breakfast with Benny and Sister Katherine and told them this was my next stop."

"Two people on your don't trust list."

I shook my head. "If they're on the list, it's at the bottom. And I had taken Sister off the list."

"You didn't notice anyone following you?"

"Nope."

"But then you weren't looking."

"I'm always looking."

"But you're not perfect."

"Pretty close when it comes to my job."

"So what else?"

"Somebody who saw me pull into the lot."

"Which could be anyone."

"Yup, anyone attached to Nadem's finger snap."

There was a knock on the door, and Bast came in. He looked at me sitting in his chair and smiled.

"I'm afraid you're not going to be quite as comfortable. It's cocaine. I've got to book you."

He turned to Ben. "Counselor, you can see him when we're done."

Ben stood. "No need, Detective. I have all I need. Spencer, should be a couple hours."

"Thanks, Ben."

Before we left his office, I thanked Bast for the hospitality.

"No problem, Spencer. This is obviously a frame. But you seem to be in good hands."

"A frame that happened in your parking lot. That raises some questions, not the least of which is how did they know I was here."

"Already working on it. I'll let you know if I come up with anything."

"Appreciate it."

The prints and photo took twenty minutes and then I was escorted to the cellblock. There were two others there, but we all had our own cells... high-class joint. But then I *had* ordered a private room. The cell was clean, and the bed was spartan but comfy. I sat on it and leaned back against the wall. I had been in jail cells before, but that was in the army when I was doing the escorting. This was my first looking from the wrong side.

I looked across the aisle at the other two occupants. One was obviously younger than me, the other older. The younger one was asleep. The older was staring at me. I was dressed better and obviously not from around there. He looked like someone I didn't want to mess with, and like he was certainly capable of doing whatever it was he was in for. It was also obvious that staring was all he intended to do. There was none of that jail cell comradery you see in the movies... "Hey, Buddy, what're you in for?" And I would have a bit more consideration the next time I heard someone say they were framed. I had already done all the thinking I was going to do about how this could have happened, so I found a comfortable spot on the wall and took a nap. That was easy to do... I knew I was getting out. I was pretty sure my people were as good as Nadem's.

# Chapter 31

I pulled into Stosh's driveway at ten to twelve Saturday morning and could see something on the front door. When I got up to it I saw it was a copy of my arrest sheet. Nice. I tore it off and let myself in. He was in the kitchen laying out the sandwich fixings.

"Thought you wouldn't have time to get lunch ready what with being so busy decorating your door."

"Thought you might like to have it for a souvenir."

"Very considerate." I took a plate and a roll and decided on pastrami.

"And maybe a reminder of what you got yourself into. Maybe time to put your feet up and read a book."

"Don't need a reminder. And Bast told me the same thing when they released me. He thinks I'm better off not playing with matches. Said he's got better things to do than arresting me."

"He's right, you know."

"Sure. One better thing is finding out who planted the drugs in my car."

We brought our sandwiches into the living room, and he settled in his recliner. I took my usual spot on the couch.

"I'm sure he'd like to find out too, Spencer. A bit embarrassing for him. I'll ask some discreet questions. Tell me about the frame."

We ate and I talked. I started with the surveillance and ended with the officer walking into Bast's office with the baggie.

"You think Nadem is behind this," Stosh said. It wasn't a question.

"Of course. Don't you?"

"I'll remind you. I don't think. I leave that up to juries. We just follow the trail and see where it leads."

"Exactly what I'm doing, and if I backtrack it ends up at Nadem's doorstep."

"Yeah, the doorstep surrounded by federal agents."

"Mom always said life wouldn't be easy."

As he set down his bottle of Schlitz, Stosh said, "You said Wednesday that you had an idea you didn't want to share. Anything more on that?"

"Sort of. I gave a couple of people a heads up in case something happens."

"Well, that clears that up. Thanks for sharing."

I laughed. "It's still not a great idea, and I get enough crap from you without adding this to the list."

He bit off about a third of the sandwich and chewed for a bit. "So you know I wouldn't like it, and even you don't like it… yet still you plod ahead."

"All I got at the moment… except of course for an arrest record."

"Your dad would be proud." He finished his beer and looked at my almost empty bottle. "You want another?"

"No, maybe later. Let's play some gin."

After two hours I was down over two bucks at a penny a point. My mind wasn't really on the game. The more I thought about it, the angrier I was about being framed. After three hours I had decided to put my plan into action.

A little before five Stosh said he was getting hungry and suggested going out for steak.

I declined and told him I needed some time to myself to think. He gave me a questioning look and told me to stay out of jail.

***

was glad Sunday was the next day. That gave me time to think some more. I took a long walk in the morning and ran in the afternoon. By the end of the day I hadn't changed my mind. Monday was going to be a busy day. That night I made calls to Williams and Sister Katherine and told them we were on. They both were ready.

# Chapter 32

I was in the office at nine when Carol arrived. I had instructions for her, too, that called for her asking no questions. She didn't ask. I left at a quarter after as she wished me good luck with whatever was up my sleeve. I took it... I needed some luck.

A little after ten Monday morning I parked across the street and down half a block from Nadem's office. The Maserati was elsewhere. The sun lit up Nadem's plate glass windows, and I couldn't see in. I wondered what color Mrs. Stadler's nails were. I was taking a chance on him being there and had already decided if he didn't show up by eleven I'd move on to my other stops and come back. He pulled in at a quarter to eleven. I watched as he stopped to smile and chat with a voter and then walked into his office. I gave him two minutes to get settled.

Mrs. Stadler looked surprised to see me, like she had been told I wouldn't be bothering her again.

Her "Can I help you?" was definitely flustered.

"Like to see the senator." I got the standard line.

"The senator isn't in this morning."

I raised my eyebrows. "Oh? Oh, I see the problem. I didn't mean that other senator who isn't here. I meant the one who drove up in the Maserati and walked in your front door less than five minutes ago." I wasn't smiling... neither was she.

"Well, he's in a meeting and can't be disturbed."

"Ah, I see. Not being in there, I'm not sure about the meeting, but I am definitely sure he's going to be disturbed. Now, why don't you pick up your phone and tell him Spencer Manning is here, and he can have the door open by the time I get back there."

There was a look of fear on her face as she pushed a button on the phone. As I started for his office I heard her tell Nadem that I was there and coming down the hall. Then she asked if he wanted her to call the police. Her only response was "Okay." I didn't hear her start another conversation, so his answer must have been no. But even if they did come I didn't plan on being there long, and I didn't plan on causing trouble. And besides, the Glencoe jail had to be better than Bast's.

Nadem was standing in the open glass doorway by the time I got to his office halfway down the hall. I smiled and said, "Good morning, Senator."

He sneered at me. "You evidently haven't been paying attention."

I thought that was an interesting comment. "Paying attention to what?"

He ignored the question. "I'll make it more clear. If you don't leave now, my secretary will call the police. And keep your nose out of my business."

I smiled. "Make you a deal, Senator. I have something to say that will take one minute. I say it… and I leave. That'll be the last time you see me unless you call me."

He laughed. "And why would I call you?"

"At the moment I have no idea. But you never know where paths lead."

He looked at me with hatred.

"You're getting to be a liability, Manning."

I smiled. "Perhaps it's your lifestyle that's the liability."

"What do you mean by that?"

"I keep looking around, and your name keeps coming up. Like Halley Rundel. She has a grudge she's holding against you. You didn't treat her so well. All—"

"Hey, she knew what she was getting into. She wanted the glory. She wanted—"

"Oh yeah, the glory of being turned into a drug addict while basking in your sunshine."

He started to reply, and I stopped him. "The state of your character is irrelevant. All I know is she gives me a name... I go check out that name, and I find him dead."

"And you're saying that somehow has something to do with me? What dots are you connecting that have my name in them?"

"Just stating the facts, Senator. I go where the facts lead me."

He stared at me, saying nothing. But his face was red, and his fists were clenched.

I nodded toward his office. "We talking out here in the hall?"

"You have one minute."

Out of the corner of my eye I saw Mrs. Stadler peeking around the corner. This was making her day, maybe her week. She'd be on the gossip phone all day.

"I got involved in this with Reynolds Margot being arrested for drug possession and sales. He knew your son, and his mother donated to your campaign."

"Lots of people donate to my campaign. That doesn't mean—"

I held up my hand and stopped him. "Of course. I'm not saying that has anything to do with anything... just pointing out the connection. And you cut into my minute. He was offered a plea deal and then ended up murdered. His body was found in an alley on the west side. Shortly after that your son was also found murdered."

I paused, expecting him to interrupt. He didn't, but his face was turning darker shades of red.

"Then I have a chat with you and an acquaintance of yours, and a suspected drug dealer in Highwood is found dead... strangled. Three people dead, lots of maybes and loose ends, and I only have one clue to follow up on."

His fists were still clenched. I wasn't concerned. I figured punching people wasn't something he was used to. He let other people swing his fist. If he tried to swing, I'd have plenty of notice and wouldn't be where his fist was swinging. I waited patiently for him to ask. I could tell it was killing him, but I knew he wanted to know. It was only ten seconds, but it seemed longer.

"What clue would that be?"

Someone came in the front door.

"Well, it seems there was a witness when Reynolds' body was dumped in the alley."

That changed his attitude.

"A witness?" He stepped back from the doorway, motioned me into his office, and closed the door. He didn't offer me a chair and didn't take one himself. I wouldn't be staying long.

"Yes. He saw the whole thing."

"He saw who did it?"

"No… too dark. But he went down after they left and picked up something they dropped."

"Which is?"

I shrugged. "I don't know. Our talk was cut short before I could find out."

He didn't ask what cut our chat short. "What's this person's name?" he asked with a hard stare.

"Rafael Melendez."

"I assume you intend to follow up?"

"I do."

He nodded. "I also assume the police have talked to this person?"

"They have."

"So they know about what he found."

"They do not. It's a recent development."

"I'm sure they'll be interested once you tell them."

"I'm sure they will."

He walked to the door and opened it. "Your minute is up, Manning. And I don't see that any of this has anything to do with me. I have run out of patience with you. This had better be the last time you visit this office."

I let myself out. Mrs. Stadler was giving pamphlets to a young woman. She didn't even look up as I walked by.

# Chapter 33

I headed downtown, hoping Thward would be in. I grabbed a hot dog and got to his office a little after one. He was in, but Mrs. Mitchell told me he had given her orders not to be disturbed. She was sorry about it. I figured he was probably getting in a nap after lunch, making good use of my tax dollars. I asked if she would be willing to tell him I was there, had some information for him about the Margot case, and that I had come to him first. She said he wouldn't be happy, but she didn't much care anymore whether he was happy or not, so she'd be glad to.

When she buzzed him he asked angrily why she was bothering him and wondered if the instructions he had given her weren't clear enough. She calmly said they were, but something had come up. She gave him my message. After a few seconds of tense silence he told her to let me in.

As I walked past her desk, I said, "I can think of better jobs… like the snake pit at the zoo."

She smiled. "I might look into it."

I took a deep breath of semi-stale air, let myself in, and walked to the closest chair.

"Don't sit, Manning. You're not staying that long. What information?"

So far this morning I wasn't making any friends. But then, for my purposes it was better to make enemies.

"I talk better when I sit." And when I don't have to breathe smoke, but I kept that to myself. He held a stub of a cigarette, and there was another going in the ashtray. God forbid he take the time to light a new one without inhaling.

He waved at the chair.

"You getting anywhere with the Margot drug case and murder?" I asked.

"That doesn't sound like information."

"Just wondering. I know you were interested in the drug end of the case, but I figure the drugs and the murder are all part of the same bad story, and I have information about the murder no one else knows."

"And why are you telling it to me?"

"I trust you… figure you could use a break."

"Sure you do." He sat back in his chair. "I make my own breaks."

I shrugged. "So you don't want to know?"

"Not particularly, but as long as you're here…"

I told him the same story I had told Nadem. He seemed a little more interested than Nadem had been.

"And you haven't told this to Bast?"

"Nope."

He thought for a bit. "What cut your conversation short?"

"Someone else came in. He clammed up, and that was the end of our talk."

"I see. But you have wasted my time. I don't see how this is any of my concern."

"Sometimes things take time to be relevant. I figured you'd want to know."

"Next time do your figuring somewhere else."

There was no mistaking that exit line. I left without being asked. Before I got to the door I coughed and turned back. "You know, they passed the Clean Air Act a while back." I quickly opened and closed the door to keep as much smoke in as possible and stopped next to Mrs. Mitchell's desk.

"What's the name in front of Mrs. Mitchell?"

She smiled. That was probably more interest than Thward had ever shown in her.

"Gretchen."

"Good luck, Gretchen." She had kind eyes that deserved better than Thward. "I'll keep an eye open at the zoo."

She laughed. "You do that. Good luck to you also, Mr. Manning."

***

I had one more stop to make. A cloudy morning had given way to bright sunshine. I was driving right into the sun as I made my way west on Randolph to Ogden and then south. It only took fifteen minutes to get to the station. This time I locked my car. Bast wasn't in but was expected shortly. I waited and watched the parade of customers. I thought about asking if I could see my cell… just for old time's sake.

My pager beeped at 3:10 with the office number. I went back to the car and called. Carol had found a computer she wanted to buy and wanted my okay. I told her it was all up to her. If she thought it was a good improvement, go for it. While she was telling me about it, Bast pulled into the lot in his tan Buick. I honked, and he walked over to the Mustang. I hung up and asked if I could have a few minutes of his time. I could.

When we got to his office he said, "Sorry for Friday, Spencer. I'm sure you'll get that all worked out. My hands were tied."

"I realize that. No problem. I can check that off my list of things to do. But you need to get cameras in your lot."

"It's been requested several times. Your car hasn't been the only one broken into. Extra points to steal something from a cop's car. But I'm sure you are aware of the budget problems. You got something?"

I shrugged. "Two things." I told him about my chat with Nadem.

"You concerned about that?"

"I find it interesting. If you have nothing to hide why make threats?"

"Good point. Second?"

"Not helping me much, but I figured you should know." I told him about Rafael.

He sat with his elbows on his desk, his fingers steepled, and his thumbs supporting his chin and listened. He only frowned twice.

"And you're only telling me about this now?"

"I just learned about the evidence he picked up. Before that it was just a crazy story by a guy lost in time. And he only told me the story because I could play the role."

He nodded and seemed to agree.

"So what do you think this evidence is?"

"No idea. Might only be something that exists in 1943 outside a farm house in France."

He thought some more. "And where do you think it is?"

"Again…" I raised my arms, palms up. "Might just exist in his head."

"But if it doesn't, where?"

"Well, he never leaves the apartment."

"Except to pick up the evidence," he said with a smile.

"Yeah, except for that."

The room went quiet. He was thinking. I was thinking about what he was thinking. While we were busy doing that his phone rang. He said to put the call through. I started to get up, and he waved me back into the chair. I listened to a few "I don't knows" and a few "we're looking into its," and he ended with "call me back in a couple hours." He hung up and gave me a stare that meant something. Five seconds later I found out what the phone call was about, but I wasn't sure what the stare meant.

He took in and let out a long breath. "That was the *Trib*. They're wondering about a report they got about a missing person."

"Sorry to hear that. Those don't usually end well."

"No, they don't. But this one maybe even more so."

"How so?"

"The missing person is Rafael Melendez."

I'm sure I looked more surprised than he did. "That's not good. But missing is better than dead. Who reported it?"

"No, it isn't. Anonymous caller. Who else have you told about this evidence?"

"No one."

He looked skeptical. "Not even your friend Lieutenant Powolski?"

"Not even him."

He thought again. "Then who else could Melendez have told?" It was a rhetorical question. He thought some more. "Maybe told his sister."

"Maybe. But I guarantee you she wouldn't have passed it on. She takes everything he says as the ramblings of a man whose mind is gone."

"By the way, his sister is missing also."

"Ah, well that makes me feel better," I said. "She probably took him somewhere."

"Maybe. But the *Trib* is wondering what we know. I'd like to know *some*thing. They also gave me his address and asked if it had anything to do with the body of Reynolds Margot that was found near that location in the alley."

My eyebrows went up.

"You wanna come along?" he asked.

"Absolutely."

"And while we're looking for evidence of whether or not they left willingly, we could be looking for whatever else we might find."

"We could do that," I said. I expected him to get some help, but he didn't. It was just him and me. That was all right with me, but I didn't think it would have been all right if one of his detectives had done the same thing.

While we were driving I asked a question. "You're the head of detectives. Why aren't you handing this off to one of your team so you can take care of all that paperwork that's piling up?"

He laughed. "You got that right. But this interests me, and when something interests me I like to take care of it myself if I can. Besides, it's not like they're sitting around waiting for something to happen. We're swamped."

Sounded reasonable to me. I'd have done the same thing. Then I thought about my list. I knew that no one on my list had been in that alley that night. Guys get hired for things like that. But guys talk, and if I was right, someone on my list would be interested in whatever evidence had been found. Bast sounded interested, but then that was his job.

# Chapter 34

We were in Bast's unmarked car. As we turned onto Rafael's block, I got a knot in my stomach. The alley where Reynolds had been left was a half block ahead. The sky had clouded over, and the buildings looked even shabbier than they had in sunlight. Boarded up windows, trim that needed painting, dirty concrete, and no place for kids to play left me wondering how people lived like that. There weren't any hopes and dreams… it was just getting through the day.

One of the buzzers in the foyer was marked "Super." Bast pushed it, and a woman answered. He identified himself and told her why he was there. She let us in and met us in front of Rafael's door with the key. She was a short, plump woman who was probably younger than she looked. It was that kind of neighborhood. After several glances between Bast's ID and his face, she let us in without asking for a warrant. She didn't ask about me. Bast asked her when the last time she saw Rafael and his sister was.

She shook her head and said, "I ain't no den mother."

She didn't come in and told us to make sure the door was locked when we left. Bast asked if she wanted to know what we found. She didn't. It was that kind of neighborhood too.

The apartment was empty. The only sounds were from cars on the street. It looked exactly as I remembered. I followed Bast around as he looked in closets and opened drawers. I didn't touch anything, and neither of us spoke. I saw everything he saw, and what we saw told us that Rafael and his sister, if they had left for any extended period of time, hadn't left of their own accord. The drawers in the bedroom dresser and the closet next to it were full of clothes. There was food in the refrigerator and in the cabinets. And there was mail on the kitchen counter. There was one odd thing that I didn't mention to Bast—Rafael's binoculars and notebook were not on his table. It had only taken fifteen minutes to look through the apartment.

"Okay, Manning. Let's look for something else."

"Like what?"

"Hey, you're the one brought this up. You tell me."

"Well, we've already checked drawers and closets. Let's think where we'd hide something if we needed to."

"Under, behind… maybe in plain view. Be nice to know how big it is."

I laughed. "It would be nice to just know that it *is*."

It's hard to find something when you have no idea what it is. It is even harder when that something might very well be a figment of someone's imagination. I didn't expect to find anything, and that's exactly what we found.

A half hour later we were back at the station. I headed for the public lot, and Bast went in to call the *Trib* and tell them what he had found.

***

It was time for part two of my plan, and I needed Ralph's help. He was the best operative I had. One of the character traits that made him valuable was that he didn't ask questions unless he needed to know something that would help with what he was doing. He didn't need to know why. And he didn't mind doing things that were illegal, as long as my neck was as much on the line as his. He once told me over a few beers that it didn't make sense that the bad guys were the only ones with the advantage of illegalities. I wondered at the time if the beers had helped that viewpoint.

The Q Ball pool hall was on Clark on the near north side, and I think Ralph used that as his mailing address. That was the phone number in my records. I didn't have to wonder if he would be there. There would be something wrong if he wasn't.

I took a stool at the bar and ordered a Rolling Rock. There were only three balls left on the table, and Ralph was shooting. Only one of them might be difficult, and that depended on how he set it up. What separated a great player from a good player was being able to look many shots ahead and not only sink balls but leave the cue ball and the rest of the balls in the right places to run the table. Ralph was great, and everybody knew it. But they played anyway, always hoping. If anyone ever beat Ralph they would be the neighborhood hero.

He sank the six ball, and as he was walking around the table I caught his eye. He barely nodded. The next shot was the tough one, or at least it would have been for me. He hit the two on the left side. As it fell into the side pocket the backspin on the cue ball drew it back to a pretty easy location for the eight in the corner. I had never seen any money change hands, but I knew somewhere along the line it did. He took the stool next to me and leaned his stick against the bar.

"Hey, Spencer. Something urgent?"

Usually I called. "Not terribly, but I was in the neighborhood."

"So I can have a drink?"

"Sure." Ralph did his share of drinking, but never on the job.

He nodded to the barkeep, who brought him a Scotch on the rocks.

"Booth?" he asked.

"Yeah." We relocated.

We both took a drink and then I said, "I need an apartment with a street view from the living room. Not the first floor. Has to have a separate bedroom. Nothing fancy."

Another good thing about Ralph was that he knew people. If he couldn't get something directly he would know someone who could.

"How long?" he asked.

"Don't know where this is going. Might as well get a month."

"Any particular neighborhood?"

I took another drink. "Around here would be fine."

"Price range?"

"Whatever the going rate."

He nodded and took a drink and didn't ask why. But since I needed his help, I told him the plan.

I had told three people about the evidence that Rafael had. I figured that one of those three people would be concerned about that because I figured one of those three people was involved. If they weren't, then I was out of luck.

My plan was loosely based on the old scam called the "blind blackmail." The blackmailer sends out letters saying "I know what you did. If you want it kept quiet, send money to…" Almost everyone has done something, so it might get results. The payoff was small, maybe a hundred or two. Most people throw the letters away, but some bite.

In this case, I figured I was guaranteed results. Once Ralph found a room, I would send a message to Thward, Nadem, and Bast. The note would say that the writer had the evidence and that it was for sale for whatever dollar amount. I figured all would bite, and my gut was telling me Nadem was the guilty party. Or maybe I was just hoping. If he was, he'd send a hired hand with a briefcase or maybe a gun. Either way, we'd have it covered. And since Bast and Thward were law enforcement, they'd show up with the troops to catch whomever was pulling this scam.

Ralph pointed out that there were holes in the plan, such as how did I know who was going to show up when. I had already thought of that. I'd send out notes one at a time with specific times to meet.

Another problem was that Nadem might just not show. But we reasoned that if he was clean he'd call one of his friends in high places and *they* would show up with the troops.

We both finished our drinks, and he said, "It might work… and it might not. But whatever happens, it'll be interesting." He also pointed out that there would be holes we hadn't thought of. There always were, and I'd always been able to work them out.

I thanked him for the rousing vote of confidence. He said he'd
start working on a place right away and let me know.

*** 

He called a little after eight. He had a place within walking distance of the pool hall… 322 West Dickens. I picked him up an
hour later, and we took a look at it. It was perfect. It was a tiny one
bedroom at the street end of a hallway on the third floor. Two windows overlooked the street. The only furnishing was a set of thin,
white curtains that had turned a bit yellow on one of the windows.
The air in the room was a bit stale, so I opened the window with the
curtain. It fluttered like a wisp of smoke.

"So how you wanna work this, Spencer?"

"We need to be here before they get the note so they can't stake it
out and see us arrive. I'll courier a note to Thward at nine tomorrow
morning and tell him to be here between two and four. That should
give him enough time and window to be able to make it. You'll answer the door. I'll be in the bedroom with a tape recorder running."

"And if he can't make it? Or isn't in the office tomorrow?"

"That's one of the holes. We'll have to play it by ear."

"And what if the guy with the troops decides to arrest us for
any one of a list of things that keeps getting longer the more I think
about it?"

I gave him my best smile. "Is that all you can do? Think about
the holes?"

"I tend to wonder about things like that when it's my butt we're
talking about. So what time do you want me here?"

"Let's shoot for ten."

He handed me a key. "See you in the morning." As he reached
for the doorknob, he asked, "Are we carrying?"

"We are."

Before he turned the knob, he said, "This may be your craziest
concoction yet."

I laughed. "No *may* be about it."

# Chapter 35

I brought the Tuesday paper in from the driveway at six thirty and started scanning. The story about Rafael was on page 6.

> Two weeks ago, the body of Reynolds Margot was found in an alley on Madison Avenue. There may have been a witness to that crime. Rafael Melendez and his sister live in an apartment building across the street from the alley where Margot's body was found. Melendez and his sister have been reported missing. Detective Bast of the Chicago Police says that they are looking into the missing persons report, and he does not know of any connection to the murder of Margot.

At nine I sent the following note to Thward by a special courier I used now and then. Special meant there was no way it could be traced to the sender. I paid a bit extra for that service.

> I have Rafael's evidence. If you want it come to 322 West Dickens, apartment 3a, between 2 and 4 this afternoon. Come alone.

Short and to the point. I left as soon as the courier picked it up and stopped at a deli for sandwiches and cokes.

Ralph was already at the apartment when I got there. I also had Paul stationed in the alley with a two-way radio. I wanted to know when Thward arrived, and there was an alley door to the apartment building. Ralph and I would take turns watching the street. We started watching at ten in case Thward sent an advance team, and we made two bets, each ten bucks. The first was whether or not Thward would show. I had yes. The second was, if he did, would it be before or after three. I had after. Ralph wanted to add a third—whether or not we'd be in jail before the day was over. I thought that was bad karma.

I won both bets. Thward arrived at 3:20. He parked on the opposite side of the street and looked up at our building over the roof of his car. I didn't notice any other cars stopping, but I did get a call from Paul. Two cars had pulled into the alley. Two men had gotten out of each car and were just entering the rear door. It looked like Thward wasn't the one I was after, but I'd wait to see what his play was. Ralph had heard Paul's message.

Ralph and I had decided beforehand about the guns if one person showed up... one person who we had laid the trap for. If someone showed up with troops, we wouldn't need or want the guns. So I took his gun and put it along with mine at the back of the high shelf in the bedroom closet. I stood behind the partially closed door to the bedroom. I'd be able to hear but not see.

A few minutes later there was a knock at the door. I turned on the tape recorder.

"Come in," Ralph said. Someone entered, but the door didn't close. "Who are you?" Ralph asked.

"A guy who got a strange note. Who are you?"

"A guy who sent the note. Let me see some ID."

It was quiet. And I smelled cigarette smoke. It was soaked into him.

"Okay," Thward said. "Now you know who I am... who are you?"

"Name's not important. I appear to have something you want."

"And what is that something?"

"You'll see when you see."

"I'm getting tired of twenty questions," Thward said with a snarl. "You got it with you?"

"I can get it within twenty minutes."

"And what are you getting in exchange?"

We hadn't rehearsed what Ralph should say beyond the basics. But I trusted his being able to roll with the punches. I was interested in what he would say next. The conversation had gotten to the arrestable offense point.

"We can talk about that if you're interested."

"Okay, let's say I'm interested. How much?"

I held my breath.

"Let's start at twenty."

I smiled. Ralph was trying as hard as he could not to mention money.

I could almost hear the exasperation in Thward's voice. "Twenty what?" he asked.

*Go ahead and say it,* I thought. *Gotta happen sooner or later.* He did.

"Twenty thousand… dollars."

Ralph yelled, "Gun!" and all hell broke loose.

I came out of the bedroom, and the troops came in the front door. Thward looked surprised and confused.

"Manning! What the hell are you doing here?"

I stood with my arms away from my sides and partially raised and didn't answer. I could see the thoughts bouncing around in his brain. And I could see five guns pointing at us.

Thward moved his gun to me and said, "Either you're dirty as hell or you set me up. I hope it's the first."

"That's not very friendly," I said. "And would you mind lowering the guns?"

"Yes, I would."

I responded. "Philip Marlowe said, 'Guns never settle anything. They're just a fast curtain to a bad second act.'"

His gun stayed pointed. "Philip Marlowe isn't real."

"Doesn't make it any less true."

"Two of you search them," he said to his troops.

They did. Not having guns had been a good decision.

"Okay, you two have a seat." He and his troops holstered their guns.

"There aren't any chairs," I said.

"Ask me if I give a damn. Sit on the floor... right next to each other."

We sat.

Thward stood looking down on us from five feet away. "I'm starting a list of things to charge you with. Being a pain in the ass is near the top, along with illegal possession of evidence in a crime investigation and interfering with a federal officer. I'm sure I'll come up with more. You and your friend here will be in jail before all this is over."

"I've already been in a Chicago jail once over this case. Another isn't going to—"

"You won't like a federal jail, Manning. We don't have all the amenities these city jails have. And the clientele isn't quite as nice."

I resisted the urge to call him Peggy. Somehow I realized that wouldn't help any. "Well, to tell you the truth," I said, "I wasn't all that thrilled about the Chicago jail either."

He dismissed half of his troops. "You've got one minute to explain with something besides Raymond Chandler quotes."

Ralph was looking at me with his usual blank stare. Any other person might be a bit worried. But if he couldn't do anything, he just became a disinterested bystander. There was nothing he could do... the rest was up to me. He knew he'd either be in jail waiting to be bailed out or playing pool an hour from now, and it didn't really matter to him which one it ended up being. There was a jail clause in his deal with me. It was worth a good chunk of money. He also knew I hadn't let him down yet. Of course we had never been sitting on the floor of a bare room with a trio of FBI agents.

I pulled my knees up to my chest. "What I have to say is for your ears only."

"And why would that be?"

"Nothing personal, but the people I trust in all this are on a very short list."

"And you trust me?" he asked.

"That's part of my story."

He thought for ten seconds and then told his two men to wait in the hall.

"And down the hall… not by the door," I said.

They stopped short of the door.

"Not by the door?" one of them said.

"And Ralph goes with them to make sure."

Thward threw his hands up. "What is this… Watergate?"

"Up to you what you do with the information after I tell you, but it starts with just you or I go to jail."

"Jesus, Manning. This better be good." He waved his men out and pointed to Ralph. "You go with them. Keep each other company." When they had left he said, "One minute."

I started. "First of all, there isn't any evidence, so you can forget about that. I—"

"What!" He shook his head. "Okay, I'll forget about that, but that adds a few more charges."

"Does you talking count in my minute?"

He just stared at me with controlled anger.

"As I already told you, I'm looking into the drug case and murder of Margot. I'm betting those two and the murder of Michael Nadem are related. I have a list of possibles that I'm not getting anywhere with. So how do I get somewhere? My usual method is to stir the pot. The only plan I could come up with was to plant the seed that Rafael had evidence and see what jumped out of the pot."

"Why the hell would you do that?"

"Because I'm not good at standing on the sidelines waiting for something to happen. It's not in my DNA."

He crossed his arms over his chest. "I must have missed something. You thought I was a suspect?"

I shrugged. "Cops on the take, politicians being indicted. Who do you trust? I know nothing about you except that you're addicted to cigarettes. Who do *you* trust, Thward?"

"Maybe my mother, but I'm not always sure about her."

"See? There are several people possibly tied to this case, and I only trust two of them."

"Which two would those be?" he asked.

"Sister Katherine is one."

"Hard not to trust a nun."

"You said you didn't trust anybody. Do *you* trust her?"

"Nope."

"You've proven my point. I had to see who would bite. If you showed up here by yourself this would have been a different conversation. Now I can cross you off my list."

"Who else do you trust?"

I shook my head. "You wouldn't believe it, so let's skip it."

"Okay… for the moment. Who else is on your list?"

"Nadem and Bast and Mrs. Margot and Benita Landez, another cop who works with Bast."

He looked out the window before he looked back at me. "The senators's son was murdered, and you think he is involved?"

"Could have been. But then things turned south."

"And your own client?"

"Until I find out otherwise."

"Who else have you sent this note to?"

"No one, yet. But all are possibilities."

He shook his head. "This is the craziest damned thing I've ever seen. And I've got several charges I could make stick with no effort at all."

"Are you open to a deal?"

"From the guy sitting on the floor with a list of charges hanging over his head?"

Putting it that way didn't sound so good.

"I'm doing something you can't... at least legally. Give me a week to see what happens. I'll keep you informed. If I have nothing by the end of the week, we can have another chat."

He shook his head again. "The only thing you have going for you is I don't need the paperwork. And there's a good chance you'll end up in somebody *else's* jail... or dead."

I stretched out my legs. "Thanks for the cheery thought."

He stared at me some more. "I read in the paper that Melendez is missing. Is that bogus too?"

"Beats me. Bast is looking into it."

"Right. Good luck with that."

*No love lost there,* I thought.

"Mind if I stand up?"

He motioned me up.

"We have a deal?" I asked.

"You have a week, and you keep me informed. And if you find something, I get the credit. You don't get crap."

"Never have needed credit, Thward. But I do have a question."

He just stared at me with a blank look that didn't say okay or not, so I asked.

"What was the deal you offered to Reynolds?"

"I don't see where that's either relevant anymore or any of your business."

"I'm trying to find out what was going on and why he ended up in that alley. It may have a bearing."

He thought for a few seconds and then decided it didn't matter if he shared it. The kid was dead.

"Nothing you probably haven't already guessed. I wanted to know where he was getting the drugs. I wanted someone higher up the ladder. Pretty simple."

"In exchange for...?"

"No jail time. Two years probation."

"And he didn't take the deal."

"We were talking. But no, he didn't jump at it."

"Doesn't that seem strange? Should have been a no-brainer."

"Very."

I filed that away. I'd think about it later.

"Send my man back in," I said.

He held out his hand.

"What?" I asked.

"I'll take the tape."

"What tape?"

"I don't walk out of here without it, Manning."

I tried to intimidate him with my stare, but he wasn't fazed.

"You could be in a holding cell in twenty minutes."

I gave in and let out a sigh. I went into the bedroom, rewound the tape, and handed it to him.

He took it and turned and left without saying goodbye. I retrieved our guns and handed Ralph's to him when he came in the room. The only question he asked was if I needed him again. I did. I asked him to meet me here at ten tomorrow. He gave me a two-finger salute and headed for the pool hall. The radio crackled that the cars in the alley had left as I watched Thward get into his car and pull away. I wasn't a fan of Thward, but I was glad to cross him off my list. Stosh had often told me not to let emotions or personal opinions into a case… just let the facts run their course. I often had trouble with that advice. The guy I really wanted was Nadem. He wasn't worth the price of a bullet, and I would love to see him behind bars. There was still hope.

# Chapter 36

Wednesday morning I sent the same message to Bast. The only difference was it was raining… a light spring drizzle that smelled clean and refreshing. When I got to the apartment, I discovered I had forgotten to close the window. The sill was a little wet, but the rain was out of the northwest and the window faced south, so the rain wasn't coming directly in the window. I pushed it shut.

Same routine. Paul was watching the alley, and Ralph and I took turns at the window. The routine changed when I saw a tan Buick drive by a little before eleven. It drove by a little slower a few minutes later and then a third time. From my angle I couldn't see the driver, but it looked like the same tan Buick Bast had. Odds were pretty good it wasn't a different tan Buick. I let Paul know and had Ralph join me at the window after the first pass so he'd know what the car looked like.

Ralph spotted the car again at 2:10. It kept going down the block, and he lost sight of it three buildings to the west. I let Paul know. If it was Bast, the fact that he got there near the start of the time window showed he was anxious. Guilty people are anxious. Paul radioed that there was no activity in the alley.

I took up a position at the window and saw Bast walking back up the street. I took up my position in the bedroom and started the tape.

Ralph answered the knock with, "It's open… come on in."

After thirty seconds of silence, Bast asked, "So what the hell is this all about?"

"Pretty simple. Reynolds Margot's body was dumped in an alley. Fellow across the street saw it. After the car left, this fellow went down to the street and found something. I have what he found."

"And what would that be?"

So far Bast was asking what a cop would ask.

"Not till we get this worked out."

More silence that was broken by Bast with, "Take off your jacket."

"Pardon?"

"Simple request. Take off your jacket."

That exposed Ralph's gun, but it wasn't the gun Bast was interested in.

"Now unbutton your shirt."

I heard Ralph sigh and realized what was going on. I was sure Ralph did also.

After ten seconds, Bast's next request was, "Now pull up your undershirt."

After a few more seconds he told Ralph to get dressed.

"So?" Bast asked.

"So, I've got something you want. When you give me something I want... I give it to you."

"And what is it you want?"

"Money."

"How much?"

"Twenty-five thousand."

Bast laughed. "And where am I going to get twenty-five thousand on a cop's salary?"

"Really? You wouldn't be here if you were just living on a cop's salary."

Silence for ten seconds.

"When would I get this evidence?"

"When will you have the money?"

"I need a few days."

"Okay. Friday."

"Here?" Bast asked.

"Nope. I'll let you know Friday morning."

"What if your evidence isn't?"

"Isn't what?"

"Isn't meaningful evidence… isn't worth twenty-five thousand."

"Then don't buy it."

Another ten seconds of silence.

"I want your tape," Bast said.

I rolled my eyes up to the ceiling. Dealing with cops was getting to be a pain in the ass.

There was a sound of Ralph starting to say something, but he was interrupted by Bast.

"Don't even think of denying it."

Ralph didn't argue. He came into the bedroom, shrugged at me, turned the recorder off, picked it up, and walked out.

More silence for about a half minute. The next thing I heard was the door opening and closing.

Ralph came back in a few seconds after that.

"He's gone."

I went over to the windows and watched Bast walk down the block. I turned to Ralph.

"So much for taping," I said. "It goes so well on TV."

He laughed. "At least you have a shiny new tape recorder. Now you just need something to play on it."

"Nice."

Ralph was smiling. "We doing this again?"

I shook my head. "Nope, we're done."

He gave me a questioning look, and I knew why.

"Technically," Ralph said, "he hasn't done anything illegal. From one point of view he's a cop waiting for enough evidence to make an arrest. And even if you had the tape, he didn't say anything incriminating."

"I know. But he came here alone." And if it was Bast, that explained the drugs in my car. And there was the fraternity connection. But I hadn't shared those with Ralph.

"And if he is involved, what if there's others on your list who are in on it?"

"Then, being the great detective that I am, I'll find out."

He was smiling again. "I hope you're a better detective than taper."

"Used to be the hired help had more respect for the boss. You know, when I was a kid, I was always a good hitter with two strikes. Next time I bring an extra tape."

He gave me his two-finger salute and headed for the door.

"Check's in the mail," I said.

I let Paul go and headed for Stosh's for dinner. I'd be early, but I needed some time to sit and think. Now I knew who it was, but I didn't know how or why, or maybe even what. It appeared to be about drugs, but appearances could be deceiving. I was missing something and needed the string that tied the pieces together.

# Chapter 37

Stosh usually got home around six. Tonight he was late. It was a little after six thirty when he pulled into the drive and parked next to me.

"Tough day at the office?" I asked.

He dropped his jacket on the couch. "Like yesterday and the one before that. I'm hungry. We're going to Carson's for ribs."

"Good by me."

"I'm going to wash up, and then I'm going to ask you a question."

I closed my eyes and waited for him. I didn't hear him come back in until he spoke.

"Article in the *Trib* about Melendez and his sister being missing along with evidence. What did you have to do with that?"

I knew I couldn't say *nothing*. He knew I had something to do with it, and we weren't going to leave until he had an answer. And I was hungry too.

"I'll tell you on the way."

We took his Ford and headed north. Before he made the turn at the end of the block, he said, "Let's hear it."

I told him about my plan to use evidence that Rafael had found to shake things up.

After he was done yelling, I said, "I made up the part about the evidence."

"What! This just keeps getting better. We'll ignore the illegality of that for the moment. Why would you do that?"

"Because I was getting nowhere. I needed to start a fire and see who ran out of the burning house."

"And you didn't think that you'd be putting an innocent person at risk?"

"I did."

"And you did it anyway?"

"Well, yes. But—"

"Jesus, Spencer! What the hell is wrong with you? You—"

"Hang on, Stosh. You don't have the whole story."

He turned onto the Edens Expresssway and headed north.

"So? Who were you going to tell about this evidence?" he asked.

"I figured I'd tell the people on my list… Thward, Nadem, Bast… maybe Benny and Mrs. Margot."

"Your client? The mother of the kid who was murdered?"

"It doesn't sound so good when you say it, but yes."

"And a detective and an FBI agent."

"Yes."

"I must be dreaming this. Your willingness to forget about the law seems to be growing."

"Helps to catch the bad guys," I argued.

"The laws that are there to protect citizens," he continued.

"And the bad guys, evidently," I pointed out.

"Bad guys are citizens too," he said.

"Not a perfect system," I said. "I can do things that are illegal for you."

"Last time I checked they are illegal for you too."

"Technicality," I said.

He was shaking his head. "And what did you expect to happen when you told them?"

"I expected different things to happen depending on who I told."

"How are you telling them? Have you told them all?"

"So far I've only told two. I had an anonymous note sent."

"This keeps getting better. We may skip dinner. I'm losing my appetite. Which two?"

"Thward and Bast."

"And what did you expect to happen?"

"See if you follow my reasoning."

He laughed. "You gotta be kidding! Any reasoning is long gone."

I took a deep breath. "I'm looking for whoever is behind all this."

"And you think that could be a police officer."

"Falls under your rule about not trusting anybody. Wouldn't be the first bad cop."

"Odds are against it," he said.

He turned off the expressway onto Touhy and in a few blocks pulled into Carson's lot. He turned off the engine and looked at me. It wasn't a friendly look.

I continued my explanation. "If either of those two showed up with backup I'd know they weren't the one I was looking for. But if someone showed up alone and bit on the blackmail…" I spread my hands, palms up. "I started with Thward. That was Tuesday. He showed up with four agents and a drawn gun and threatened to arrest me."

"I wish he had. But since you're sitting here, my wish didn't come true. What happened?"

"I explained the possibilities and asked him to give me a week. He said he'd rather not do the paperwork anyway and agreed. But he took my tape and said jail was only a step away."

"Jesus. Who were you raised by… a pack of wolves? Oh yeah, a police chief. Unbelievable."

"And then there was Bast… this afternoon. He showed up by himself and looked for a wire on Ralph. He asked how much and didn't argue. Asked when and where. Ralph told him he'd get another note. He asked what the evidence was. Ralph told him he'd find out when he got it."

He shook his head some more. "I haven't heard anything illegal yet. He's not going to pull out his badge until an exchange is made."

"He came there alone, Stosh. He checked Ralph for a wire. He acted guilty."

He shook his head. "Suspect but circumstantial. You've got a good cop who is being careful and has no idea who he's dealing with, or a bad cop who isn't stupid."

"Not enough to put him in jail, but enough to point me in his direction and start tying this together with him in the middle of it. I make informed guesses."

"Sometimes. Most the time you make gut guesses."

"And most the time they're right." I thought about beer and ribs. "Actually, all the time."

He shook his head and let out an audible breath. "Why is it always so hard to stay mad at you?"

"Because I'm so lovable," I said with a smile.

"Right… that's it. Let's eat."

When we got our beers and had ordered we continued the conversation.

"Well, if it *is* Bast, that solves one mystery," Stosh said. "We know who planted the drugs in your car."

"Probably. But he had help. Someone else had to do the actual planting. I was with him the whole time except for a few minutes when he went to the head. That didn't give him enough time to plant the drugs, but it did give him enough time to tell someone else to."

"So maybe Bast is the guy up the ladder Thward has been trying to catch," Stosh said.

"Looks that way. And Bast knew about the deal Thward wanted to cut with Reynolds, and there was only one way to make sure he didn't talk. And that's why Reynolds was reluctant to make a deal."

"And pretty easy to blame it on the Prophets," Stosh said.

"Yeah, sitting ducks."

"But how did Reynolds get involved with Bast? And what about Nadem's kid?"

The ribs arrived.

"Good questions. There's obviously something I'm missing."

"Puzzles don't make sense if you're missing pieces," Stosh said. "So what's next?"

We ate and talked. The ribs were, as usual, delicious.

"I'll have to start another fire."

"Are you done with your blackmail scheme?"

I nodded while I ate.

"So where's the next fire?" he asked.

"There's the fraternity connection. Bast said he didn't know the Margots before this, and Mrs. said she didn't know Bast. But with Bast and Mr. Margot being back-to-back presidents of the same fraternity that's hard to believe. There's some connection there that I'm missing."

"Well, if it's there I'm sure you'll find it. But maybe Bast isn't the only one on your list involved in this."

"Maybe. I'd like Nadem to be."

"You don't get to pick."

"Too bad. And I'm not happy that Thward isn't."

"It's not about you, Spencer. You know, Thward has every right to arrest you."

"I know."

"You gotta stop putting yourself on the line, kid. Not all bad guys get caught."

"I know. But I'll do what I can to get the ones that cross my path."

He finished a rib and said, "This wouldn't be the first time you put yourself in the line of fire."

I thought about my folks and my sister and my health. "I don't have much to lose, Stosh."

"Sorry you feel that way, kid."

"I know. It's okay."

"Just be careful what fires you light. You've got people who care."

I nodded and unwrapped a wet wipe.

# Chapter 38

**M**y car phone rang Thursday morning as I was on the way to the office.

"Spencer, are you coming in?"

Carol sounded flustered.

"Yes. Be there in ten minutes."

"Could you make it five?"

"What's up?"

"Someone dropped a sheet of paper in the mail slot."

"And?"

"It says 'You're still not listening. We have Rafael, and we know who is important to you. We can get them too.'"

I ran a yellow light.

"Go next door to the deli and ask Marco if you can wait for me in his office. I'll make it five. We'll go get Billy."

"Spencer, I—"

"Go now. Lock up."

I hung up and pulled around a cab and ran another light. That one turned red as I was in the intersection. I needed to get protection for Carol and Billy. But I couldn't do that if I was working on the problem. I thought about Larry Maggio. Joey the Juicer had two hired hands who sat around the ice cream parlor all day trying to stay awake, and either one would be willing to put a bullet in someone who threatened my friends, or anyone else if the price were right. But then, as I thought about Aunt Rose and Maxine, I had a better idea.

I parked two doors down from the office in front of a fire hydrant and found Carol in Marco's office. I thanked him on the way out.

"Is Billy in danger, Spencer?"

"Not yet," I assured her as we climbed the stairs to her apartment. "It's probably just a scare technique, but if they are serious they'll wait to see if I back off."

"But they said they have Rafael."

"They don't."

"How do you know that?"

"Because I'm a detective. I know stuff." She unlocked her door as I told her to pack bags for her and Billy for a trip to Door County. Easier to protect your loved ones if they're all in one place.

"For how long?"

"I don't know. But put as much in a suitcase for each of you as you can."

"I'm afraid, Spencer."

"I know. I'm sorry. But I'll take care of you."

"How do I know we'll be safe up there?"

"Because I have friends who will see to it." I took ahold of her shoulders and told her to look at me. "You'll be fine, Carol. If need be, I'll back off, but I don't think that'll be necessary."

She closed her eyes and said, "Okay."

As she was packing, I told her we'd get Billy and then head for Enterprise to rent a car she could use to drive to Wisconsin. I wrote down directions while she was packing. It was a pretty simple drive. And I gave her the two hundred dollars I had taken out of petty cash. On the way out we grabbed the bag of dog food, and Watson jumped in the back seat.

The drive to the school took only a few minutes. No one was following. I waited in the car. Billy seemed excited to be getting out of school and got in the back seat with Watson.

Carol turned to him and said, "You don't have to be so happy about missing school."

"What did you tell them?" I asked.

"That there was a family emergency."

"Good."

"What emergency, Mom?" Billy asked as he was petting Watson.

She turned to the back seat. "Well, it's not really our emergency, sweetheart. It's something for Spencer. We have to go up to Aunt Rose's in Door County."

Billy and Carol had spent time at my cottage and with Rose last summer, and Billy had begged to go back.

"That's great, Mom! That'll be fun! I thought I was in trouble. Miss May came in our room and said something to our teacher, and she called my name. When I went by Jimmy's desk he said, 'You're in trouble *now*.' He said it was about time."

"Ah, the Jimmy's of the world," I said.

"What does that mean?" he asked.

"That means your mom's got a good kid."

Carol put her hand on my thigh and smiled and said, "I've got two good kids."

I pulled into the Enterprise lot. Carol and I went in, and Billy sat with Watson on a bench outside. There were two people in front of us. While we waited I took Carol to chairs by the window, and we sat.

"I'm so sorry for getting you into this, Carol."

She put an arm around my shoulder and said, "It's okay, Spencer. I could have gotten a job at Enterprise, but I took a job working for a private investigator. That comes with some risk… everything comes with some risk."

"The risk is considerably greater. I don't see anyone threatening to kidnap those clerks behind the counter."

"So far I've loved my job. And the guy I work for is great."

"But, I—"

She squeezed me closer. "Look what you're doing to protect us. I'm not concerned."

\*\*\*

got Carol a car and saw them off. Then I sat in the rental parking lot and called Chief Iverson in Door County. He was just leaving the station.

"How's things, Spencer?" he asked with a cheery lilt.

I told him about the letter and that I'd fill him in on the rest later. I told him Carol and Billy would be staying with Rose, and I needed a man at the inn around the clock.

"When will they be here?" he asked.

"They just left, so five to six hours. But I want someone there ASAP to cover Rose and Maxine."

"Do they know?"

"They will as soon as we hang up."

"Okay, I'll have someone there within a half hour."

"Great. Thanks, Chief. Would you call Rose and tell her who you're sending? Let me know too."

"Sure," he said. "Call back when you can and fill me in. Good luck."

I hung up and called Aunt Rose. Maxine answered. I cut her off in mid-sentence.

"Is Rose there, Maxine?"

"Yes. Do you want to talk to her?"

I told her no and explained the situation and told her that Carol and Billy were on their way.

"Don't either of you go anywhere until help gets there. Iverson is going to call you and let you know who's coming."

"Okay, Spencer."

"And don't take any new reservations. If anybody calls, you're full for a week."

"Got it. Will you call later?"

"Yes. Don't worry, Max."

She laughed. "It's whoever wrote that note should worry if they wanna mess with *me*."

"That I know. Just keep your eyes open."

"Will do."

*\*\*\**

**S** tosh was next on my list. I waved to the desk sergeant on my way into the station and took the stairs two at a time. He was in the hall outside his office talking with a detective. I walked past them and sat opposite his desk.

"Just make yourself at home," he said as he sat. "Order you some breakfast? Eggs? Pancakes?"

I took the note out of the envelope I had put it in and slid it across his desk. I had folded a piece of paper over the top of the note to avoid touching it. I told him not to touch the note, and he quickly lost the attitude.

Shaking his head, he said, "Jesus, Spencer. This isn't worth it. Time to quit and let the guys with the badges figure this out."

"Yeah, they're doing a great job so far."

He started to say something, but I interrupted him.

"The circus of agencies involved in this is spending more time arguing about who has jurisdiction over what than solving anything."

"While I'll give you some of that, you don't know what they're doing. More goes on than what's in the papers. They want this solved, too, Spencer." He drummed his fingers on his desk and said, "It's one thing to put yourself in danger. This is another."

"I know. And I've taken care of it." I told him about Carol and Billy and Rose and Maxine. "And I figure you can take care of yourself."

"That's no guarantee."

"And what do you suggest?" I asked. "Turning this over to the cops, one of which looks like he's involved with drugs and two murders?" I let that sit for five seconds. "And asking the police to protect all these people around the clock? That better?"

He just took a deep breath and slowly let it out.

"And there's no guarantee they'd quit even if I backed off," I said.

"You done?"

"Hey. You don't have to get snotty just because I'm right."

"No, but it's more fun that way." He leaned forward and read the note again. "I do have to admit you did all the right things. Put all your people in the same spot and get them some hired help. I wouldn't be surprised if Iverson showed up himself from time to time."

"At around dinner time," I said.

"Of course. And this confirms the Melendez kidnapping."

"It appears to."

He looked at me sideways. "Why do I have the feeling there's some hidden meaning there?"

"Maybe because you're a suspicious government employee. What's hidden? I agreed with you."

"I'm not sure I like it when you agree with me."

I nodded toward the note. "Would you check it for prints?"

"Sure. But I doubt if we'll find any."

"Other than Carol's, probably not." When she started working for me, I had her printed and put on file just in case something like this happened. "And would you see if you can find anything on Bast?"

"Yeah, but again, I doubt there's anything. He has a good reputation."

"Doesn't hurt to look."

He nodded and looked at his watch. "Got a meeting in five. Anything else?"

"No. I'm going to do some digging on the Margots."

"You want some help with that?"

I smiled. "No thanks. I have better sources than you."

He shook his head with a hint of a smile. "I don't want to know."

"No, you don't."

# Chapter 39

I was surprised at how empty the office felt without Carol and Watson. I missed the look of disdain he gave me every time I came in.

I dug through Carol's files and found the folder on background checks. She had a number and a password. She had to say the password first or the person would hang up. It was a contact Ben had given me, so I assumed it was some kind of government connection that most people didn't have access to... even people in the government. Carol had told me that the password changed, and there was a complicated system of notification. I assumed she kept the password in the file current. I had once asked her what the cost was. She couldn't answer. The cost varied depending on how soon I needed the information and how involved it was. She said we'd just get a bill. I also assumed that whoever had set this up was operating not entirely legally.

I dialed the number, and a woman answered with a very curt "Hello."

"Reindeer."

"Go ahead."

I identified myself and told her I wanted whatever she could give me on the Margot family and gave her the address. She asked how soon I needed it. I said twenty minutes would be nice. She hung up. I held the receiver in front of me and looked at it, surprised at what had just happened. Carol hadn't told me about the lack of... I didn't know what to call it... humanity, friendliness, civility?

But the service was always accurate and helpful, so I guess I didn't need friendliness.

I sat at Carol's desk watching traffic and then went to the deli for a sandwich. The last few days had been perfect weather-wise. Temperature in the seventies, sunshine, white fluffy clouds. But when I was driving back from the station the sky was clouding over, and as I walked to the deli a drizzle started. I brought an Italian sub back to the office.

I hadn't expected results in twenty minutes, but there was a fax waiting when I got back. I wondered what that bill would be. There was nothing on the fax to identify the sender. I stayed at Carol's desk and read the two-page report. It was well worth whatever it cost. I ate while I read.

There were the normal facts about addresses and phone numbers. But there was also a bombshell. Jeanne had told me Reynolds was their only son. There was another... Raymond. He was four years older than Reynolds, which made him twenty-two. I'd seen family pictures in their den and the library, and the only picture of a son was that of Reynolds. The second page had a paragraph on the car accident that had killed Jeanne's husband, Robert, four years ago. Raymond had been driving. A car had run a red light and broadsided the passenger side of his car. The report listed his current location as Lone Star, South Carolina. There was an address from a speeding ticket five months ago in Charleston. I needed to have a chat with Jeanne.

As I was getting ready to leave, the phone rang. It was Iverson.

"All set, Spencer. My man is at the inn."

"Cop?"

"Retired CIA."

"In Door County?"

"He's trying to get away from it all."

"Good place to do that. Retired? But still young enough to be effective?"

"Seventy-eight."

"Ah hell, Chief. I need somebody—"

"Nobody better," he interrupted. "He could whup your sorry ass. And he blends in nicely on the porch with the inn look. He has a cane he uses for hiking. And a sawed-off fits nicely under an old man's blanket."

I took in a deep breath. "If you say so."

"I do."

"I'm just leaving the office. I'll call you from the road and fill you in."

***

It was almost one thirty by the time I got to Kenilworth and rang the Margot's bell. Maddy answered the door.

"Hello, Mr. Spencer." She looked happy to see me.

"Hello, Maddy. Mrs. Margot in?"

"No, sir. She's out for the afternoon."

"Would you mind if I came in and talked with you for a few minutes?"

She hesitated and looked flustered. "Well, I... Mrs. Margot doesn't—"

"It's okay, Maddy. How about we sit out here?"

She looked past me toward the street. "I suppose that would be all right."

We sat in the afternoon sun on one of two matching wrought iron benches that framed the front doors.

"I only have a few minutes... I have work to do."

"That'll be fine, Maddy. How long have you been with the Margots?"

She looked thoughtful. "I guess it's going on eight years now."

I nodded. "So you were here during the good times."

"Yes. Times were better."

"And you were here when Raymond was here."

"Yes, he was..."

She quickly realized what she had said, or rather shouldn't have said. She looked afraid and clasped her hands over her chest.

Shaking her head, she said, "I shouldn't have said that. Mrs. Margot would fire me if she knew I said that. Please don't—"

"Don't worry, Maddy. I won't say anything. Why would she fire you?"

She shook her head some more. "I shouldn't say any more. It's not something to be talked about."

"Maddy, I already know about the accident. I know where Raymond is."

She looked surprised as she dropped her hands to her lap.

I spoke calmly. "I'd like to know something about him."

She looked out over the yard with tears in her eyes. "He was a good boy. Quiet. Never any trouble with him."

"Unlike Reynolds?" I said.

"I don't say bad things about people."

"From the time I was with him I got the feeling Reynolds was a handful. Rebellious."

She just nodded and asked quietly, almost in a whisper, "Where is Raymond?"

"He's in South Carolina. Didn't Mrs. Margot tell you?"

She shook her head. "After the funeral he just disappeared. No one said anything about Raymond, and I didn't ask."

"Why do you think that was, Maddy?"

"I truly don't know."

"Raymond must have felt terrible."

"He must have."

The mailman pulled up to the box at the front of the driveway as I decided Maddy had given me all the information she had. I thanked her and wished her well.

As I got into the car I reached for the phone to call Carol to ask her to make plane reservations to South Carolina. Then I remembered she wasn't there. I'd have to make them myself. All the way back to the office I tried to talk myself into driving rather than flying. I hated flying. I knew the statistics… it was far safer than driving. But I hated giving up control. I understood the science of thrust and lift, but it seemed to me that something that heavy didn't belong up in the sky. And being in something that could fall out of the sky didn't seem like a good idea either. I had only flown three times, and each one was not pleasant. At some point it was worth spending extra time to drive. But South Carolina was way past that point. I'd have to bite the bullet.

I made the reservation when I got back to the office. Then I called Ben and invited him to dinner at McGoon's. He'd meet me at seven fifteen.

# Chapter 40

I was getting out of the car when he pulled in. Jack waved to us from the bar as we were shown to our table. We each ordered a Guinness, and Jane asked if we needed menus. We didn't. Two ribeyes medium rare. I brought Ben up to date on everything that had happened since he had bailed me out of jail… my notes to Thward and Bast and their appearances at the apartment, the threatening note, my discovery of Raymond Margot, and my plan to try and find him.

"So where has this kid been hiding?" he asked.

"Charleston."

"Illinois?"

I grimaced. "No. South Carolina."

Jane arrived with the beer.

After raised glasses, he said, "That's a long drive."

"Yeah, which is why I'm flying."

He almost choked on his beer. "In an airplane?"

That didn't merit an answer.

"Wow. You should be walking away from this. It's not worth the risk. Instead you're getting on an airplane. I thought you said after the turbulence of the last flight the only way you'd get on a plane would be if you had lost your mind."

"I think I have."

"You must want this bad."

I didn't answer that either. A couple was seated next to us. The restaurant was busy for a Thursday night.

"What are you hoping to get from him?" Ben asked.

"Answers to questions."

"Which are?"

"I know next to nothing about his brother. I'm hoping he knows what was going on. How did he get involved with drugs? Why is he in South Carolina, and why are there no pictures of him in his house?"

Ben set his glass down. "I'm guessing the answer to the last is he wanted to disappear. And if that's the case, he won't be happy about you finding him."

"Probably not."

"But you're doing it anyway."

I took a long drink. "His brother is dead. I'm hoping he cares about that."

Ben nodded. "Maybe he does… and maybe he doesn't."

I cocked my head. "Only one way to find out."

He nodded again as the food arrived. I was famished.

After a few bites, he said, "As you know, I spent many years working for the state's attorney's office as a prosecutor."

I just looked at him as I savored the steak.

"I've learned a few things about the law," he said as he ate.

Knowing what was coming, I kept chewing and looking at him. I could do both at the same time.

"Bast hasn't done anything illegal," he said.

"I've been told that. You law guys have a one-sided view of things."

"Yeah, the side of the bench the judge sits on."

I took a bite of garlic mashed potatoes and said, "I'm aware of the law. But I can do things the law can't. And the way he went about that smelled bad. And there's the drugs that were planted in my car. Easy explanation if it's him."

He cut another piece of meat, juice running onto his plate. "First, you shouldn't do things the law can't. You just choose to ignore that fact. And some day bailing you out will be a lot more complicated.

Second, I agree with you. Worth taking a closer look at him. If he is involved in drugs, he's doing it for the money. So where is it?"

I shrugged.

"Fancy car?"

"Tan Buick sedan, at least three years old."

Ben laughed. "Nothing says drug money like a three-year-old Buick. Fancy house? Expensive wife?"

"Don't know."

"Okay. I've got nothing to do while you're risking your life in the friendly skies. I'll look into it."

"Thanks. Appreciate it."

"And I appreciate the steak dinners."

We finished eating and chatted about the Cubs, hopeful for a series run this year.

# Chapter 41

I didn't want to leave the Mustang in the lot at O'Hare, so I took a cab to the airport Friday morning. My flight left at 10:20. I had a return flight Sunday afternoon. I was being optimistic. I wasn't a white-knuckle flyer, but as we sat waiting for clearance I wondered if I'd ever see Rosie again. But I had been wondering that anyway. And I had always thought there was nothing Stosh would keep secret from me.

I actually enjoyed the rush of power as the plane roared down the runway and took off. And once we got in the air, I resigned myself to whatever was going to happen and read or slept. Ben had once told me that it didn't matter where I was or what I was doing, if it was my turn to go, it was my turn to go. My argument to that was what if it was the pilot's turn to go? All in all, I'd rather be on the ground. To make matters worse, it was cloudy when we took off. Again, I understood radar, but I'd like the pilots to be able to see where they're going.

We had a tail wind and landed in Charleston at 1:40, twenty minutes early. The pilot announced that the skies were clear, and the temperature was eighty-two degrees. The temperature made me happy, but not as much as the clear skies. I also liked the pilot to be able to see the runway well before he landed on it.

***

I rented a car from Enterprise and got a map of the Charleston area. We had taken a vacation every summer when I was a kid and seen a lot of the country, but we had never gotten to Charleston. For my birthday when I was ten my parents got me Bruce Catton's three-volume series on the Civil War, and I spent the summer reading. I had always wanted to see Fort Sumter, but with Aunt Rose's inn being guarded I didn't think I should be sightseeing. I'd have to come back.

Lone Star was less than an hour north of the airport off of Route 26 and southwest of Lake Marion. I got a room at the Holiday Inn next to the airport and then headed north to Lone Star.

Based on the Margot's lifestyle, I expected an expensive neighborhood. I was wrong. I came into town from the lake side where there were expensive homes. But a quarter mile from the lake the homes were modest. The homes along the lake were probably modest at some point too, before money discovered Lake Marion. Most of the homes away from the lake were ranches with detached garages, and most needed some work. Raymond's was no different. It was pine clapboard that had been painted white, not recently, with dark-green trim. His lawn needed mowing, and there were no flowers or bushes. And there was no car in the driveway. I pulled off onto the verge two houses down from Raymond's and watched for a half hour without seeing any sign of life, either in Raymond's house or anywhere else on the street.

At ten to four I decided to be nosy. I walked slowly up the walk and rang the bell. There was no answer. I looked in the front picture window and saw nothing out of the ordinary. I went around back and looked in the kitchen window. Nothing. No answer at the back door either. The backyard was in worse shape than the front... lots of red clay patches. I walked across them to the garage and peeked in the window. It was empty.

As I turned back toward the driveway, I heard, "Hey, fella. What are you doing?" A grizzled, hornery-looking man who looked to be in his seventies was peering over a wood fence.

I figured the truth was the best answer. "I'm looking for Raymond. Do you know when he'll be home?"

"There's no Raymond here. Try again."

He didn't look menacing, but I didn't need him calling the police. "Maybe I have the wrong address." I gave it to him. And I realized that Raymond probably wasn't using his right name.

"Right address... no Raymond. Why don't you mosey along."

I figured that was the best thing to do when I heard, "What's going on, Zeke?"

"This guy says he's looking for Raymond. I suggested he look somewhere else."

The kid looked the right age and looked a lot like his mother.

"Thanks, Zeke. I appreciate it. I'll take care of it."

Zeke slowly made his way back into his house as the kid turned to me.

"Want to tell me what this is about, mister?"

Again, I figured the truth would work best. "You look just like your mother."

"That tells me nothing," he said.

"Reynolds was arrested for drug dealing. I was hired by your mother to help."

He shrugged. "And what does that have to do with me? My brother likes getting into trouble."

That was present tense. He didn't know. And I wasn't sure that I should be the one to tell him. But I was the only one there. I took a deep breath and just said it.

"Well, he won't be getting into trouble anymore."

"What does that mean?"

"He was murdered."

That got his attention. He lost his balance for a second. I reached out, but he waved me away.

He shook his head. "Murdered. How?"

"That's what I'm trying to find out." I told him what I knew. "Look, Raymond. I don't know why you ended up down here, and it's none of my business. But I'd like to find out who killed Reynolds, and I have a lot more questions than answers."

He didn't respond. He was just staring past me.

"You knew about the drug charges?" I asked.

He nodded.

"But you didn't know about his death. How do you explain that?"

He stared at nothing for a couple more minutes. I let him stare.

When he turned to me, he said, "The only contact I have with my mother is when I call her. I haven't called her since the drug arrest."

"She can't call you?"

He shook his head. "I don't have a phone. That was the... um... arrangement."

"Seems odd. Why?"

He had looked away but now looked right at me. "Because if she didn't know where I was no one else would either." His look changed from sad to hard and angry. "Which brings up a question."

I knew what it was, but I let him ask.

"How did *you* find me?"

"You got a speeding ticket six months ago."

His anger disappeared, replaced by concern and acceptance of something he didn't want to accept.

"So if you found me, so can anyone else."

"Not necessarily. My sources are broader and deeper than most."

He thought about that for a moment and didn't appear convinced. He asked for my ID. I showed it to him.

"So what do you want from me?" he asked.

"I was hoping you could fill in some blanks."

He slowly came back to me and, in a quiet voice, said, "I don't know anything about a murder."

"I didn't think you did, but I could use some family background."

He didn't respond. I persisted.

"There might be something that rings a bell." I looked over the fence. The neighbor was standing on his back porch looking in our direction. I didn't know if he was nosy or concerned.

"Can we go inside, Raymond? Not too private out here." I looked to the left toward the neighbor.

He followed my nod and said, "Zeke's okay. He kinda looks after me. We play checkers. I'd rather not go inside. The place isn't very homey."

I was ready to give him a card and ask him to call me if he wanted to talk when he said, "Getting on dinner time. Wanna join me?"

"Sure. What do you have in mind?"

"There's a tavern in town that has good burgers. We can sit outside and talk."

"Sounds good. I'll drive."

"Is that your car on the street?"

"Yup."

"Why don't you pull it in the driveway. It's only a fifteen-minute walk."

"Fine by me."

As we walked down the driveway I asked if he had a car.

"Yeah. A seventy-nine Chevy." He laughed. "With a few dents."

His laugh told me a lot about him, as did the house he was living in. But there were two clues to his former life... an expensive pair of sunglasses and designer jeans that were a lot nicer than mine, and I was wearing my best pair. When I flew I always tried to impress the flight attendants in case they'd have to make a choice about who to save first.

Raymond stood at the edge of the road while I pulled the rental into the drive.

"So where's your car?" I asked as we walked up the street.

"In the shop for an oil change. I left it there this afternoon and walked home."

We turned left at the first side street, and a collie ran out to make sure we didn't need watching.

"Your brother drove a BMW. You don't miss that?"

He laughed again. It was filled with disdain. "Can't miss what you never liked in the first place. I drove an Audi when I had to drive, but that was only because my father wouldn't have allowed a Chevy in the driveway. What would the neighbors think?"

I thought that was funny, but he wasn't laughing.

"We both grew up with money and everything we could want. Problem was I didn't want it. I wanted something more simple. He liked adventure and did dangerous things. I guess that's what got him killed. I liked to sit and look at the lake and read. He was perfectly happy with the things money bought. I would have liked time with my mother and father."

I felt sorry for this kid. I'd had the things he wanted, which made it all the harder when they were taken away from me.

"I can understand your father not being there," I said. "People who work the trading floor tend to be driven by that. It consumes them. But your mother didn't have to work. Surely she was around."

He laughed a bitter laugh. "She was, but not for me. She was busy being a socialite, either giving parties or going to them or hobnobbing with the people who mattered. That's what consumed *her*."

The conversation was beyond my expertise. Family matters were something I had learned didn't have easy solutions. So I changed the subject.

"Weather always like this down here?" I asked.

He laughed. "It's pretty nice. This is usual for spring. But it gets a little hot and humid in the summer. Not much worse than Chicago though. And the ocean is a nice escape. Then there's the threat of hurricanes, but the tradeoff is worth it."

"How did you end up here?"

"We came down here when I was a kid. Stayed in a big house on the beach. But I'd take the car and explore. I liked neighborhoods like this. People would talk to me like I belonged there... not like they had to because we had money."

That didn't answer my question. I wanted to know what had made him leave Chicago. I'd follow up on that.

I could see the tavern after we turned the next corner. It was flanked by a bakery and a bicycle shop. There was only one other couple outside on the patio. We sat five tables away from them and ordered beer and burgers.

# Chapter 42

After the waitress left, Raymond said, "I don't know how I can help you, but I'll try and answer your questions."

I figured I might as well start with the hard one. "Why did you leave home?"

"The easy answer is my mother begged me to."

I stopped my glass just as I was about to take a drink. "Begged?"

"Didn't make any sense to me either. But she was insistent. I needed to get away and disappear."

"From what?"

He shrugged and took a drink. "Don't know. I thought about it a lot at first, but now I just don't care anymore."

"When was this?"

"About a month after my… after the accident."

I set my glass down. "Sorry about that, Raymond. That must have been awful."

He slowly turned his glass on the glass-topped table. "Yeah, would have been horrible even if it wasn't my fault."

I stretched out my legs under the table and said, "I heard someone ran a red light and broadsided you."

He nodded.

"How's that your fault?"

He was silent for a moment, staring at the glass. "I should have been paying better attention. I should have swerved or something."

"You weren't paying attention?"

"No. We were arguing."

"About what?"

He stared at the glass some more. "My brother. I was trying to get my father to pay attention to something I thought was a problem."

I finished my beer and waited. The waitress came out, and I got her attention and held up a finger.

"My brother got into a lot of trouble in high school. He hung around with people who did things I didn't agree with. It wasn't the first time I brought something up. But my father was too involved in his own life to pay attention, and my mother thought the sun rose and set over Reynolds. Neither one of them paid much attention to me."

"Probably because you were the good kid. They knew you'd be okay."

He shrugged. "If being ignored by your parents is okay."

I figured I should leave that alone. Family counseling was above my pay grade. "What was the problem you were arguing about?"

"There was a friend of my father's from his fraternity in college who was a part of my parents' social circle. He'd be at every party. Reynolds and I were expected to make an appearance... I guess to show what a great family we had. This guy paid a lot of attention to me and my brother. Thought a lot of himself. He told me he had plans for me that would lead to a big future. I assume he told Reynolds the same thing. I couldn't stand him... he was pretty sleazy. But Reynolds ate it up. Then one night I was out at a restaurant with friends, and this guy was there... in a booth. When I went to the bathroom I saw Reynolds sitting across from him. They seemed to be having a pretty serious conversation."

My radar had clicked on when he said fraternity. "Did you say anything to Reynolds?"

The waitress brought my beer and asked Raymond if he wanted another. He shook his head. "Your burgers will be right up," she said.

As she walked away, he said, "No. I'd given up on talking to him. He just laughed at me when I would show any concern. Said I'd never get anywhere in life hiding behind a book."

"And that's what you were arguing with your father about?"

"Yeah. I thought something strange was going on, and I wanted him to talk to his friend."

"Do you know the friend's name?"

He tried to think but came up empty. "No. I was obviously introduced to him at some point, but I was introduced to so many they all just became a blur."

"Does the name Bast ring a bell?" I asked.

He looked like he was trying to remember. "Might be," he finally said. "Yeah, I think that's it." Then his thoughtful look turned to puzzled. He looked at me with squinted eyes. "How do you know that?"

"I told you I've been looking into your brother's drug problem. The name came up."

"I thought you were investigating his murder."

I nodded as the waitress brought the burgers. They were served in plastic baskets with wax paper liners. A stack of fries filled half the basket. She asked if we wanted anything besides the ketchup and mustard she set down. We didn't. She glanced at the beers, saw they were more than half full, and walked away.

I poured ketchup on the fries and said, "I always figured this all started with the drug arrest. The murders are part of that."

In the middle of a bite, he said, "Murders? Plural?"

"Don't you get any news down here?" I wasn't surprised he hadn't heard about his brother. But the murder of a senator's son should have made nationwide news.

"I don't pay much attention. Don't have a TV."

There were several things about being that disconnected from the world that sounded nice. "Lucky you."

I told him about Mark Nadem. He sighed and looked far off.

"He was someone my brother hung around with. They both liked the same things... all of them expensive."

"And maybe dangerous."

He looked confused. "What does that mean?"

"I had your brother followed. He met Mark at a restaurant. My man sat close enough that he could hear them talking about daring each other. Sounded like each time the stakes would be raised."

He sighed and nodded. "Sounds like my brother. The more dangerous the more fun it was."

I had more questions but wasn't sure how far I should push him. So far he was doing okay. He seemed to have accepted his family and the role he played in it. And he seemed to be doing just fine down here in Lone Star.

We were both done eating. The waitress stopped and asked if we wanted dessert. Raymond recommended the peach ice cream. I held up two fingers. As she walked away the street lights came on. I hadn't noticed it getting dark. The sky was a darker blue over the houses to the east, and the temperature had dropped. But I was still comfortable in a short-sleeved shirt. Several people had come and gone, and we were now alone on the patio. I had one more question.

"Who are you hiding from?"

The ice cream arrived, and he shook his head.

"I have no idea."

We each took a bite. His recommendation was a good one.

"I thought about it a lot when I first got down here and came up almost empty."

"Did you ever ask your mother?"

"Yes. She didn't answer... just told me it would be the wise thing to do. But she knew. How could she not?"

"She couldn't," I agreed.

He took another bite. "Then why do you think she's not saying?"

"She's afraid. And she thinks that's the best thing to do to protect you."

He scooped his spoon around the edges of the ice cream. "I'm sure she does, but I think if you know what a challenge is you can better face it. Wouldn't you agree?"

I told him I did. "You said you came up almost empty."

He took a big bite and stared at the spoon as if it had answers. "I only came up with one thing. Someone was holding something over her head."

He paused. I let him think and finished my ice cream.

"And if I put several things together I came up with an answer I didn't like, so I stopped thinking about it."

He paused some more, and this time I prompted him.

"What were the things?"

"I didn't like Bast. And I didn't like him meeting with my brother. And nobody wanted to talk about that. And somebody had something that threatened my mother."

This time I let it lie. He knew what it was, and I knew what he thought it was. Nobody wants to know that their mother was having an affair. But I thought there was more to it than that.

I was done asking him questions. I was surprised he had answered all the ones I had asked. But I had more questions for his mother... more questions that Mrs. Margot probably wouldn't answer truthfully. And the more she didn't answer, the more I would know the answers.

When we got back to his house I handed him a card and told him to call me if he wanted to know how things were going. He said he probably wouldn't call... he was happy not knowing. I couldn't blame him. It looked like he was pretty happy in Lone Star without all that money.

***

I got back to my hotel room at a little before ten, called the airline and booked a seat for Saturday early afternoon. I called Stosh and asked him to pick me up. Then I called Ben, and we chatted about Bast. Ben had found nothing out of the ordinary. No big bank accounts or fancy toys. He lived a normal middle-class life. I was hoping for more. He pointed out that maybe Bast was setting himself up for early retirement with a hidden account somewhere.

I turned on the TV and let it keep me company while I thought about all the pieces. I put them together in a way that made sense and then wondered what I'd do about it. I had no clue. After an hour I still didn't, so I switched to thinking about Rosie, missing her, and wondering what she was up to. I fell asleep wondering.

# Chapter 43

S tosh was waiting for me as I walked out of the glass doors at O'Hare into weather that wasn't anywhere near eighty and sunny. The pilot had said partly cloudy and fifty-two. I threw my bag in the back seat and climbed in.

"So you tempted fate and survived another flight, eh, kid?"

"I did. I love living on the edge."

It was a bit early for dinner, but we decided to head for Gino's for pizza, talk over a few beers, and get out of there before the Saturday night crowds showed up. We picked up my car, I drove to his house, and I drove to Gino's.

Traffic was already heavy on the Kennedy, but we weren't in a hurry. I wanted to wait until I had his full attention to tell him about my evening with Raymond.

While we drove, he asked, "Wanna hear about my Friday?"

"I'm on pins and needles."

"Of course you are. The calls started coming in again yesterday. Six stores, all within two blocks of each other, and five blocks from the last robberies."

"Imagine that."

"But this time we were ready. I figured they were testing our response in that neighborhood, but they wouldn't be after a grocery store or a shoe repair shop. I figured they would be after something more high-end. So we walked the neighborhood and identified two jewelry stores. We've had those two under surveillance all week.

They're three blocks away from the other six. They hit both, and we got them on the way out."

He looked very proud of himself.

"You figured all that, did you?"

He glanced at me quickly out of the corner of his eye and said, "I may have had some help."

"You *may* have. I seem to vaguely remember something about all that."

"Whatever… it all worked out good."

"Great! Anything else you need help with feel free to call."

We spent the rest of the drive talking baseball and weather.

I found a spot on the street only a block from the restaurant.

***

We slid into a booth, and the waiter brought waters and menus. We ordered beer and a half-and-half sausage pepperoni and mushroom green peppers pizza. I was trying to be healthy. Sometimes I succeeded.

After the beer came, I told him about my trip and what I had learned.

"So you're thinking the mother was sleeping with Bast."

"Wouldn't be the first time. Husband working long hours, not paying attention. At the house a lot for parties. Starts with an innocent cup of coffee and pretty soon…"

"Yeah, nothing like frat buddies." He took a long drink and said, "Your expertise with psychology aside, you still got no proof."

"Why must you always dredge up the technicalities?"

He laughed as a couple was seated at the table next to our booth. "In my line of work it's not exactly a technicality."

"Why I'm not in your line of work," I said.

"So, Mom having an affair, kid involved in drugs, two dead kids. Tie all this together."

"And drugs planted in my car at a police station, and a senator who'd rather not talk about all this, and ten other things that keep me awake at night. I thought it started with the drug arrest, but it looks like it started with the affair." We both sipped while I talked.

"Try this. Mom hooks up with Bast. Bast at some point gets into the drug business, maybe back in his college days, and it becomes a nice sideline when he becomes a cop. She tells him about Reynolds, her problem child. Doesn't know what to do with him. Bast knows and sees it as a chance to expand into the burbs. So he recruits Reynolds, who thinks it's a great idea, and he has a friend, the senator's kid."

I picked up my beer, drank, and looked at Stosh who was listening with only a slightly furrowed brow.

"The kids have this dare challenge going on to make their boring life in the high-rent district more interesting, and Reynolds ends up on the west side of Chicago, picked up in a federal stakeout. Bast talks to Thward and tries to work out an easy way out for the kid. But Thward wants bigger fish than Reynolds and pushes for names. Bast can't risk the kid talking and has him killed."

Stosh had been slowly turning his glass on the table. He took a drink. "What about Nadem's kid?"

"I'm not as sure of that. But his name must have been thrown in the pot at some point, probably by Reynolds."

"And how does Raymond fit into this?"

The waiter arrived with the pizza.

I took a bite of the veggie side. It didn't taste as good as the other side looked. "At some point Mom wants to break off the affair and is overwhelmed with guilt. And she suspects Reynolds is involved in something with Bast. She tells Bast she is done and is going to say something about the affair and his relationship with Reynolds. He threatens her with harm to Raymond if she says anything. She gets Raymond out of town."

I watched him finish a piece of sausage and pepperoni.

"Why would the mother implicate herself in an affair?"

"Maybe she's tired of it hanging over her head. Sometimes the threat is worse than reality. What better way to stop a threat but to make it public?"

"And then she gets set up for the murder," he said.

"Lots of reasons for her to be afraid, which she definitely is. But deep inside she has some motherly instinct that protects her kid."

"And she hires you but doesn't tell you about any of this… even denies knowing Bast."

I shrugged. "It ain't perfect. If I'm right, all these things happened. Not sure about the timeline."

"Seems to me you should be unsure of more than that. It's all conjecture."

I fell off the healthy wagon and picked up a pepperoni. "But pretty solid conjecture. The pieces all fit."

"You think Bast is in bed with the Prophets?"

"Nope."

He looked surprised. "You seem sure of that."

I nodded and took a drink. He didn't ask how I knew.

"So, if you're right, what do you do about it? Those of us in law enforcement like to have proof before we arrest people."

"Yeah, that's the part I haven't worked out yet."

"If Bast is into the drug trade on the side, there should be money somewhere," he said.

"I had Ben look into that. Nothing."

"We catch people because they're dumber than rocks. But a cop knows the ropes. Dirty doesn't mean stupid."

I caught the waiter's eye and ordered more beers. "No. But there's someone else in the department in on this. Someone planted the cocaine in my car. Maybe that person isn't as smart."

He laughed. "You want me to look into the finances of a whole department?"

"No. Just the day shift."

"Ah, well, that's better. I thought you were being unreasonable."

We chatted over the rest of the pizza and finished our beer. By the time we were done we had come up with a skeleton of a plan. If a mouse likes cheese, bring him more cheese.

As I motioned for the check my pager vibrated.

"Stosh, it's Iverson."

"Go call, kid. I'll take care of the check."

I grabbed my jacket and ran to the car. Iverson answered on the second ring.

"I didn't want to hear from you, Chief."

"No. They made a run at Billy."

My stomach turned, and I tried to keep the pizza down.

"Tell me."

"He's okay. About an hour ago, a guy walks up the porch steps of your aunt's inn. No car. Young guy wearing a light jacket and a ball cap. He walks carefully and silently by my man napping on the porch. As he walks into the lobby he pulls out a gun. He stops dead in his tracks when he hears the shotgun cock."

"That's always an attention getter."

"My man has him turn around and lay the gun on the floor, which he does. Then all hell breaks loose from the back of the inn."

"Two men. Jesus. We should have had two on watch."

Iverson laughed. That made me feel better.

"Well, as it turns out… seems another guy went in the back door. He finds Billy in the kitchen sneaking a piece of cherry pie and grabs him by the collar. Billy yells, and your dog appears out of nowhere and clamps onto the guy's leg. He's screaming and pulls his gun. As he's trying to aim it at the dog Maxine runs in, grabs an iron skillet, and bashes him in the head."

By the time he was done, I was laughing too. I would have loved to have seen that.

"Extra biscuits for Watson," I said. "Are either of these guys talking?"

"Front door just wants his lawyer. Back door is a bit out of sorts. Doc says he has no idea how long he'll be unconscious."

"I'm having dinner with Stosh. I'll fill him in and see what we can find out on this end."

"Probably nothing, but I'll keep working on this guy."

"Thanks, Chief. I owe you."

"Add it to the list. You want me to keep my man there?"

"I think so. Probably over, but doesn't hurt to be safe."

"You got it. He'll be happy. He's raving about the food."

We hung up, and ten seconds later I saw Stosh walking toward the car. He got in, and I filled him in. By the time I was done, we were both laughing.

"These guys aren't your top-of-the-line thugs," Stosh said as I pulled out of the spot. "Beaten by an old guy in a rocker and a lady with a skillet."

"And Watson the wonder dog," I said.

He nodded. "And Watson the wonder dog."

*** 

When I got home, I called the inn and got the story again from Aunt Rose... with a few embellishments. She couldn't wait to tell her bridge group.

# Chapter 44

figured the pool hall would be crowded on a Saturday night. I was right. Ralph was sitting on a barstool watching two games and sipping a scotch on the rocks. If given a choice, that was his. He saw me, nodded, and joined me in the last booth before the bathrooms. Not exactly the best ambience, but more private. He set his drink down, and a waitress showed up. I ordered a Pabst.

"You want to do act three?" Ralph asked.

"Yes, but it's a different scene. As you and others have pointed out, Bast did and said things that are suspicious and perhaps incriminating, but they won't hold up in court. Everything about this has his name all over it, so we're going to up the ante."

He was sipping his scotch, waiting for me to explain. I told him about Raymond and the affair I was sure Bast had with Jeanne and the incident in Door county.

"If I'm right, Bast has been behind everything, including trying to get rid of me. And I think Nadem is in it with him."

"So every time you poke Nadem, Bast hears about it."

"And Nadem tells Bast to do something about it."

He nodded. "Makes sense to me."

"We need a different trap, one that's more alluring. He has two interests, drugs and me. I'm hoping he'll think he can kill two birds with one stone."

"And where do I come in?"

"He already knows you're a blackmailer. So I figure he'll have no trouble believing the story you give him."

He finished his drink and signaled the waitress.

"Speaking of which," he said, "I told him I'd get back to him yesterday. Probably wondering what the hell is going on."

"I think that works in our favor. You're going to tell him something better came up. We'll give the mouse a piece of cheese he can't resist."

I explained the plan, part of which was I needed a building somewhere on the near north side for a meet, a warehouse with cover. He said he'd start looking.

Ralph wasn't one to sit and chat. I downed the rest of my beer, and he took his drink back to his barstool.

I was tempted to stay and watch him play, but it had been a long two days. An early evening sounded good.

# Chapter 45

I was in the office when Ralph called on Tuesday. He had found a building he thought would work. It was two blocks south of North Avenue on Pierce in the first block west of Ashland. It was a warehouse owned by a friend of a friend who was willing to provide access for a mere two fifty. The location was perfect... not in Bast's precinct but in Stosh's. If the layout was right, we were on. I called Stosh. He was available at three. I picked him up and then drove to the pool hall and got Ralph.

Ralph had the key to the rear entrance off the alley. I drove through the alley first. There were warehouse or manufacturing buildings on both sides. I parked on the street, and we walked around the back. The meeting would be at night, but even in the afternoon we saw no one else in the alley.

There was enough light to see during the day from high windows along the rear wall. But at night we'd need lights. I sent Ralph to find the switches.

The layout of the warehouse was perfect. There was an open space with tables in the middle of several aisles with twenty-foot-high shelves stacked with boxes. Plenty of spots for cover.

Stosh and I stood and waited. The place was dead quiet... as quiet as a Monday church.

A minute later a bank of lights came on, and Ralph joined us a minute after that. It was too bright for my liking, and I asked Ralph if some could be turned off. He said he had flipped two switches and would try one. The lights dimmed to what I thought would work.

The three of us walked the aisles and laid out a plan. The open space was perfect for meeting Bast, and there were spaces between the boxes on the shelves that would let someone in adjacent aisles see the open space. Stosh and Ralph agreed that it would work. They then added the opinion that if I was wrong about all of this, there would be hell to pay on many fronts.

I went over my plan again. We had the same options we had in the apartment. There were only two possibilities. Either Bast was guilty or not. If he was and bit on the cheese, then Stosh would be there with the troops. If Bast pulled out his badge and acted like a cop, then Ralph and I would plead guilty, and Stosh and his troops would stay hidden and slip away.

Stosh pointed out that Bast would probably come with backup either way. I agreed.

"So, what's next?" he asked.

"The first step is to send another note to Bast inviting him to a meeting."

"And if he ignores it?" Stosh asked.

"Can't see him doing that. The cop would want to catch the bad guy. The bad guy wants the cheese. Either way, he shows up. And second, I drop in on him and see if he shares the note with me."

Stosh smiled. "You do like to poke at hornets' nests."

"Might tell me something," I said.

Ralph was leaning against a large steel table pretending he didn't have a horse in the race. But I knew he was paying attention. The table top was just above his waist and had a shelf halfway down to the floor.

"Won't tell you crap," Stosh said. "He reacts the same way no matter which way he leans. You won't know until he plays his cards at the warehouse."

"Maybe not. But a fellow's gotta have some fun."

I looked at Ralph. "You have any questions?"

He stood away from the table. "We still have our go-to-jail deal?"

I assured him we did.

"Great, looks like I'm going to need it."

On the way out he turned off the lights.

While I was driving them back I told them I'd send Bast a note Wednesday morning and stop by his office in the afternoon. The note would say there would be a meeting Thursday at nine PM. He'd find out the location Thursday at five. We wanted to be set up before he had a chance to look at the warehouse. So we'd be in and ready by five. I told Ralph I'd pick him up at four. Stosh would meet us.

After I dropped Ralph, Stosh asked, "What the hell's a go-to-jail deal?"

I told him if any of my people were ever arrested they would get a bonus large enough to make it worthwhile... and a free attorney. He said that was a benefit most companies didn't offer. I pointed out that I wasn't like most companies. He agreed, but he didn't sound like he thought that was a good thing.

I pulled into the station lot and said, "I haven't gotten the usual lecture about the crazy things I do."

He took his hand off the door handle. "Nope."

"And not only are you not lecturing, you're participating."

"Yup."

"Can't help wondering why."

"Because they went after our family. This is personal."

I couldn't have agreed more. This wasn't about Reynolds anymore... it *was* personal.

"And you're doing it without any hard evidence," I said.

"Nope. Listen, kid... I don't usually agree with how you do things, and you haven't been doing it very long in the grand scheme of things. But you've been right every damn time. I'm going with your gut. If you say this is Bast, and it does look like it, this is bad... it's worse than bad. And I want part of it."

"Thanks, Stosh. That means a lot to me."

He smiled and popped the door open. "And if it ain't him, I ease on out of there like fog and you're on your own."

"Nice."

As he walked away, I thought about what he had said. I had grown up thinking Stosh was part of the family, kinda like an uncle.

But the word family had never been mentioned by him until now. I smiled as he walked into the building.

# Chapter 46

I sent a message to Bast Wednesday morning.

> There's a new plan. We are in control of a large shipment. We don't want to do business with the gangs and need help with marketing. We believe we can reach a mutually beneficial agreement. The evidence in our possession would be part of the agreement. If you are interested, meet us at nine PM tomorrow evening. Come alone. The location will be sent to you tomorrow.

\*\*\*

I walked into Bast's office a little before three. His desk was covered with a map of the west side and several files.

"Looks like fun," I said.

"Not much fun, but good job security. Close the door, and have a seat."

I pushed the door closed and pulled the wooden chair in front of his desk. "If I'm going to be coming here this much I'm gonna buy a better chair."

He ignored that, pulled out a drawer, and handed me a piece of paper. "What do you think of this?"

What I thought about it was that *something* I was hoping for had appeared. It was obviously a copy of the note I had sent, but the sentence about evidence had been removed. That would have prompted questions he didn't want to answer, if anyone saw it, like me. But if he wasn't dirty it wouldn't have mattered.

"Who was this sent to?" I asked.

"Me."

"Really? Pretty vague. Any idea what it means?"

"No clue."

"Large shipment of what?" I asked.

He shook his head and looked confused. "My guess is drugs, but it could be clown hats for all I know."

"Okay, let's assume drugs. This is worded like whoever it is is cutting you in on the deal."

"It is, isn't it."

"And you have no clue?"

"None."

"Could be tied into whoever planted the drugs in my car."

"Could be."

Someone knocked on his door.

"Later," he said.

"How was it delivered?"

"It was in this envelope." He pulled an envelope out of the same drawer with Bast's name and "Personal" written below it. "It was left with the desk sergeant. Nobody needed a signature… just dropped it off and left."

"Prints?"

"None."

"It says they'll let you know the place tomorrow."

He nodded.

"Could you detain whoever delivers the next message?"

"Already got it covered. But it probably won't help. Just a messenger service, and my guess is there's a paper trail that won't lead anywhere."

There was another knock with the same response from Bast.

"So are you going to meet?"

"I am. Would you like to come?"

"Wouldn't miss it. What about the come alone part?"

"They got that from TV."

"Maybe. But you gotta assume these people aren't stupid. Probably be watching."

His phone rang. He answered and told whoever it was he'd get back to them.

"Probably, but I can say you're my partner. No deal without you."

I nodded.

"Manning, last week you said you hadn't told Lieutenant Powolski about the evidence."

I nodded again.

"How much have you shared about all of this?"

"Nothing. I haven't seen him much since all this started."

"Good. Keep this under your hat, okay?"

"Sure." I smiled. "You want all the credit, eh?"

He smiled back. "Doesn't hurt. I wouldn't mind moving up. I've got retirement to think about."

***

I'd have to call Stosh and Ralph and let them know about the change in plans. Bast was going to let me know when the meet time would be, and he wanted me to meet him a block from the location and walk in with him. I didn't like that idea, but I didn't see any way around it without making him suspicious.

# Chapter 47

I was sitting in the office waiting for Bast's call with the luxury of knowing when that call would come. The message with the location would be delivered at five. I was sure Bast wouldn't leave the office before then. I was also sure he had been lying about giving the desk sergeant a heads up about the delivery service... unless, of course, I was completely wrong about all this. Then Ralph would get his bonus, and we'd all have a good laugh.

Bast called at ten after five and gave me the address and time. He wanted me to meet him a block away from the building at eight thirty. That gave us a half hour to talk about strategy. I figured the strategy had already been decided on with whomever else he was bringing to take care of his hidden agenda... hidden from me, that is.

I called Stosh and Ralph and told them the bait had been taken. I had no worries that both of them would take care of their end of things.

***

I turned onto Pierce and parked at twenty after eight. I got out of the car and adjusted my shoulder holster with the .357 Magnum in it under my jacket. Then I reached back in and took my Taurus out of the glove compartment and snugged it into my belt in the small of my back. Bast pulled up behind me five minutes later. He sat in his car until another car pulled in back of him two minutes after that. Bast got out of his car, followed by two men from the car behind him. They were both bigger than me or Bast. I joined them on the sidewalk next to Bast's Buick.

"I thought you were told to come alone," I said to Bast.

He laughed. "Right. Like this guy's gonna be alone. I'm not walking into a trap without backup."

"You think this is a trap?"

"Wasn't born yesterday, Manning. If it goes down smooth, I'll be pleasantly surprised."

I glanced at the two thugs. They were just staring at me with blank expressions.

"You carrying, Manning?"

"Yup. My .357 Magnum in a shoulder holster." I showed him.

He nodded. "Good. Might come in handy."

"Let's hope not."

As we walked, I asked, "These two guys cops?"

"Sort of."

I just nodded.

\*\*\*

The alley door was unlocked.

"You stay right behind me, Manning," Bast said.

He didn't have anything to say to the other two. They'd already been told.

The lighting was dim, and there was no noise. Bast led the way slowly down an aisle toward the center of the floor, walking like he owned the joint. His confidence made me nervous. As we walked out of the shelving units into the open area the light brightened a bit. I looked behind me. The two men had disappeared. Bast had a plan that he hadn't shared with me. And I was sure dealing with me was part of that plan.

Ralph and another man I didn't know were standing on the opposite side of the table from us. On the table was a clear plastic bin filled with several baggies full of some white substance. My guess was powdered sugar.

Bast walked to within twenty feet of the table with me at his side.

"So, we meet again," he said to Ralph. "Okay, I'm here. I hope you have more to say than last time."

"Last time?" I asked.

He ignored me.

"I told you to come alone," Ralph said.

Bast laughed. "Right. I'm just as alone as you are. Who's the goon next to you?"

"I could ask you the same thing."

"And both answers are meaningless. Let's just say insurance. So talk," Bast said.

"I have the evidence that puts someone away for the killing."

"But you're keeping that in your pocket," Bast said. "So you either don't have any evidence, or you want something else."

Ralph nodded. The man next to him was slowly scanning the area.

"As I said in the note, we have come across a deal that's too good to pass up." He nodded at the bin. "This is a sample. But we need help, and we don't want to go to the Prophets. Your name came up."

"Yeah? How did that happen?"

Ralph shrugged. "Doesn't matter. All that matters is whether you want in or not."

"And if I say yes, the evidence comes along with the deal?"

So far, no one had mentioned drugs. Bast already knew Ralph was fond of recordings.

"That's the deal," Ralph said.

"Uh huh. Let's see the evidence."

"We make a deal first," Ralph said.

"Well, here's the deal. I don't think you have any evidence. I think you're just a cheap blackmailer who saw more dollar signs with whatever's in that bin. Never did like blackmailers."

At that point, Bast's two thugs stepped out of aisles on either side of the space. They both had guns leveled at Ralph.

"And I have a good thing without cutting you and your pal in."

"But you don't have the connection."

Bast shrugged. "If it's that big, I'll find out. And if I don't find out, I don't much care. Like I said, I don't need you or your connection."

Ralph started to talk, but Bast pulled his gun, and Ralph stopped. He was probably thinking the go-to-jail clause wasn't much good if he was dead.

"We'll take your bin. But first, both of you put your guns on the floor under the table."

"We don't have guns," Ralph said.

"Then we'll just shoot you to make sure."

Ralph and the man next to him reached into their jackets and pulled out guns which they laid on the floor.

"Very good. Now, Manning, you join them. He turned his gun on me. But first, hand me your Magnum. And don't try anything. This is a nice quiet place. Whoever picked it did a good job. Nobody is going to hear you die."

I guessed I didn't have to wonder anymore. I handed him my gun as I said, "You and your two thugs aren't going to get away with this." I wanted to let Stosh know that Bast only had two men with him.

He tucked my gun into his belt and said, "Seems to me you're not exactly in a position to be cocky. Now move. All three of you behind the table. It's going to look to your buddy Powolski like these two jumped us, and you tried to be the hero. This is perfect. I showed you the note, and you insisted on coming along. Nobody will question that what with your loose cannon approach to things. And your car is parked conveniently down the street. You'll have a nice recognition ceremony. I'll look real sad."

I watched Ralph and the other man as I walked to the table. They were both looking around the room. I guessed they were wondering where Stosh was. So was I.

I joined Ralph, and Bast took a few steps toward the table. "Any last words?" he asked.

"Just wondering how someone who puts on a badge ends up with drugs and murder on his hands," I said.

He shrugged like it was nothing. "Shit happens." As he glanced at his two thugs, we all heard the sound of shotguns cocking. I couldn't tell how many there were, but there were more than two. That got the attention of Bast and his thugs as Stosh stepped out of one of the aisles.

"The three of you point your guns at the floor, bend down slowly, and lay them down. Then step away ten feet and lie down on your stomachs with your hands behind your heads."

They hesitated with shocked looks.

"Each of you has two shotguns aimed at your torso. Won't matter where you get hit. You have no idea where my men are, but they sure as hell know where you are. You've got two seconds."

The thugs responded before Bast, but Bast wasn't far behind.

"Okay," I said. "Now the Magnum, Bast."

I started walking around the table toward Bast. As I did, I pulled the Taurus out of my belt and held it at my side. Bast started to lay the gun down and then suddenly turned the gun toward his head.

In a split second, I raised my gun and fired. I hit him in the wrist, and he dropped the gun.

I walked up to him and kicked the gun away. He was holding his right wrist, blood smeared between his fingers.

"You're not getting off that easy, Bast. There's three people dead, two of them kids, not to mention framing me and going after my family. You're going to spend the rest of your life thinking about this from the wrong side of the bars."

He looked up at me and managed to sneer. "You're dreaming, Manning. You've got nothing. If you did, you wouldn't have set up this sham. There's nothing that would hold up in court."

"Get up," I said.

As he got to his feet, he turned to his left and threw a punch at my stomach. I turned quickly enough that it landed on my side. I snapped a straight right onto his nose, and it immediately started to bleed. He put his left hand to his face and looked at the blood on his fingers. Blood was streaming down his face… noses bleed a lot. I figured he was done, but he raised both hands in fists and threw a left at my face. I ducked left, and it missed as I turned to my left and kicked his left kneecap with my right foot. As he was falling, I hit him on the back of the head with my left forearm. He slid to the floor and didn't try to get up. *Now* he was done.

As Bast gasped for breath, I turned from him to the two thugs lying on the floor and told them to sit up.

"How about you two? You want to keep him company? Or do you want a deal?"

The balding one started to talk.

"Shut up, you fool!" Bast yelled, still gasping for air. "He's got nothing."

The bald one did shut up. I walked over to him and told him to stand up... easier on the knees and a more compassionate bargaining position. I smiled at him. "I gotta admit, free room and board sounds appealing, but I hear the food's not that good."

"Don't listen to his crap, Harry!" Bast yelled.

I slowly shook my head. "He's not worth it, Harry."

Harry looked from me to Bast. His eyes were open wide with a look of fear. But I couldn't tell who he was more afraid of, me or Bast. The other thug was watching intently.

Stosh walked over to the other thug. "What about you?" he asked.

He looked like he wanted to answer, but after glancing at Bast he didn't. Bast looked smug.

I rested the Taurus in the palm of my left hand.

"Okay, here's the deal," Stosh said. "The first of you to talk gets the deal, probably no jail time, depending on what you have to say. We're not after you... we're after the upper end of the food chain."

"Don't say anything," Bast said. "He's all talk. And he can't offer you a deal. He's just a cop, like me."

Stosh started to say something but was interrupted as Thward stepped out from one of the aisles.

"He can't, but I can." He walked over to each of the thugs and introduced himself, showing his ID. Both of them started talking at once. He stopped them.

"Okay, hands behind your backs. We'll continue this at the station."

Bast had lost the smug look.

As one of Thward's agents walked toward Bast, he said, "I'm not the top of the food chain. Same offer apply to me?"

"Always willing to listen," Thward said. "But a cop involved anywhere in the chain stinks bad."

Bast finally looked defeated. "I've got nothing to lose."

"And not much to gain," Thward said.

***

**W**hile the agents were reading rights and snapping on cuffs, I walked over to Stosh.

"That went pretty well, don't you think?" I said.

"Coulda been a lot worse," he said.

"And it coulda been better."

"How so?"

I shook my head. "I was hoping he'd get up again."

He took in a deep breath. "So was I, kid. So was I."

"And I still got it!" I said.

He laughed. "Got it, my ass. I could beat up a guy, too, if I *shot* him first."

"You're just jealous," I said.

He was still laughing. When he calmed down, he said, "One thing that didn't go so well... you used Rafael and his sister."

"I know. It was the only plan I had."

He just shook his head sadly.

"What are you doing in the morning at a quarter to nine?" I asked.

"Working... like every other day. Why?"

"Meet me at St. Agatha's."

"Why?"

"There's a nun I'd like you to meet."

"I've met nuns."

"Not this one. Humor me. And debrief tomorrow night at McGoons at seven. Steaks on me."

He agreed. Ralph and I left Thward and Stosh to clean up the mess. When I got home, I called McGoons and reserved the private room.

I then called Iverson and filled him in. I asked that he keep his man on for one more day just in case somebody didn't get the message. I told him Stosh would call him about the prisoners. I didn't ask about the guy with the dent on his head. I didn't care. I then called the inn. Aunt Rose answered, and Maxine got on the extension. They were thrilled and said they had no doubt I would take care of everything. I talked to Carol and told her it was all over, and they could head back. She said Billy would be disappointed.

After two more calls I took a hot shower and called it a night.

# Chapter 48

Friday morning was bright and sunny and held every promise of spring. I got to the church and parked in the lot at a quarter to nine. Stosh pulled in five minutes later and got in the passenger's seat.

"This better be one special nun," he said.

"I guarantee it."

We got out and sat on the front steps of the church and watched the neighborhood come alive. At five after, the front door opened and Sister Katherine and Benny joined us. After introductions and small talk Stosh looked at me like he was ready to go and wondering why he had made the trip. I didn't bother explaining.

At twenty after, a black Mercedes pulled up in front of the steps. Stosh's brow furrowed. After ten seconds, the driver's door opened, and Renald Williams got out and looked at us over the top of the car.

Stosh looked very confused, and I was enjoying every second if it.

"What the hell is he doing here?" Stosh asked.

No one answered.

Renald walked around to the passenger side and opened the rear door. He offered his hand and helped out Maria Melendez. He did the same for her brother Rafael, and Maria and Rafael walked over to where we were now standing. She hugged Sister and Benny and me, and I introduced them to Stosh.

Renald walked back to the driver's side and gave me a two-finger salute. I returned it with a nod.

Stosh was watching it all, shaking his head. He turned to me and said, "What the hell?"

Sister Katherine turned to him with a smile and said, "The Lord works in mysterious ways."

I smiled. "McGoons at seven. Don't be late."

"Oh, I won't. And I'll be real hungry."

I laughed.

Maria gave me another hug and a kiss on the cheek. From Sister Katherine I just got a hug, but it was one of the best hugs I ever got.

"You want a ride home?" I asked.

"I'll see them home," Sister said.

"Okay, but hang on a minute. I've got something for Rafael."

I walked to the car and came back with a box and handed it to Rafael. He opened it, looking like a kid at Christmas, and pulled out a new pair of binoculars. He immediately started looking around the neighborhood. I got another kiss from Maria.

I gave her my card and said, "If you ever need anything, you call me."

She nodded with tears in her eyes.

# Chapter 49

The front page of the *Tribune* covered the story but left a lot of questions that would probably never be officially answered. Some of them had to do with deals that were yet to be made. Thward had shared the confessions with me.

McGoons was crowded. I stopped at the bar and wasted two dollars throwing darts. Jack thanked me for the contribution. Stosh and Ben were already at the table. Ralph arrived ten minutes later, followed by Benny and Sister Katherine.

"Glad you're here, Spencer," Ben said. "Stosh has been grilling me for the last fifteen minutes. I told him I gave up trying to keep track of what you do a long time ago."

"I bet." I was enjoying keeping him in suspense.

Jane took drink orders, and we ordered appetizers. When the drinks arrived, I took questions. Stosh wasn't about to let anyone else get in first.

"I'm sitting in front of a church and Williams pulls up in a Mercedes and drops off two people who were supposed to have been kidnapped. Let's start with that."

"Remember that chat we had about who I could trust? Well, I figured if I couldn't trust a nun the world was in big trouble. And in order for my plan to work I needed help from someone else. That someone else just happened to turn out to be Williams."

"And what made you decide you could trust him?"

"He told me I could."

"Where's that waitress? Maybe more alcohol will help."

That brought a laugh.

He continued. "How do you even find yourself having a conversation with the head of the Prophets?"

I knew this answer wasn't going to make any more sense than the last one, but it was the only answer I had. I took a deep breath and said, "Larry Maggio set up a meeting."

He just stared at me, picked up his glass, and emptied it. Then he went back to staring at me.

"Sister, remember when we were having breakfast and I said I never know where ideas come from?"

"I do."

"Well, the idea that rolled around was to make whoever the culprit was think there was evidence that had been found at the scene by Rafael. But I knew that would put Rafael at risk, so I had to make sure he and Maria were safe. Someone had to keep them safe. Then Maggio called and wanted a meeting. Turned out the meeting was with Williams, who said he was getting some heat over the murder and wanted to assure me that he had nothing to do with that or Reynolds."

"And of course, why not believe the head of the biggest gang in the city," Stosh said. "How does that happen?"

"Because Sister told me I could."

She started to say something, but I cut her off.

"I know, not in so many words. But you did say he did a lot of good things for the neighborhood. I had to make a gut decision, and that was it."

"But the note stuck in your mailbox said they had Rafael, and they could get your family too," Stosh said. "What about that?"

"That was just serendipity, and it was actually pretty smart of them. Bast read the article in the paper about Rafael and Maria being missing. He knew he didn't do it, but obviously someone had. So why not use that to threaten me?"

"So how did the *Trib* get the story about them being missing?" asked Benny.

"My secretary, Carol, and a friend I have on the paper who didn't need more than my asking him to do it in exchange for the story."

Stosh caught Jane's eye and asked for another round. When she brought the drinks we all ordered.

"Where did Williams keep them?" Stosh asked.

"No clue. But I had Sister Katherine work everything out with Maria. I wanted the apartment to look like they had been taken. So their clothes were still there, and the place looked like they had left suddenly. I gave Sister money to buy them clothes and anything else they'd need. There was only one thing that might have caused a problem."

"What was that?" Benny asked.

"Rafael took his binoculars with him. But luckily Bast didn't know about those."

"What about the gun that killed Nadem?" she asked.

Stosh answered. "Bast and his two cronies haven't stopped talking. Bast ordered the killing of Reynolds and Mark Nadem. He gave us the killer's name, but so far he hasn't been found. Reynolds was shot with his own gun, and the killer used that gun to kill Mark and then left it next to the body. As you know, Mrs, Margot's prints were on the gun, and she was questioned."

I took a drink. "This all went back to the drug arrest," I said. "Seemed odd that Reynolds wouldn't agree to a deal. But the deal would have been to turn in a cop, and he was afraid of doing that."

"So if he wasn't going to make a deal, why kill him?" Sister Katherine asked.

"I don't know," I said. "The only answer I have is that Bast couldn't be sure the kid wouldn't talk. Only one way to be sure."

"And how was Mark Nadem involved?" she asked.

Stosh answered. "Bast knew the Margot family through the fraternity connection and was having an affair with the Mrs. He had a small drug operation on the west side and wanted to expand into the suburbs where all the money was. He needed someone to work the sales. He had met both Margot boys and knew Reynolds liked danger and wanted to be a big shot. He was an easy target. Reynolds and Mark played a dare game where they kept raising the ante. One of the raises evidently was to sell drugs on the west side."

Jane brought the appetizers, and we passed the plates.

"Doesn't make sense," said Benny.

"What doesn't?" I asked.

"Bast isn't going to get a drug business going with one kid."

"No, Reynolds was just the hired help."

"So who else?"

Stosh started to answer, but I wanted this one. With a smile, I said, "Our servant of the people, Senator Nadem. Seems he and Bast met somewhere along the way, and one thing led to another and they went into business. Things were evidently shaky on the home front for our wonderful senator. His wife found out about an affair and wasn't too happy. All the money in the family was hers, and the senator perhaps saw that money drying up. He needed some extra income."

"But his son couldn't have been part of the deal," Sister said.

I looked at Ben and Ralph, who were sitting next to each other. I didn't expect to hear any questions from them as long as there was food on the table.

"No, certainly not," I said. "He had no way of knowing the trail would lead to Mark."

"How sad," she said. "But I haven't heard anything about the senator."

Stosh took over. "Senator Nadem seems to have disappeared. His wife said he was gone when she got home last night from a bridge game. The girl at his office hasn't heard from him, and he hasn't shown up for any of his appointments. Several agencies are looking. And we're checking the airport. He may be long gone by now."

"I'd love to see that bastard behind bars," I said.

"Well, you may have to settle for a life in ruin," Stosh said.

"If that's what you call lying on a beach somewhere spending your drug money."

"Can't get them all," Stosh said.

Two busboys arrived with platters of food and passed out the steaks. Sister Katherine had shepherd's pie.

"And I assume the drug charges will be dropped against you, Spencer," Benny said.

"Already in process," Stosh said. "Although he probably deserved those few hours for all the lines he's crossed over the years."

I didn't agree.

"What about the two up in Wisconsin?" Ben asked.

"One is still in a coma." I said. "The other isn't talking yet. He doesn't believe Bast was arrested. He thinks it's a trick to get him to talk. He'll talk eventually when he figures it out."

Jane got refill orders, and we all started eating. I thanked everyone for their help.

When I asked if anyone had anything else to say, Ralph finally stopped eating long enough to say, "A couple hours in jail would have been nice." Stosh and I laughed. Everyone else looked confused. I decided to leave it that way. If they knew what his contract said, they'd all want to be arrested.

I answered a few more questions as we finished eating. Jane started to clear and said she'd be right back with the check.

Two minutes later I heard commotion behind me and turned around. Jack was walking toward our table carrying a cake with one big candle in the middle. I stared hard at Stosh who was doing a good job of looking shocked. If looks could kill…

As Jack set the cake down he started singing, and the rest joined in. By the second "happy birthday" I was laughing. In red and blue icing was written "Happy 29th!"

They all wished me a happy birthday, and I smiled at Stosh.

"Hey, kid, if it's your birthday, you gotta have a cake."

***

As I drove home, I thought about the case. I was usually left with a good feeling that I had done something good for someone, that someone had come out on the plus side. But not this time. I had solved the case, but my client, Mrs. Margot, had lost everything… her husband, her son Reynolds, and perhaps her son Raymond. She was left with a very expensive, lonely house. Mrs. Nadem was better off without her senator husband, but she had lost her son.

Perhaps the only one who was in a better place was Raymond. He was leading the simple life he wanted to live with a neighbor who cared about him and someone to play checkers with. Perhaps that simplicity was worth more than all the money on the north shore.

Please go to the *Drug Affair* page on Amazon and post a review.

For news about Spencer, go to rickpolad.com and click on "Contact Us."

# Acknowledgements

This book would not exist without the help and support of several special people. To my readers and friends, Mike Polad, Carol Deleskiewicz, John Zelman, and Ellen Tullar Purviance, thanks for your edits and input. Any remaining errors are the property of the author.

Special thanks to my publisher, Gary Lindberg (best-selling author of *The Shekinah Legacy*) for his ongoing support and expertise.

And, as always, to all my friends and readers who have asked for more Spencer, my undying thanks.

# About the Author

Rick Polad worked as a geologist, taught Earth Science and Astronomy at a junior college for twenty-nine years, and volunteered with the Coast Guard Auxiliary on Lake Michigan. Rick edited the English version of Living With Nuclei, the memoirs of Japanese physicist, Motoharu Kimura, and currently works as chief editor for his publisher, Calumet Editions. Rick also worked at Fermilab, the country's highest energy particle accelerator, and currently volunteers at Microtrace, one of the world's premier forensic chemistry labs. You can find more information on the Spencer Manning mysteries at rickpolad.com.